ALL THINGS UNDYING

ALL THINGS UNDYING

A Hannah Ives Mystery

Marcia Talley

This first world edition published 2010
in Great Britain and in the USA by
SEVERN HOUSE PUBLISHERS LTD of
9–15 High Street, Sutton, Surrey, England, SM1 1DF.
Trade paperback edition first published
in Great Britain and the USA 2011 by
SEVERN HOUSE PUBLISHERS LTD.

British Library Cataloguing in Publication Data

Talley, Marcia Dutton, 1943–
   All Things Undying. – (The Hannah Ives mysteries series)
   1. Ives, Hannah (Fictitious character) – Fiction. 2. Women
   mediums – Crimes against – Fiction. 3. Detective and
   mystery stories.
   I. Title II. Series
   813.6-dc22

ISBN-13: 978-0-7278-6879-4   (cased)
ISBN-13: 978-1-84751-263-5   (trade paper)

All Severn House titles are printed on acid-free paper.

Severn House Publishers support The Forest Stewardship Council [FSC],
the leading international forest certification organisation. All our titles that
are printed on Greenpeace-approved FSC-certified paper carry the FSC logo.

Mixed Sources
Product group from well-managed
forests and other controlled sources
www.fsc.org Cert no. SA-COC-1565
© 1996 Forest Stewardship Council

Typeset by Palimpsest Book Production Ltd.,
Falkirk, Stirlingshire, Scotland.
Printed and bound in Great Britain by
MPG Books Ltd., Bodmin, Cornwall.

In memory of
the 946 American servicemen who died
off the coast of Devon in April 1944 during Operation Tiger.

'That Others May Live'

ACKNOWLEDGEMENTS

Thanks to:

Charles and Marilyn Mylander, who shared tales of Charles's time as a faculty exchange professor at Britannia Royal Naval College in Dartmouth (as well as a huge box of memorabilia!), and especially for introducing me to:

Jill and Ian Rowe, David and Maralyn Norman and Richard and Anna Alexander, who adopted me when I came to Dartmouth and made sure I lacked for nothing. Chauffeurs, tour guides, lunch, tea and dinnertime companions extraordinaire. Come to Annapolis! *Mi casa es su casa.*

MaryLou Symonds, who graciously loaned me a copy of her unpublished journal, *Brilliant! Adventures of an Academic Wife Abroad*, which is . . . well, brilliant!

Dr Richard Porter, Curator of Britannia Royal Naval College, who took me on a behind-the-scenes tour of the college and supplied me with guidebooks, photographs and a pair of cufflinks, too.

Robbie Robinson, Curator at the Brixham Battery Heritage Centre, Devon, who told me the 'real' story of Slapton Sands.

Jean Parnell of Strete whose girlhood memories of the Evacuation of South Hams in November and December of 1943 remain vivid, and whose book, *The Land We Left Behind*, published in association with The Blackawton and Strete History Group (BASH) was an invaluable resource.

Sarah Glass, who was there from the beginning, when Susan Parker was born.

Brent Morris for Paul's book; Eileen Roberts for Samantha and Victoria's story; and Dot Lumley, for a blustery but delightful after-noon at Greenway House.

Kate Charles, the best of friends, who held my hand throughout, and helped keep my Brits from sounding too much like Americans.

The Annapolis Writers Group – Ray Flynt, Lynda Hill, Mary Ellen Hughes, Debbi Mack, Sherriel Mattingly and Bonnie Settle – for tough love.

That said, all mistakes are mine alone.

Dear! of all happy in the hour, most blest
  He who has found our hid security,
Assured in the dark tides of the world that rest,
  And heard our word, 'Who is so safe as we?'
We have found safety with all things undying,
  The winds, and morning, tears of men and mirth,
The deep night, and birds singing, and clouds flying,
  And sleep, and freedom, and the autumnal earth.
We have built a house that is not for Time's throwing.
  We have gained a peace unshaken by pain for ever.
War knows no power. Safe shall be my going,
  Secretly armed against all death's endeavour;
Safe though all safety's lost; safe where men fall;
And if these poor limbs die, safest of all.

Rupert Brooke, *1914: Safety*

ONE

'One of the longest standing and best known galleries in Dartmouth is the Simon Drew gallery in Foss Street. Famous for his fantastic combination of humour and design it is almost impossible to visit the gallery without being tempted into buying a gift for someone (or maybe even yourself!)'
Nigel Evans, *Reflections of Dartmouth*,
Richard Webb, 2008, p. 29

When it's late July and so hot you could fry an egg on the sidewalk, I find it hard to look seriously at fall fashions in shop windows.

Except I was in Dartmouth, Devon, UK, and the only fried egg I was likely to see that day had been at breakfast at our B&B at the top of Horn Hill.

'You'd look good in that, Hannah,' Alison said, nudging me with her elbow.

'That' was a knee-length, nubby-knit sweater coat in tweedy, earth-tone, crock pot colors that had been all the rage back in the 1960s. We were vacationing in Devon, and I'd forgotten to pack the brown leather belt that I liked to wear with my favorite pair of jeans, so Alison and I had poked our noses into every boutique and charity shop along Duke Street looking for a replacement.

'*You* can wear orange,' I said, considering my friend's neatly bobbed, fashionably fringed, coppery-blond hair and green eyes. 'Me, I look like the Great Pumpkin in orange.'

Alison seized my upper arms with both hands and spun me around gently until I was standing with my back to the window. She squinted at me in the mid-afternoon sunlight, then stared into the window, sizing me up against the coat. 'You're right,' she agreed, dropping her hands to her sides.

'I'm remembering you from before, back when you had dark hair and pale English skin.'

I turned to study my reflection in the glass. 'This tan will fade soon enough,' I said. 'I slathered myself with SPF thirty-five in the islands, wore hats, but . . .' I shrugged. 'The price one pays for six months in the Bahamas.'

Alison grinned. 'Poor you.'

'Tragic,' I agreed.

'As for the hair,' I continued, combing through the curls with my fingers, fluffing them out, 'I was getting panicky about the gray. Before we left Annapolis, I let my hairdresser talk me into highlights.'

'Goes with the tan,' Alison said. 'I like it.'

'Me, too,' I confessed. 'Until my pale English skin returns and I get roots.'

'We *do* have hairdressers in England, you know. Remember Beautopia?' she said, naming a hole-in-the-wall salon where we once had our faces done on a particularly fine Girls' Day Out.

'Eeek! How you talked me into that eye shadow, I'll never know. Acid Rain?' I said, remembering a particularly vile shade of yellow sold by an upstart cosmetic company called Urban Decay.

'You made *me* buy the roach-colored lip gloss, as I recall, so nobody's vying for sainthood here.' Alison punched me lightly on the arm. 'We had fun, didn't we, Hannah? I'm already missing you, and you've only just arrived. Three weeks isn't much of a holiday, if you ask me.' She looped an arm through mine. 'Jon and I haven't seen you in ten years. I wish you could stay longer.'

We turned right and strolled down the center of Foss Street, an ancient thoroughfare that had been neatly cobblestoned and pedestrianized. Upscale galleries, shops and restaurants stood cheek by jowl on both sides of the narrow lane. 'Alas, Paul has to teach,' I said, stopping for a moment at the corner of Flavel to admire a watercolor in the window of Baxter's Gallery. 'Classes begin again on August twenty-fourth.'

'Rotten luck. You're going to miss Regatta, and the fireworks, and the Red Arrows!'

'And the beer barrel roll, and the trolley race. I know.'

The Royal Regatta, an extravagant three-day city fair, featured sailboat and rowing races, too. Regatta had been a highlight of the year we spent in Dartmouth over a decade ago, when Paul had participated in the faculty exchange program between the United States Naval Academy and Britannia Royal Naval College. Sadly, the program had been discontinued in recent years, so Paul's newer colleagues wouldn't benefit from the same broadening opportunity.

'I'll have to make do with the Blue Angels, I suppose,' I said, referring to the US Navy's own precision flying team.

'Ah, yes,' Alison said with pardonable pride, inclining her head close to mine. 'But there are only six Blue Angels. We have nine!'

As far as places to live go, Annapolis is about perfect – historic colonial seaport, vibrant cultural life, temperate winters. Yet all those years ago, when the taxi carrying me, Paul and a mountain of luggage from the train station in Totnes had popped out of the hedgerows over Jawbones Hill, and I first laid eyes on the ancient town of Dartmouth sprawled along the Dart River valley below me, it had been love at first sight. A steam locomotive slowly chug-chug-chugging its storybook way up the opposite bank from Kingswear to Paignton had been the proverbial icing on the cake.

For the exchange all those years ago, Robert and Sally Gardner (now retired to Ludlow) had moved into our home on Prince George Street in Annapolis, and we'd taken over their spacious Victorian on Dartmouth's Vicarage Hill. 'I'm teaching Robert's courses, living in Robert's house, and driving Robert's car,' Paul had quipped at our first drinks party. 'And this,' he had added, throwing his arm around my shoulder, 'this is Robert's wife.'

Men! Jon Hamilton had laughed so hard he'd dropped a Pringle into his sherry, until Alison's evil eye silenced him in mid-guffaw. Alison and I have been friends ever since. So when an email arrived from the Hamiltons urging the Ives to consider a return visit, it had not been a question of when, but how soon.

Alison and I wandered into Baxter's where I pawed
through a basket of ceramic buttons, selecting interesting
shapes and designs for a sweater I planned to knit for my
granddaughter, Chloe. Alison sought out my opinion on a
colorful Chas Jacobs print of the Dartmouth boat float
(*Fabulous, you must have it!*) then I gathered up my
purchases and wandered over to the register. To the buttons
I added a whimsical Lynn Antley rabbit pin with a red heart
for a tail that the savvy shopkeeper had displayed all too
temptingly next to the till.

'I like your hair,' the shopkeeper said as she toted up my
purchases.

'You do?' I felt a blush coming on, thinking that the highlights had been a good idea after all.

Alison slapped my arm playfully. 'Your *hare*, Hannah!
The brooch!'

I burst out laughing. 'Lifts, bonnets, boots, lorries, braces,
and now hares. George Bernard Shaw was right. Two coun-
tries separated by a common language.'

'Two friends separated by an ocean,' Alison pouted as
she reached out and gave me a one-armed hug.

Carrying our neatly wrapped purchases we moseyed along
Foss Street to the Kitchen Shop where I browsed for gadgets
I couldn't live without. Herb scissors! Milk frother! Lemon-
saver! A canned tuna fish drainer! Who knew? 'I'll worry
about how to pack them later,' I told Alison. 'Another thing
charity shops are good for. Second-hand luggage at rock-
bottom prices.'

At Simon Drew's gallery Alison and I were greeted by
the black-hatted, white-bearded artist himself, resplendent
in a pair of khaki shorts, and wearing a red and gold vest
– what the Brits would call a waistcoat – over a turquoise
shirt. A neon yellow bow tie completed the ensemble.
Through spectacles that rose like bat wings over his eyes,
Drew twinkled like Santa Claus as he introduced us to
Rabbit, the black and white sheepdog eyeing us lazily from
a prone position under a display case.

Alison stooped to give Rabbit a good scratch behind the
ears, then checked her watch. 'Crikey! Where did the time

go? My daughter's got a bridge game, and I agreed to watch the kids. If I don't hustle, I'll be late.' She kissed the air next to my cheek, promised to call me around teatime the following day, and vanished through the door.

From the great man himself, I bought two 'Cat-a-Tonic' coasters, a 'Prawn to be Wild' tea towel, half a dozen greeting cards, and a pack of playing cards that featured some of Drew's most popular drawings. After admiring the ceramics on display in all three of the gallery rooms, I thanked the artist, bid him a cheerful goodbye, and wandered further along Foss Street to the Dartmouth Canvas Factory. I was staring into the window admiring a cleverly designed six-pocket canvas beer bucket that I thought would make a great birthday gift for Paul, when I sensed someone standing close behind me. Without turning around, I refocused my eyes, and peered at the reflection in the window.

'Excuse me?' the reflection said.

I turned, expecting to have a hand thrust in my face, wrapped around a charity can decorated with dogs, cats, horses, foxes, maybe even anchors. But instead of begging for donations to the animal rescue league or some aged sailors' home, the owner of the reflection said, 'You don't know me, but my name is Susan Parker. I'm a medium and clairvoyant.'

One might expect such a conversation-stopper out of the mouth of some fresh-faced, gauzy-skirted New Age flower child wearing her hair in dreads, but with the exception of a single purple lock that quivered gently over her left eyebrow as she talked, Susan Parker, Medium and Clairvoyant, looked perfectly normal to me. She wore an embroidered jacket over a crisp white blouse tucked into the waistband of slim black slacks, and a pair of fashionable, sling-back, low-heeled sandals. 'I don't know whether you believe in mediums or not, but when I saw you standing there just now, I just had to speak to you. Do you have a minute?'

'Do you always stop people on the street like this?' I asked.

She answered me with a grin, not at all spoiled by a slight gap between her two front teeth. 'It's what I do.'

I had plenty of experience with mediums like Susan Parker. When my grandson was kidnapped, psychics crawled out of the woodwork like termites fleeing a burning building. It would be interesting to see where this was going. Since I didn't have anything in particular that I needed to be doing, I introduced myself and said, 'I guess I can spare a minute. Maybe even two.'

'It's just that there's an aura around you,' Susan began. 'I see a female figure. A sister. No, wait a minute . . .' Her eyes darted away, focusing on a spot somewhere beyond my right shoulder. She shook her head. 'No, not a sister. A mother.'

Everybody's got a mother. So far, I was unimpressed.

'She passed away, didn't she?'

Bullseye. Yet that, too, could have been a lucky guess. In spite of my new youthful do, I was no spring chicken. 'Yes,' I said, struggling to keep my face blank.

Susan raised a hand, palm out, and cocked her head as if she were actually listening to someone. 'Your mother's apologizing. She says she's sorry for not being around when you needed her.'

I nodded dumbly. Tears pricked the corners of my eyes.

Once again the medium glanced away. Listened. Nodded. I followed her gaze, by now so unnerved that I half expected to see my mother posing in the shop window wearing one of their handmade fishermen's jackets. I shook off the feeling. It was an act, had to be, but a good one. And the envelope goes to . . . Susan Parker, Best Performance by a Medium Conversing with the Dead.

'Does the name George mean anything to you?'

My father's name is George! But before I could recover my breath and answer in the affirmative, Susan squinted through the shop door, as if having a conversation with someone standing just inside. 'Thank you!' she chirped, then turned back to me. 'Not George. Georgina.'

I stumbled back against the window glass, grabbing the sill for support. Georgina was my baby sister back in Baltimore. How could a total stranger an ocean away in England know about Georgina?

'My sister,' I stammered, instantly buying into this woman's act one hundred and one per cent. 'Georgina is my sister. Is she all right?'

Susan touched my arm, squeezed it gently. 'I'm sorry, I didn't mean to alarm you. But your mother is here with me, and she has a message for your sister. She's saying, "Tell Georgina it's not her fault." Does that mean anything to you?'

I nodded, too stunned to speak. Oh, it meant something all right.

Suddenly Susan winced. She inhaled sharply, pressed one hand tightly against her chest, then let her breath out slowly. 'I'm feeling pressure. Here. In the chest area. Did your mother die of a heart condition?'

Again, I nodded. This was getting too weird for words. If Susan Parker wasn't talking to my mother, she had to be reading my mind.

'I'm feeling cold,' Susan continued. Both hands were at her waist now, thumbs forward, fingers flexing, working her lower back. 'I feel like I'm lying on something cold. And hard.' Her eyes, crystalline blue, widened. 'Why do I keep seeing a refrigerator?'

'Jesus!' I blurted. I couldn't help it. My mother had died in a Baltimore hospital, but the heart attack that killed her had happened in my kitchen, during a knock-down, drag-out screaming match with my sister Georgina. When I could breathe again, I said, 'You're freaking me out.'

'It's OK to freak out.' Susan smiled. 'Do you want me to go on?'

I clutched the shopping bag from Simon Drew to my chest, wrinkling the heck out of the caricature of Rabbit printed on its side, and considered Susan's question for maybe two and a half seconds. 'Yes,' I said, blinking back tears.

'Your mother's saying she's fine, she's not in pain anymore . . .' Susan paused for a moment, just long enough that I began to worry. 'There must be another sister.'

Oh. My. God. Susan Parker knew about Ruth, too. I'd walked out of the fanciful world of Simon Drew and straight into the Twilight Zone. 'Uh huh,' I croaked, trying to swallow the lump that was suddenly taking up too much space in my throat.

Susan laid a gentle hand on my arm. 'Your mother wants you and your sisters to know that she loves you very much.'

'Uh huh,' I sniffed.

'Do you need a tissue?'

'Thanks.' While I wiped my eyes and blew my nose with the tissue thoughtfully produced from the depths of Susan's leather handbag, I tried to make sense out of what had just happened.

'Are you OK?' she asked.

'How . . .?' I began.

Susan shrugged. 'I don't know,' she said. 'I honestly don't know. It just happens.'

As if to punctuate her comment, the bells of St Saviour's Church began to chime the hour. Susan jumped as if she'd been shot. 'Sorry, I've got an appointment. Have to run. Are you going to be all right?'

'I think so,' I said, tucking the soggy tissue into my shopping bag. 'It's just a lot to take in all at once.'

'It was lovely to meet you,' Susan said, extending her hand, smiling. 'And your mother!'

Rabbit appeared just then, checking out the shoppers, no doubt, snuffling noisily around my ankles as if I'd recently misted them with Eau de Boeuf. I bent to give the dog a pat. By the time I'd ordered Rabbit not to be such a beggar and sent him back to his owner, the embroidered sunflower on the back of Susan Parker's jacket was disappearing around the corner of Union Street.

'Wait a minute! There's something I want to ask you!' Gathering my wits about me once more, I set off at a trot in the direction of Market Square searching for Susan, but she had vanished into the crowds that clustered around the market stalls selling everything from fresh raspberries to 'designer' handbags.

Still in a fog, I made my way to the market tea room where I bought a cup of cappuccino, sat down at a table by myself and sipped it very, very slowly, feeling sorry for myself.

I was sprinkling a second packet of demerara sugar over the foam when it occurred to me. Susan Parker sounded exactly like Sue Scott playing the Lutheran Lunch Lady on *Prairie Home Companion*. She was an American.

TWO

'Horn Hill House is a fully restored Grade II listed Georgian townhouse perched on a hill overlooking the River Dart. Four en-suite bedrooms are offered, each with a colour television, a mini-cooler and a hair dryer. Fresh milk, leaf tea, ground coffee, and tea cakes are also provided. Natural cotton bedding and non-allergenic pillows have been specifically chosen to ensure each guest a good night's sleep. Special diets are catered for using, when available, organic produce.'
www.DiscoverDartmouth.com

I honestly don't remember how I got back to our B&B on Horn Hill, but I must have made the right turn on to Anzac Street, skirted St Saviour's Church, and passed right by the Singing Kettle without even thinking about stopping for tea, which only goes to show how preoccupied I was because a cream tea at the Singing Kettle is a near religious experience, even if you've just finished a cappuccino.

Somehow, I made my way into Higher Street and turned right for the long climb up Horn Hill, one of the many stepped thoroughfares for which Dartmouth is famous. Horn Hill House was near the top, on the left, through a gate and up five additional steps along a narrow alleyway that opened into a well-tended garden.

When I snapped out of my daze, I found myself standing on the doorstep of Horn Hill House, fumbling in my handbag for the old-fashioned key with its unusual Buddha-shaped fob. Unlocking the door required two hands, so I tucked my packages under my arm, slotted the key into the lock, and turned both the key and the doorknob at the same time.

The door swung open on noisy hinges, and I stumbled

into the tiny vestibule. I'd taken two steps in the direction
of the narrow, twisting staircase that led to our room on
the floor above when a door opened to my right. 'Hannah?'
   It was Janet Brelsford, our proprietress, looking super
smart in a fuchsia scoop-neck T-shirt tucked into fashionably faded jeans with a razor-sharp crease.
   'Sorry, Janet. I didn't mean to disturb you.' I jingled the
key. 'I'll get the hang of the door eventually!'
   Janet laughed. 'I have no doubt of that. Can you come
in for a moment? I've got something to show you.'
   Paul and I had been in Dartmouth only a few days, but
Janet and I had already become friends. From the minute we
stepped over the threshold of Horn Hill House, Janet Brelsford
and her husband, Alan, had made us feel like family. Janet
cooked for us like family, too, if your family includes a Paris-
trained Cordon Bleu chef among its members. Alan, a
Francophile himself, managed to complement every meal
with a fine Savigny Les Beaune Cuvee, a Sauvignon de Saint
Bris or some other nearly unpronounceable *vin extraordinaire*, produced with a flourish from the depths of a wine
cellar he kept locked with a key the size of a handgun.
   'I hope you don't mind,' Janet continued, easing the door
to their sitting room a bit wider, 'but when I was changing
the linen in your room just now, I noticed your knitting.'
   I had been contemplating a hot bath – a long, brain-
sorting think in the claw-foot tub tucked into an alcove of
our comfortable en suite – but suddenly, talking about knitting seemed a pleasant distraction. I dropped the keys into
my bag. 'It's not a particularly ambitious project,' I told
her. 'Slip one, knit one, pass stitch over on the even rows.
It's called a healing shawl. I knit them for cancer survivors.
Almost as good as a hug.'
   'We make them here, too,' Janet said. 'Comfort shawls we
call them.' She waved a hand toward a flowered chintz-
covered sofa. 'Speaking of which, make yourself comfortable. I've just put the kettle on. Would you care to join me?'
   After all the coffee I'd had at the market, my eyeballs
were floating, but I found I was craving company, so I
caved. 'Tea would be perfect. Lady Gray, if you have it.'

Janet smiled. 'My favorite, too. Just a tick!'

While Janet bustled around in the kitchen of the ground floor apartment she shared with her husband and two young daughters, I sank gratefully into the sofa, rested my head against the upholstery and stared at the coffered ceiling, embossed with curling vines. What had happened only minutes before already seemed like a dream. Still, it unnerved me. I should tell Paul, of course, but he'd groan, roll his eyes and make *Twilight Zone* noises. Ruth would be right on board, of course, but my older sister was back in Maryland, probably *feng shui*-ing the heck out of somebody's house. For a woman who believed that mirrors could repel evil spirits, talking to ghosts wasn't a huge leap.

'Here we go!' Janet returned, carrying a tray on which she'd arranged a teapot, two mugs, a sugar bowl and a jug of milk. Balanced on top of the milk jug was a plate of chocolate digestives, a kind of flat, round graham cracker frosted with chocolate. She set the tray carefully on the footstool in front of me. 'Shall I be Mother?' she asked.

'Absolutely. I'm dangerous. Whenever I pour, the top of the teapot has a tendency to fall into the cup.'

Smiling, Janet filled my mug with tea. 'Milk?'

'No thanks,' I replied. 'A weird American thing, I know, but I like my tea plain. No sugar either.'

'Black, then. Here you go.'

I accepted the steaming mug, wrapped both hands around it, and sipped carefully. 'You wanted to show me something, Janet?'

'Right!' Janet groped about in the space between the sofa and the wall, retrieved a basket by its handles and set it on her knees. 'Since you're a knitter, too, I thought you'd be interested in this project I've just finished. It's knit from the wool of a sheep I met up in Somerset.' She lifted a sweater from the basket and spread it out on the sofa between us, smoothing it gently.

The sweater was an oatmeal-colored turtleneck; intricate cables snaked across the chest and down each sleeve. 'Gorgeous!' I set my mug on a coaster on the end table, picked up a sleeve and rubbed the wool appreciatively between my fingers. 'I love how you can feel the lanolin.'

While I fondled the material, Janet rose, crossed the carpet to the fireplace and picked a snapshot off the mantle. 'This is Sheila. She's a North Ronaldsay.' Janet handed the photograph to me. An animal – half sheep and half shaggy dog – gazed out of the frame with dark, soulful eyes. 'It's a fairly rare breed originally from Orkney,' she explained. 'A friend of mine keeps a small herd on her farm near Bradford on Avon.'

I looked up from the photo. 'This is her wool?'

Janet chuckled. 'The sheep's, not my friend's!'

'I'd rather be working with Sheila's wool than the synthetic crap you saw upstairs,' I said. 'But some people are allergic to wool, poor things. Not that I'm going to be working on anything in the immediate future, anyway. Some humorless Neanderthal confiscated my knitting needles at the security checkpoint at BWI.'

'You're joking! I thought they rescinded that rule.'

'Maybe the agents at BWI didn't get the email. I don't suppose there's a yarn shop nearby?'

'Sorry.' She returned the snapshot to its place on the mantle, propped up next to a framed photograph of her twins, Samantha and Victoria, age six. 'What size needles do you need?'

'Eleven.'

'Eleven? For that shawl?' Her forehead creased in puzzlement.

It took me a couple of seconds to figure out what the problem was. In the States, the fatter the needle, the higher the number. In the UK, the same rule applied, but they used metric numbers. I wondered if I was asking for a needle the size of a walking stick, useful if you're knitting socks for Bigfoot, I suppose, but not much else. Fortunately, I remembered a second number that had been stamped into the steel of the knitting needles now likely resting under a ton of garbage at the bottom of some dumpster back at BWI. 'Eight millimeters?'

'Not a problem, then. I'm sure I have a pair around somewhere. I'll leave them in your room, shall I?'

'Would you? That would be very kind!' I reached for one of the digestives. 'Is Paul back yet? He went off to share a pint with two former colleagues. By my estimation, that was three pints ago.'

'I haven't seen him, but I went to fetch the girls from their piano lesson, so he may have slipped in while I was out.' Janet sat down, picked up her mug and studied me over the top of a pair of pink plastic reading glasses, perched precariously near the tip of her nose. 'You look worried. I'm sure he's just fine.'

I managed a smile. 'Paul's a big boy. I let him cross the street by himself and everything now. It's just . . . well, the craziest thing just happened to me.' Setting my tea aside for a moment, I told her about my encounter with Susan Parker on Foss Street. 'It so unnerved me that I don't even remember walking back here. I hope nobody saw me,' I added quickly. 'I was probably reeling like a drunk.'

'Susan Parker? I'm surprised you haven't heard of her.'

'Really, why?'

'She's rather famous. Even has a television show on ITV.'

'Get out!'

Janet selected another digestive for herself and bit into it. 'I haven't seen every broadcast, of course, too much going on around here most times, but she can be jolly amazing.' She licked a crumb from her lip. 'Her program's called *Dead Reckoning*.'

'She talks to the dead for a living, then.'

Janet smothered a laugh with her hand.

'What'd I say?'

'Sorry. It just struck me as funny.' She waggled a hand. 'Dead. Living.'

I chuckled, too. After a moment I asked, 'Do you really *believe* in that sort of thing, Janet?'

Janet shrugged. 'Fake mediums are a dime a dozen. But Susan? She's the genuine article.' Before I could digest that remark, she hurried on. 'You wouldn't know she's such a star, would you, when you see her in person?'

'True. At first, I thought she was collecting for charity.'

Janet chuckled. 'Susan is so down to earth. She lives on

Ridge Hill Road. If you're up and out early enough, you'll meet her walking Bruce along the Embankment just like regular people.'

'Bruce?'

'Her dog. A border terrier.'

I'd always liked border terriers, ever since Puffy upstaged all the human actors in the movie *There's Something About Mary*. 'Bruce? What an odd name for a dog.'

'He's named after Bruce Springsteen,' Janet explained. 'You know, "Born in the USA".'

I had to laugh. Naming a dog after The Boss would never have occurred to me. 'You sound like you know her.'

'Sorry? Oh, yes, I do. We volunteer for the Christian Aid Lunch at St Saviour's Church. It's at noon on Tuesday, by the way, if you'd like to come. Not much of a meal, if you want to know the truth. Sandwiches, veggies, tea and cakes, that sort of thing. Only a pound, but I like to chuck in another quid or two for the cause.'

'I'd love to,' I said. 'Will Susan be there?'

'I doubt it. She stopped coming a while back. Could have been her busy schedule, of course, but I know she found some of the parishioners a bit off-putting.' Lifting the teapot with one hand and securing the lid with two fingers of the other, Janet topped off my mug. 'Susan ruffled quite a few feathers when she bought St Anthony's and converted it into flats.'

I remembered St Anthony's, a solid, Victorian-era church near the intersection of Clarence Street and College Way, not far from the river. 'It was made redundant?'

Janet drew quote marks in the air. 'Surplus to requirements. Available for disposal. It just about broke my heart.' She helped herself to another biscuit. 'A pity, that, but what can you do?' She shrugged. 'St Anthony's was down to a handful of parishioners. If they ever got double digits at a service, Christ himself would have climbed down from the cross to congratulate the vicar. A beautiful old building, really. Neo-Gothic. Forty-five hundred square feet, give or take, so Susan's architect had a lot to work with. It's four flats now.' After a moment, she added, 'Susan surprised us, didn't she?'

'How's that?'

'Everyone thought she'd be taking the flat with the rose window, the one that faces east over the Dart, not that you'd get much of a view out of it, but the sunrise would be spectacular. But, no. Her flat's on the south side where the special windows are.'

The way Janet emphasized 'special' made me wonder if said windows were endowed with supernatural powers, like the Grotto at Lourdes. I had to ask. 'What do you mean, "special"?'

Janet leaned toward me and lowered her voice, speaking in a reverent whisper. 'When the builders started pulling down the interior walls, they uncovered a pair of Byrne-Jones windows that somebody had covered up with plasterboard during the Second World War. A Miriam and a David, they were, smaller versions of the ones up at St Michael's and All Angels in Hertfordshire. They're part of Susan's sitting room now.'

Byrne-Jones windows? I was astonished, and said so. 'How could anyone simply forget a Byrne-Jones window? They're classic! Trinity Church in Boston has one of his windows. The Adorations of the Magi. I've seen it, and it's glorious.'

Janet shrugged. 'Alan claims that Byrne-Jones was hopelessly out of fashion by the 1930s. Perhaps nobody missed them.'

'What brought Susan Parker to Dartmouth, do you know? It seems a long way out of London. I presume that's where she tapes her show.'

'Three hours. But you'll remember that from before, Hannah. Catch the eight-fifteen out of Totnes and you're in London well before noon. People have been commuting from London to Dartmouth for at least a century of weekends.

I remembered that, too. 'The English Riviera,' I said, quoting a popular guidebook.

Someone says 'Dartmouth' and you think 'sailing'. But sailors aren't the only types attracted to this splendid little corner of the world. Writers, poets, artists, and musicians have *all* found inspiration in Devon – it's that kind of place.

'We certainly have had our share of celebrities buying

holiday homes down here,' Janet continued, ticking them off on her fingers. 'Samuel Taylor Coleridge. Rudyard Kipling. Edmund Crispin. Daphne du Maurier.' She paused for breath. 'No, hold on. Du Maurier lived in Cornwall, didn't she? And Agatha Christie, of course.' She caught her breath. 'Hannah!'

She spoke my name so sharply that I sloshed tea over the rim of my mug. Was there a spider crawling up my sleeve? A rattlesnake coiled at my ankles ready to strike?

'Sorry! Didn't mean to startle you,' she said, handing me a napkin. 'I suddenly remembered that the National Trust opened Christie's home to the public just last month, and I know what a fan you are of mysteries, so I wanted to make sure you knew.'

'Greenway House is on the top of *my* to-do list,' I said with a smile. 'Cut my teeth on Nancy Drew, then graduated to Christie. Never looked back. Visiting Greenway is a kind of pilgrimage, I suppose. Not sure about Paul, though. He's more of a Grisham fan.'

'When you go, take the ferry,' Janet suggested. 'It's a wonderful trip. Besides, Greenway gives you a discount if you travel by green transport.'

'We've got National Trust membership,' I told her, patting the outside pocket of my handbag where I kept the magic National Trust get-into-just-about-anything-free card.

'No worries, then. In any case, don't miss the gardens! The rhododendrons should be glorious this time of year.'

Before Janet could take a long detour on to a botanical tangent, I asked, 'Susan's an American, isn't she?'

Janet nodded. 'From your American Midwest. She did a year abroad reading medieval English at one of the red bricks. University of Warwick, I believe it was.'

'Gosh! I wonder how she got from Beowulf and Chaucer to . . . to . . .' I thought for a moment. 'Well, from reading about dead people to talking to them.'

'Why don't you ask her yourself?'

'Oh, sure. What do you suggest? That I walk up to her flat and simply knock on the door?'

Janet's smile took on Cheshire Cat proportions. 'What are you doing on Thursday evening?'

'Recuperating, I imagine. Paul wants to take the lower ferry to Kingswear and hike to Coleton Fishacre and back.' Coleton Fishacre – the name, I learned, was a corruption of something bucolic in old French and had nothing to do with fish – was the holiday estate of the famous Sir Rupert D'Oyly Carte whose father was the impresario behind the operettas of Gilbert and Sullivan. Built in the Roaring Twenties, my guidebook gushed, the house was an Art Deco masterpiece redolent of the Jazz Age, set in acres of glorious gardens sweeping down to the sea.

'I'll ring her up and see if she's available for dinner.'

'Who? Susan Parker?'

'Of course,' Janet said, as if inviting celebrities to dinner was an everyday occurrence. 'Anyone else you'd like me to invite?'

I thought for a moment. 'Jon and Alison Hamilton, our friends from the college. You've met them, haven't you?'

Janet nodded. 'Indeed. Dartmouth's a small town.' She began stacking our empty mugs on the tea tray. 'I'll confirm with you later, then. Will you and Paul be wanting dinner in tonight?'

'Thanks, Janet, but no. We've booked a table at the Royal Castle Hotel. When I walked by this morning, they had *moules frites* on the menu board outside. I am crazy for mussels!' I stood up, too, and waved toward the remains of our tea.

Janet raised a hand. 'You leave the washing-up to me.'

'You sure?' I gathered up my purchases. 'Fingers crossed Susan will be able to come on Thursday. There are some things I'd like to ask her.'

Janet twisted the knob and held the lounge door open until I'd passed through it into the hallway. 'She'll probably be expecting my call.'

'Why do you say that?'

Janet winked. 'What kind of psychic would she be if she didn't?'

THREE

'In the course of a successful reading, the psychic may provide most of the words, but it is the client that provides most of the meaning and all of the significance.'

Ian Rowland, *The Full Facts Book of Cold Reading*, p. 60

I was licking garlic butter off my fingers in the cozy, dark-timbered ambiance of The Royal Castle Hotel's Galleon Bar, when Paul said, 'Too bad you didn't like the mussels.'

'Mmmmmussels!' I moaned.

With the exception of a mound of empty, wing-shaped ebony shells piled haphazardly in a bowl next to my elbow, there was no evidence that mussels had ever been served.

Between bites, I'd retold the story of my encounter with Susan Parker. Paul had listened politely, rolling his eyes only twice, which, knowing his propensity for critical thinking, must have required superhuman self-control.

Now I was finishing off my story as well as the last of the *frites* that had come with my *moules*. 'So, you see why I'm kind of freaked.'

'Hannah, Hannah, Hannah,' Paul chided, as if he were dealing with a particularly slow and difficult child. 'She's a talented cold reader – i.e. a fake.'

I decided to ignore him. I dragged a French fry though the scrumptious broth remaining at the bottom of the pot the mussels had so recently occupied, popped the fry into my mouth and chewed slowly.

'Earth to Hannah.'

'Are you going to talk to me like a grown-up?' When Paul agreed, I said, 'OK. Leaving aside for a moment the question of is-she-for-real-or-isn't-she, what I want to know

is this: what's in it for her? Why would she walk up to a total
stranger on the street, pretend to have a conversation with
that stranger's dead mother, then simply disappear?' I reached
for my wine glass. 'She didn't ask me for money, Paul.'

'No, but neither did that so-called psychic who showed
up on our doorstep when Timmy was kidnapped. Dakota
Whatshername.'

'Montana. Montana Martin.'

'Whatever.'

'But for Montana, there *was* money in it. There was the
reward money, of course. Worse case, she did it for the
publicity.' I polished off another fry and stared at the copper
pots gleaming from the walls, admiring the way they
reflected the light. I flashed back to the day Montana Martin
parked her boots on my daughter's doorstep, and in a parting
shot, claimed that my late mother wanted me to have her
emerald ring. 'Lucky guess,' Paul had insisted at the time,
but I had never been totally convinced.

'Remember the ring?' I asked.

Paul shot an exasperated here-we-go-again glance at the
ceiling. 'The opposite of cold reading, Hannah, is hot
reading. Quite simply, Montana cheated. Did her home-
work, I mean. The ring? It's mentioned in your mother's
will. The will is on file with Anne Arundel County. It's
public record. Montana could have looked it up.'

Paul had a point. I hadn't thought of that. 'But, but, but
. . .' I was stalling, organizing my thoughts. 'But Susan
Parker doesn't know me from Adam! For all she knew, I
was a tourist fresh off the Eurostar and she'd never see me
again. What you're suggesting is that she targets likely
tourists, manages to learn their names, does a bit of research
– on the Internet, I suppose – and then contrives to run into
them on the street sort of accidentally on purpose.' I puffed
air out through my lips. 'Doesn't make sense. And that bit
about my sister, Georgina. Spooky!' I dragged out the 'o'
and waggled my fingers.

'Your mother's obituary,' Paul said reasonably. 'If it
appeared in the newspaper, it would definitely be available
on the Internet.'

I had one of those duh, head-slapping moments. 'Right. "Survived by three daughters", et cetera, et cetera.' I reached across the table and grabbed Paul's hand. 'Wait a minute! Information about my sisters could certainly be squirreled away in some remote corner of the Internet, but Susan knew that my mother died of a heart attack, and I'm pretty sure that information isn't on the Internet.'

'Not in her obituary?'

'No, sir. I wrote it myself. It said "after a long illness", which could mean anything.'

'As I said earlier, Hannah, all that means is the woman's an extraordinarily skilled cold reader. Tell me. Did this Parker woman come right out and say "heart attack" or did she work up to it first, like, "I feel a pain in the chest area"?'

I closed my eyes and tried to replay the conversation I'd had with the medium, but I couldn't remember Susan's exact words.

'Think of how many medical conditions "chest area" could refer to,' Paul continued. 'Heart attack. Lung cancer. Emphysema.' He squeezed my hand. 'Even breast cancer.'

'Why do you have to be so goddamn reasonable?'

'She was fishing for details, I'll bet, and reading your body language, letting *you* connect the dots.'

I was saved from having to agree with my husband by the reappearance of our server, inquiring if Sir and/or Madam would care for pudding this evening.

'Yes, please.' I dredged up a smile for the young woman. 'It's been a stressful day.'

After she went off to fetch Paul's apple tart and a crème brûlée for me, Paul leaned back in his chair and announced, 'Anybody can be a psychic, even me.'

'Do tell.'

Paul reached across the table and captured my hand in both of his. 'First, I get you comfortable, ply you with good food and fine wine.'

I snatched my hand away. 'Where did *you* learn to be a psychic?'

'I used to wow 'em with my magic tricks in high school.

At lunchtime, I was the star of the cafeteria. And I did a lot of reading. The Amazing Randi has a lot to say on the subject of psychics.'

'Randi? The magician?' I put my lips together and made a rude noise. 'None of it positive, I imagine.'

'Like Houdini, he uses his skills as an illusionist to expose frauds. I guess you could call Randi a professional debunker. He refers to psychic shtick as woo-woo.'

Grinning, Paul reclaimed my hand. 'Next, I smile, make eye contact . . .' He stared at me, his eyes like deep chocolate pools. What with his goofy grin and wide-eyed, silent screen star gaze, I couldn't help it. I started to giggle.

'You are . . . let me see.' Paul began stroking the top of my hand as he held it over my half-empty wine glass. 'I'm getting a strong feeling about September, here.'

'Not fair! You know my birthday's in September!'

'Just play along, Hannah.'

I closed my eyes. 'OK. Yes. I was born in September, O Magnificent One.'

'Ah, yes, I can see that.'

My eyes flew open. 'Hah! But what if I'd said, "September? I can't think of anything special about September"? What would you have said, then?'

Paul raised an eyebrow, patted my hand sympathetically. 'Yes, I see that you've suppressed the memory of it. Something painful happened in September. Ah, I feel it, now. A pain, here, in my chest.'

Then it was my turn to roll my eyes. 'Well, duh!'

Paul forged on. 'You are not cooperating, Hannah! OK, try this on for size. What if I say, "You don't work with heavy machinery, do you?" What do you answer?'

'I say no, of course.'

'But here's the beauty of it! If you say no, I say, "Yes, I thought not." If you say, "Yes, that's amazing, I drive the Zamboni around the ice rink," I say, "Yes, I thought so." For the psychic, it's win-win either way.'

'Order me another glass of wine, Professor Ives, and do shut up!'

Paul waved to attract the attention of our server. 'Scientists

have been trying to find proof of life after death for over
a century,' he continued as the server trotted off in the direction of the bar to fetch us more wine. 'They've designed
experiment after experiment, but I'm quite certain nothing's
been proved.'

'Lots of things are invisible,' I said. 'Atoms, radio waves,
the wind. You don't see the wind; you see the effects of the
wind. Maybe the spirits of the dead are like that.'

'William James certainly thought that was a possibility,'
Paul agreed. 'Back in the 1880s he theorized that researchers
could be overlooking some sort of natural fact that might
explain ghostly phenomena, simply because it didn't fit into
their carefully organized system of knowledge.'

'Do I see a crack opening in your great wall of skepticism, Paul?'

Paul laughed. 'I'm willing to keep an open mind.'

'Then promise me you'll behave yourself at dinner on
Thursday night,' I said. 'No ghost busting. No trick questions.'

'You have my word.' Paul raised his wine glass and
clinked it against mine. 'But sometimes you need a reality
check, Hannah. And that's my job, too.'

'The Great Carnac has spoken.'

'Damn right, sweetheart,' Paul said, imitating Cagney.

Our desserts arrived and we dug into them, all serious
conversation replaced by a succession of yummy noises.
As I scraped the last dabs of pudding from the ramekin, I
had to admit that assuming Susan Parker *had* somehow
managed to target me in advance, Paul's arguments made
sense. But there was something I still didn't understand.
Susan had asked me, *Why do I keep seeing a refrigerator?*

And that was a question even Carnac in all his magnif-
icence couldn't answer.

FOUR

'It may seem strange but Operation Tiger, which happened so many years ago [to the Americans] is as if it happened yesterday . . . I have no doubt that this emotional feeling of loss stems also from the fact that they never got the bodies back. They never knew what had happened to them. All they had received were telegrams saying that their men were killed in the European theatre of operations.'
Ken Small, *The Forgotten Dead*, Bloomsbury, 1989, p. 197

At home in Maryland, there are no surprises at the breakfast table, just Paul hunched over a bowl of Cheerios with the *New York Times* folded open to the OpEd section and propped up against the salt and pepper grinders. At a B&B, though, every morning stars a new cast of characters and some days can surprise you, like tuning in to *Good Morning America* without checking the program guide first.

At Horn Hill House on Tuesday morning there were eight around the breakfast table, including a family of four from Nantes, and a rough-hewn Yorkshire man and his florid-faced wife who appeared to be huffing and puffing their way from Starcross to Salcombe along the coastal path. By Wednesday, the couple from Yorkshire had hiked on, to be replaced by an American who, if the noise on the stairway the previous night was any indication, had arrived late and out of sorts. It was well past eleven when she woke me with her grumbling as she bump-bump-bumped her roller bag up the staircase and along the landing just outside our room.

'Good morning,' the American chirped as she slid an

expanse of Madras plaid into the chair next to Paul, grabbed
her napkin, snapped it open and smoothed it over her bare
knees. She leaned forward. 'OK, so who are the other
Americans here?' Before anyone could answer, she held up
a cautionary hand. 'No, wait a minute. Let me guess.'

Through slitted eyes, she considered each of us in turn,
as if we were in a police line-up and she were a victim
intent on making a positive ID. 'You,' she said, jabbing her
finger at the mother of two from Nantes who had been
ignoring the whole production while helping her daughter
carve up some sausage. 'You from the States?'

The woman looked up. '*Mais, non.* I am Nicole. My
family and I, we are from France.'

'Well, can't win 'em all.' The new arrival snorted daintily, then turned to lavish a smile on my husband. She stuck
out a pudgy hand. 'So, you must be the Americans. I'm
Cathy Yates, Cathy with a "C" from Pittsburgh, PA.'

Paul laid down his fork. 'I'm Paul Ives, and this is my
wife, Hannah. We're from Annapolis.'

'Indianapolis?' Cathy inquired lazily, toying with her spoon.

'Annapolis. As in Maryland.'

'Holey moley! My brother went to the Naval Academy
in Annapolis!'

After we compared notes and determined that Paul and
her brother had overlapped, but he hadn't been enrolled in
any of the classes my husband taught, Paul and I got down
to the serious business of tucking into the full English breakfast Janet set down in front of us: two eggs – I prefer mine
soft-boiled, toast, baked beans, fried tomatoes, sautéed
mushrooms and a nicely browned American-style sausage,
not the fat, white tube of sausage-like substance one usually
encountered in British B&Bs.

'Gosh, that looks good,' Cathy said. A strand of long,
blond, stick-straight hair slipped over her shoulder and
hovered dangerously over Paul's plate as she leaned over
to inspect his breakfast. 'I'll have what they're having,
Janet.'

When a woman reaches a certain age, the hairstyle that
saw you through the peace marches of the 1960s has got

to go. *Get a haircut, Cathy*, I wanted to tell her, *or put a bag over your head*. But I held my tongue.

While we ate, the newcomer entertained us with a stream-of-consciousness account of her harrowing trip to Dartmouth from Heathrow. 'Jeeze laweeze,' she began, 'I thought I'd never get here. How on earth do you drive in this flipping country? I mean, cheese and crackers! It's bad enough that you're sitting on the wrong side of the car driving on the wrong side of the road, but you can't see a flipping thing over the gee-dee bushes. Please pass the O.J.?'

When the French couple simply looked confused, I translated for them – *jus d'orange, s'il vous plaît*. Nicole passed the pitcher to Paul who poured some orange juice into a glass and handed it to Cathy.

A sip of the juice had remarkable restorative powers, giving Cathy the energy to barrel on. 'Coming around this corner? Ran smack dab into a herd of sheep! And they kept moseying along, moseying along, all the time in the world, calm as you please. Baaa, baaa, baaa. Honestly, you think the fellow in charge would *do* something, wouldn't you, but noooo.' She set her glass down, selected a slice of whole-wheat toast from the toast rack and slathered it with strawberry jam, wielding the table knife like a palette knife, covering every square centimeter of bread evenly with the jam, working right up to the edges of the crust, as if it were an art project she'd be graded on.

'I left that rental in the parking lot down by the Tourist Center and there it's going to stay until Europcar comes to pick the sucker up,' she continued, aiming the toast at her mouth and taking a semi-circular bite. 'Swear to God, I'm not setting foot inside it again. It is a miracle I got here at all.'

'Driving in the UK can be a challenge,' I agreed. 'We lived in Dartmouth for almost a year, but when we first arrived, I thought I'd never get the hang of it. Once you master it, however, it's like riding a bike. The skill is yours for life.'

'And you have recent experience, too, Hannah, don't forget about that.'

At first I couldn't imagine what Paul was talking about.
And then I remembered. 'We drove on the left in the
Bahamas, too,' I added with a grin. 'But that was usually
in an island golf cart. I'm not sure that qualifies.'

Cathy's breakfast had arrived, and she dug in, beginning
with the baked beans. 'Can't trust a GPS, either,' she grumbled. 'Dang thing led me down a flipping dirt road, not that
I'd dignify two ruts by calling it an actual road. Where the
Sam Hill are you supposed to go when you meet somebody coming the other way?' she asked the table at large
between forkfuls. 'I faced off grill to grill with this garbage
truck, and I thought we were going to sit there all day,
glaring at each other through our windshields. I honked and
honked, and the guy *finally* backed up so I could get by.
That was enough for me!' She picked up her knife and
began sawing on her sausage. 'What I'm going to do for
transportation the rest of the week I have *no* idea.'

'Public transportation is pretty good here,' I told her.
'Plenty of trains and buses. Where do you want to go?'

'A town called Torcross,' she said. 'Somewhere south of
here.' She leaned over, retrieved her bag from the floor,
and pulled out a paperback: *The Forgotten Dead*, by Ken
Small. 'Do you know this book?' she asked my husband,
correctly pegging him as the historian in the group.

'I do,' Paul said. 'It's the story of how one man raised
a Sherman tank from the ocean floor and set it up on shore
as a memorial to the Americans who died near here during
training exercises in the Second World War.'

'During Operation Tiger,' Cathy added, her face grave.
'Nine hundred and forty-six men. My father was one of them.'

'I'm so sorry,' I said.

'So am I. I hadn't been born yet when it happened, but
do you want to know the incredible thing?' She shook the
book under Paul's nose. 'Nobody told us! Mom always
believed that Dad had died on Utah Beach in the Normandy
invasion. Until Uncle Charlie sent her this book. To find
out Daddy actually died in England during a dress rehearsal
for D-Day was quite a shock, I can tell you.'

Cathy opened to the back of the small, well-read paperback

and smoothed open a page. 'There,' she said, sliding the book along the tablecloth in our direction and pointing to what was clearly a long casualty list. 'MM2 Curtis Yates. He was on LST531 when it was torpedoed by the Germans. We never got his body back.'

'*Pauvre petite*,' Nicole soothed from across the table, although 'petite' wasn't the word I'd choose to describe Cathy's plus-sized frame. 'I know about this. El Ess Tay. Is a landing ship tank. It carries many soldiers.'

Many soldiers. That was an understatement.

One couldn't spend any amount of time in Devon without hearing about the disaster at Slapton Sands.

Shortly after midnight on April 28, 1944, two LSTs, carrying more than a thousand men each, sank in a few fiery, terror-filled minutes after being torpedoed by German subs on routine patrol that had slipped, undetected, through Allied defenses. A third LST, although damaged, had limped back to Portsmouth harbor. 'I can see why visiting the memorial is important to you,' I said.

She sucked in her lips and nodded. 'I hate the word "closure", but that's what it's all about, isn't it, Hannah? Closure.'

I couldn't think of anything to add to that, so I simply smiled reassuringly and returned to whacking the tops off my soft-boiled eggs.

'Say,' Cathy continued after a moment. Head bent, she fumbled once more in her commodious bag, coming up with a set of car keys. She plunked them down on the table in front of Paul, although they were clearly intended for me, one chair over. 'Hannah. If you can drive me down to see the Sherman tank, you'll be my BFF.'

BFF. Best friends forever. 'Your friend, certainly,' I agreed, thinking that one out of three was the best this pushy American was going to get, at least for the time being. Maybe she was an acquired taste.

Cathy's eyes widened hopefully. 'You'll do it?'

She looked so childlike, so vulnerable, that I felt my defenses weakening. 'Sure,' I agreed, figuring that there were a lot worse things than a long drive on a glorious

English summer day. 'Shall we say this afternoon, then?
Nothing else on my schedule.'

Speaking of Dads, I was thanking my own, still alive and
thriving back in Maryland, as I climbed into Cathy's Vauxhall
Corsa with . . . wait for it . . . manual transmission.

Back when I was sixteen, Dad forced me to drive stick.
'You never know when it will come in handy, Hannah.'

I'm sure he was thinking about rushing somebody to a
hospital, or moving a car, fast, out of the path of an oncoming
locomotive, or it could even come in handy should my
getaway driver accidentally lock himself in the bank vault.
But, for me the 'when' was 'now', in Devon with Cathy,
an American I had just met, taking her for a rendezvous –
of sorts – with her own father.

As she climbed into the passenger seat to my left and
buckled up, I took a moment to familiarize myself with the
controls. 'Ready?'

She nodded.

'We're off, then.' Using my left hand, I shifted into
reverse, backed out of the parking space, put the car in first
and headed for the exit on The Quay near the Flavel Arts
Centre. Fortunately, the brake and accelerator pedals are
not reversed on English cars, or I would have sent the
Vauxhall crashing through the plate glass window of the
Visitors' Center when I braked to avoid a child who darted
out from behind an SUV. After the frisky little tot had been
chased around the car park and corralled by his mother, we
continued up College Way past the Naval College to the
roundabout on the A379 where we made the turn toward
Stoke Fleming.

I was feeling pretty comfortable behind the wheel until we
got behind an articulated lorry just outside Stoke Fleming.
As the huge, double-jointed truck slowed to wind its way
through the twisting, one-lane, two-way streets of the village,
I grabbed what I thought was the gearshift and instead of
downshifting to second, rolled down my window. Next to
me, Cathy noticed and laughed out loud. 'See what I mean!'

I had to laugh, too.

Thankfully, we lost the lorry when it headed west on the road toward Bowden, Ash and Bugford. We continued along the A379 hugging the coastline. Just outside Strete, we popped over the crest of a hill to see the vast panorama of the sea spread out below us, sunlight dancing on the water like a carpet of diamonds. There was no one behind me, so I pulled to the side of the road for a moment so that Cathy could appreciate the view. 'On a clear day, you can see France,' I told my passenger.

'Is that Slapton Sands?' she asked, pointing to an expanse of beach dotted with bathers, beach chairs and umbrellas.

'Not yet. You're looking at Blackpool Sands, just north of Slapton. It's a beach club now, but this area was requisitioned during the war, too.'

After a few moments, I drove on. The road, shaded by overhanging branches, narrowed even further. I took one turn a little too fast for comfort, and Cathy yipped like a terrier as branches slapped the passenger's side door.

'Ooops, sorry,' I apologized, tapping the brakes. 'I hope I didn't scratch the paint.'

'Scratches, smatches,' Cathy said. 'That's what insurance is for.'

Eventually we popped out of the trees and over the headland, beginning the long, winding descent to Slapton Sands. Below us the sea, the beach, the road, and the Ley – a reed-dotted, freshwater lagoon – formed parallel ribbons of aquamarine, beige, slate and blue which eventually yielded to the patchwork yellows and greens of the fields in the surrounding countryside. In the bright afternoon sun, the effect was stunning. I slowed to a crawl.

Cathy rolled down her window to admire the view. 'I can see why the Allies chose this area for the rehearsal.' She propped both arms on the windowsill and rested her chin on them. 'It looks just like all the aerial photos I've ever seen of Utah Beach in France. I can't wait to walk on it.'

'Soon. But first, I want to show you the memorial.' We drove to the north end of the beach, where I swung left into the car park, slotted the rental car into one of the marked spaces, turned off the ignition, and climbed out.

Cathy followed me on to the beach. 'I thought this was supposed to be Slapton *Sands*,' she complained, tiptoeing carefully over the rocky ground in her sling-back sandals, eyes on her feet. 'This looks like gravel to me.'

'The Brits call it shingle,' I explained as she caught up to me.

Arms spread wide for balance, Cathy tottered along at my side as we made our way along the wide swath of pebbles that ranged in size from marbles to golf balls. Before long, we were standing before a chunky granite obelisk perhaps twenty feet high incised with confident black lettering.

Cathy pushed her sunglasses to the top of her head. 'This memorial was presented by the United States Army author-ities,' she read aloud, 'to the people of the South Hams who generously left their homes and their lands to provide a battle practice area for the successful assault in Normandy in June 1944. Their action resulted in the saving of many hundreds of lives. Blah blah blah. I think it's fishy,' she added, turning to face me, blinking back tears, arms folded across her chest like a petulant child. 'This ugly thing was put up in 1954, but does it mention anywhere the guys like my dad who *died* here? It does not. All these people did was lose their homes for a couple of months. It's sad that they were forced to clear out and all that, but at least they got to come back to them eventually. My dad's out there somewhere.' She swept her arm in a wide arc, indicating the fields on the hills behind us, rising up grace-fully over the Ley. 'Or maybe there,' she added, tugging her sunglasses down to cover her eyes and turning her face out to sea.

I stepped away, putting some distance between us, leaving her alone with her thoughts.

After a few minutes Cathy announced, 'I'm ready to see the tank, now.'

I fished the car keys out of my pocket. 'Let's go then.'

We crunched our way along the shingle back to the car park, then drove another five miles to Torcross at the southern end of the beach.

Finding the Sherman tank wasn't difficult. Hard to hide a thirty-two-ton hulk of metal in a tiny village. After being dragged out of the sea, the tank had been installed on a concrete slab atop a plinth of smooth round stones the size of baked potatoes. Its gun, silent now, stood frozen at a forty-five-degree angle, pointing out over the English Channel. Memorial plaques dedicated to the various military divisions who trained at Slapton Sands during World War Two were placed at various intervals around the tank.

'It's curious,' I said as I wandered about reading the inscriptions. 'You'd expect the names of the dead to be listed here, but they're not.'

'Too many names,' Cathy stated simply. 'Too many names.' As I watched, she reached into the outside pocket of her backpack and withdrew a red silk rose and a laminated four-by-five photograph. 'This is my father,' she said, handing the photo to me.

Behind the plastic, a handsome, bright-eyed sailor smiled for the camera, his Dixie Cup cap shoved to the back of his head at a jaunty, non-regulation angle. 'You favor him,' I told her as I handed the photo back. 'Especially around the eyes.'

'That's what Mom always said.' She propped both the photograph and the rose up carefully on a tread of the giant amphibious vehicle.

'It feels odd to be praying at the side of a flipping tank,' she said after a moment of respectful silence. 'Normal people have a grave they can visit. There's a space for Dad back in Pittsburgh, in Allegheny Cemetery, next to Mom.' She took a deep, shuddering breath. 'Until then, I suppose this tank will have to serve as his unofficial tombstone.'

'So,' she said after a bit, slapping her hands together in a let's-get-down-to-business way. 'Why don't you take me to the field where the bodies were buried?'

'Field? What field?'

'The one Ken Small mentions in his book. Here.' Head down, Cathy rummaged in her backpack for a moment, stopped, then raised a hand. 'Never mind, I must have left the book back at Horn Hill House. But here's the gist of

it. After the disaster, bodies began washing ashore. Hundreds
of bodies. Small says they were buried temporarily in a
field. He knew where it was, too, and so did this old farmer
he talked to.' She gazed west over the Ley, toward the
rolling green hills beyond, shading her eyes against the
brightness of the afternoon sun. 'I wonder which field it
was.'

It had been a while, but I'd read Small's book, too. 'Small
doesn't exactly say, does he? He's really rather secretive
about it. Too bad he died back in 2004, or you could ask
him.'

'Do you think that farmer he wrote about is still alive?'

'I don't know. He could be, I suppose, but since Small
never identified him . . .' I shrugged. 'What can you do?'

'I think there needs to be an investigation. I counted the
number of missing and unaccounted for. Eighty. Their bodies
have to be somewhere, Hannah! They didn't simply go
poof! Somebody *must* have seen something.'

'I'm not so sure about that, Cathy. Everyone agrees that
security was super tight back then. The Home Army kept
everyone out of the American Zone, and not even the
displaced locals knew what went on in their homes and in
their fields during the war. The US really kept the lid on.'

'I guess so,' she admitted. 'Thousands of people involved,
from Eisenhower down to the lowliest seaman, and yet they
were able to keep the screw-up that was Operation Tiger
secret for more than forty years. I'll bet that took some doing!'

I hated to mention it because she seemed so distressed,
but I wondered aloud if her father had been one of the
sailors who went down with the ship.

Cathy shook her head. 'We thought of that, but no.
Through the VFW, I was able to track down a couple of
his buddies. One of them, a guy named Jack, told me they'd
been asleep in their bunks, heard the klaxon, grabbed their
gear and were halfway up the ladder to their duty stations
when all hell broke loose. The ship was on fire, men were
screaming for their mothers, they were jumping into a sea
of burning diesel. Jack says that he and my father jumped
together, but got separated during the night in the freezing

water. Jack was picked up by a lifeboat, so Dad could have been, too. Dad could have drowned – I can concede that – but I *know* he didn't go down with the 531.'

I laid a hand on her shoulder. 'I hate to deflate your balloon, Cathy, but some people around here believe that Small made up the bit about the bodies as a publicity stunt to help drive business to his guest house.'

She ran her hand along the flank of the vehicle as if it were a prize steer. 'I don't think so. I believe it's all part of a massive cover-up.'

I'd heard anecdotal tales about bodies being unearthed while doing back garden renovations, but nobody had ever confirmed that. Alison Hamilton's father in particular had pooh-poohed the whole notion, going on and on (when Alison let him!) about the inaccuracies he'd discovered in *The Forgotten Dead*. I could tell Cathy about them now, or . . .

Looking at my new friend's hopeful face, I took the coward's way out. 'I know someone who grew up on a farm near here. Her father was one of the people evacuated back then. Stephen Bailey. He might be able to answer some of your questions.'

Cathy's face brightened like a child on Christmas morning. Santa Claus might be coming after all. 'That would be super! Would you put me in touch with him?'

'Of course.'

'How soon can you do it?' she hurried on. 'I have to fly home next Thursday.'

'I'm seeing Alison for dinner tomorrow night. I'll ask for her father's telephone number. Best if you talk to him directly.'

'I really appreciate this, Hannah.'

I didn't have the heart to tell her that I knew almost precisely what Stephen Bailey would say. If Cathy actually got to speak to him, I knew he would totally shatter her hopes.

FIVE

*'When I was a little girl, I discovered I had a gift:
communicating with those who are no longer with us.
Some people say what I do is scary. Other people say
I change their lives. I just say what I hear and see,
and I see a lot.'*

Lisa Williams, *www.lisawilliams.com*

When Alison and Jon Hamilton arrived for dinner at Horn Hill House on Thursday and we'd settled ourselves down on the sofa in Janet's cozy lounge, I asked Alison how her father was doing. I remembered Stephen Bailey as a spry, weathered man with a shock of Clintonesque white hair and hands calloused from a lifetime of farming.

Alison snorted. 'Cantankerous as always. Just celebrated his eighty-sixth, but he's still milking the cows himself every morning. He's always had help with the crops, of course. Barley mostly. Some maize.' She sighed. 'Don't know why he bothers with the bloody cows. Most of the milk comes from Holland these days.'

'That's one of the reasons we've put the farm on the market.' From behind thick lenses, Jon's smoky eyes considered me somberly.

Like a bobblehead doll, I glanced from Alison to Jon and back to Alison again in the moment it took for that news to sink in. 'Oh, Alison! I'm so sorry. That farm's been in your family for, gosh, how many years?'

'Since Cromwell's corpse was beheaded, at least that's what Granddaddy always said.'

'Which Cromwell?' I asked. 'Thomas or Oliver? There's a century difference.'

Alison made a face. 'The second one. They dug up his

body and decapitated it later. I guess they wanted to make sure the old tyrant was really dead.'

'I can't imagine your father being happy with the idea of selling.'

'Lord, no! But it was time, Hannah. He's getting too old to manage the chores on a working farm. There's Tom Boyd to help out, of course. I don't know what we'd do without Tom. Dad's been getting forgetful lately.'

'Talking him into just visiting one of those retirement communities was like pulling teeth,' Jon said.

'Practically had to kidnap him,' Alison added.

'We took him on a drive up to Coombe Hill in Dittisham,' Jon said, anticipating my next question. 'It's a historic house on Riverside Road, not far from the town center. They converted it into thirty-six one-bedroom flats. Nicer than most.'

'Dad wasn't very keen, at least not at first.'

Jon caught my eye and winked, then grinned at his wife. 'And that extremely attractive widow who conducted the tour? I don't suppose *she* had anything to do with your father's sudden about-face?'

Alison looked at her husband sideways, through her lashes. 'I think it was the fact that they'll let him keep his cat.' She waved a dismissive hand. 'Anyway, once we were over that hurdle, and he actually agreed to help assemble the Home Information Pack, it was smoother sailing.'

'With a few squalls,' Jon added, sipping his wine. 'Stephen complained that he wasn't one of those white-shorted, tennis-playing types that they seem so fond of featuring on all the brochures. He's afraid he won't fit in.'

Alison snorted. 'Did *you* see any tennis courts at Coombe Hill? Of course, he'll fit in,' she continued, without waiting for an answer. 'I'm more worried about getting him to keep the house tidy for viewings. With Jon busy teaching, that falls to me, of course, and frankly, I'm exhausted.'

'Any interest in the property yet?' Paul asked.

'We had an offer early on, but Dad turned it down.'

'The estate agent is advising him to lower the asking price, the economy being what it is . . .' Jon let the sentence die. 'But Alison's father is a stubborn old goat and we feel we can push him only so far.'

'Doesn't sound like he's serious about selling,' Paul commented.

Alison scowled. 'And he won't sell, either, if he can't keep his dirty clothing picked up off the floor when he has viewings.'

While Janet puttered about in the kitchen putting finishing touches on the hors d'oeuvres, refusing all offers of assistance, and Alison and I waited for our husbands to reappear from the wine cellar where they were consulting with Alan on the wines to be served with dinner that evening, I filled Alison in on my trip to Slapton Sands with Cathy Yates. 'She says her father's body is not at Brookwood Cemetery in Surrey, nor at Madingly near Cambridge, so she's convinced herself that he's lying in an unmarked grave somewhere in Devon, along with hundreds of others.'

Alison heaved a long-suffering sigh, filled with exasperation. 'We've heard those rumors for years, and there's not a bit of truth in them, yet Americans keep reading that damn book, coming over here, tramping all over our fields, looking for the ruins of those bomb shelters Ken Small claims he saw. If the man were still alive, I swear to God I'd strangle him. I wasn't born until after the war, of course, but as far as I know, there were no air-raid shelters out here in the countryside. Nobody considered us a target-rich environment, for one thing. Philips' Shipyard up at Noss, sure, but not South Hams. The Naval College was bombed, as you know, but everyone seems to think that was more of an accident. Some German pilot jettisoning a couple of surplus bombs on his way back to France.'

'Would your dad be willing to talk to Cathy about the war? Set her straight? I sort of volunteered him, I'm afraid.'

'He'll be flattered to be asked, but from what you say, she's not going to be easily swayed.'

'She's a Duracell bunny, that's for sure. Indefatigable. Bears more than a passing resemblance to Ken Small's Sherman tank, too, if you want to know the truth.'

'Is Cathy joining us for dinner tonight, then?'

'No.' I grinned. 'She was having a Big Mac attack, so
she went off in search of the golden arches. I didn't have
the heart to tell her that the nearest McDonald's is in
Torquay!'

Alison rolled her eyes. 'And thank heaven for that! So,
who else is coming, then?'

'Didn't Janet tell you?'

Alison considered me over the rim of her sherry glass,
shook her head. 'Maybe it's a surprise? Prince Charles,
perhaps? Sting? Sir Paul?' She flapped a hand. 'Be still my
heart.'

I laughed. 'No, but she *is* a television personality. Have
you ever heard of Susan Parker?'

Alison had relaxed into the cushions, but at the mention
of Susan Parker's name, she snapped to attention so quickly
that a bit of her wine sloshed on to the upholstery. 'Susan
Parker? The medium?' She dabbed frantically at the wet
spot on the cushion with her cocktail napkin.

'That's right.' I explained about my strange encounter
with Susan on the street earlier in the week. 'Turns out
she's a friend of Janet and Alan's.'

'I can't believe this. I love her show! I record every
episode!' She set her wine glass down on the end table and
leaned forward, hands resting on her knees. 'One of her
shows was taped at the Naval College, did you know that?'

'No kidding!'

'You have *got* to see it! The woman is incredible.' Alison
slapped her chest with the flat of her hand as if trying to
jumpstart her heart. 'I can not *believe* that she's coming
here for dinner! Maybe I've died and gone to heaven.'

'Not yet, I hope. Good friends like you are hard to find.
But when you do pass on, Susan'll be able to talk to you.'

'Very funny, Hannah.'

We were giggling like schoolgirls when Janet breezed
into the lounge carrying a platter of broiled mushroom caps.
'Susan just phoned and said she'd be a few minutes late,
but there's no reason to hold off on these. Careful. They're
hot.'

I stabbed one of the mushrooms with a toothpick, waved

it briefly in the air to cool it, then popped it into my mouth. Flavors exploded gloriously over my tongue – goat cheese, basil and another ingredient I couldn't immediately identify. When the platter came back in my direction, I skewered another mushroom, chewed thoughtfully – for research, of course – and was able to put a name to it – kalamata olives. 'These are *so* good,' I moaned.

'Dead easy, too,' Janet said. 'The recipe calls for pine nuts, but I'm not overly fond of pine nuts, so I leave them out.'

'Fine with me. Pine nuts leave a metallic taste in my mouth,' Alison said as she polished off another one of the hors d'oeuvres.

I speared a third. 'You, too? I thought I was the only person in the world to suffer from a pine mouth affliction. Weird. Last time I ate pesto, it took me two weeks to get my taste buds back in order. One thing a person definitely needs while staying with you, Janet, is taste buds in proper working condition.'

'Ooops! There's the bell.' Janet set the tray of mushrooms on the coffee table and hurried to answer the door.

When she returned to the sitting room with Susan Parker in tow, I was amused to see that the guest of honor and I had dressed in almost identical, loose-fitting linen dresses from Flax, except hers was lavender and mine was rose.

'So, you are a psychic!' I said, indicating our matching outfits.

'No, not a psychic,' Susan replied with a grin, shaking my hand. 'Psychics can see into the future. I've never been able to do that. I don't dream about fiery plane crashes, then rush off to Heathrow to start warning people not to take off on flight number whatever to Los Angeles, thank God. Think what a terrible responsibility that would be!'

Alison had captured Susan's hand and was holding on to it with both of hers. 'She's clairvoyant. She sees things other people can't. Like dead people.'

Susan extracted her hand, set her handbag down on the sofa and plopped down next to it. 'Thank you. And the medium part means I serve as a go-between, bringing messages to the living from spirits on the other side.'

I felt a chill crawl up my spine. 'Like my mother.'

'Precisely.' She might have elaborated, but I'll never know because we were rudely interrupted by the return from the cellar of the 'boys', bearing half a dozen bottles of wine, each covered with a dusting of gray. 'Here we go, ladies,' announced Alan, carrot-topped, freckle-faced leader of the pack, as they jostled one another, tumbling into the sitting room like eager puppies. 'Oh, Susan, you're here!' Alan tucked the bottle of Bordeaux he was holding under his left arm and shook the medium's hand. 'I'd like you to meet Hannah's husband, Paul. And this reprobate over here, the studious-looking chap cradling the Chateau Macquin St George, is Jon Hamilton. He belongs to Alison.'

Susan shook Paul's hand, then Jon's, holding on to it – or so it seemed to me – a bit longer than necessary upon meeting someone for the first time. She glanced from Jon to Alison and said, 'Excuse me for asking, but this isn't your first marriage, is it?'

Jon fumbled the bottle he was carrying, nearly dropping it, but he recovered quickly. 'Ah, no.'

Alison tripped across the carpet to join her husband, slipped an arm through his, squeezing tight, standing in we'll-get-through-this-together solidarity. 'Jon's first wife died more than a decade ago in a sailing accident.'

Susan cocked her head. 'I'm seeing a B. Bonnie? Barbara? Bess?'

'Beth!' Alison bounced up and down on her toes. 'Jon's first wife was named Beth!'

'Beth.' Susan stood quietly for a few seconds. 'Beth. That's right. I'm feeling . . . Oh, my gosh!' Susan's hand shot to the back of her head. 'I'm feeling pain here.' She massaged the spot vigorously, then pressed her hand against her temple. 'And here.' To Jon she said, 'Is that significant?'

'I . . . I don't know,' he stammered, the scalp under his pale hair turning pink. '*Biding Thyme* washed up on the rocks near Stumpy Steps with her sails still set. Beth's body was never found. The River Dart can be unforgiving.'

Behind me, Janet clucked her tongue and muttered, 'Every
year, the Dart takes a heart. That's what they say.'

A tremor shook Susan's body. She shrugged it off, then
turned to face the rest of us, hands raised in apology. 'Poof!
Sorry. Gone. *Do* forgive me. It's sometimes hard to turn
the voices off. That's why I plug myself into my iPod whenever I drive or walk the dog.'

'Ever try a tinfoil hat?' Paul wondered aloud.

I found my husband's foot and mashed down on it, hard.
'You promised to behave,' I hissed.

Susan dissolved into peals of laughter. 'Hannah, your
husband is a *hoot!*'

I shot said husband the evil eye. 'Oh, he's a laugh a
minute, all right!'

'Well,' Janet announced from the doorway. 'Now that
we've got that all settled, I wonder if you'd like to move
into the dining room. Dinner, as they say, is served.'

As I followed our hostess into the dining room, my
stomach clenched. Alison Hamilton and I were supposed
to be friends. But this was the first I'd heard of a previous
Mrs Hamilton.

At my house, you're lucky to get a salad accompanying
your casserole or one-skillet meal, but things were different
at Horn Hill House. I'd just polished off my starter of
smoked salmon and quail eggs and was buttering a fresh-
baked roll, when the conversation took a hard right turn.
Away from the Devon weather – if you don't like it, wait
a few minutes – to something even more interesting than
wondering about Jon's marital history.

'How long have you known each other?' Paul asked Janet,
his eyes ping-ponging between our hostess on his left and
Susan Parker across the table.

Susan laid down her fish knife. 'Janet, haven't you told
them how we met?'

Janet blushed. 'I didn't want to scare them off.'

Paul looked puzzled. 'Why would we be scared off?'

'It's a long story.' Janet stood, pushed her chair back. As
she circled the table collecting our empty plates she said,

'Why don't you tell them, Alan, while I go and fetch the main course.'

Like spectators at a tennis match, all heads swiveled obediently in Alan's direction. He squirmed in his chair.

Paul tipped his wine glass at our host. 'Yes, Alan. Do tell.'

Alan took a fortifying sip of a fine Sancerre. 'It goes back to when the twins were born,' he began.

I remembered that the twins, Samantha and Victoria, were around six years old and did the math. 'So, 2004?'

'Yes, that's right. The girls were delivered at Torbay Hospital in Torquay and everything was fine until we brought them home.'

'The girls were ill?'

'No, no, the babies were fine,' Janet interjected from the kitchen. A second later she appeared carrying three fully loaded dinner plates, one in each hand, and a third balanced on her left forearm. 'Once we got the girls home, though, the strangest things began happening.' As Alan helped pass the dinner plates around, Janet continued. 'It was little things at first. After their two a. m. nursing, I'd put the girls down in their cots and go back to bed.'

'They had separate cots,' Alan added. 'That'll be important later.'

'I'd just get back to sleep when Victoria would start to fuss. I'd ignore it, and then Samantha would chime in. So I'd go up, burp them, check their nappies, get them settled. Up and down, up and down, sometimes it seemed I was awake all night. Excuse me for a minute while I get the rest of your dinners.'

It sounded like new-motherhood-business-as-usual to me, but I figured Alan would get around to the 'strange' part eventually.

'Janet was breastfeeding, so by the end of the second week, she was exhausted,' Alan went on. 'So one night when they started fussing I told her, "They're fed, they're dry, ignore them. The girls will go to sleep eventually." But she was a new mother, and worried over every little thing.'

'As one should do,' Alison chimed in.

'*Exactly* as one should do,' echoed Janet, reappearing with the four remaining plates. She set one down in front of me and I nearly swooned: lamb with leeks and ginger. The aroma was intoxicating.

Janet reclaimed her seat at the head of the table, picked up her knife and fork and indicated that we should all do the same. 'One night, though, I was so tired that when Victoria started tuning up, I decided to stay in bed and see how long she'd cry. Five minutes? Ten? An hour? After three minutes Samantha had joined the chorus and I was crazy to get out of bed, but Alan held me back. "Do you hear that?" he asked me, and he started squeezing my arm. "What?" I snapped. "All I hear is babies screaming."'

'What I heard was singing,' Alan explained.

Janet paused, a fork full of lamb halfway to her mouth. 'I didn't hear anything, but after a minute or two Victoria stopped crying and seconds later, Samantha did, too.'

'Somebody was singing a lullaby, very softly,' Alan whispered. '"Sweet and low, sweet and low, wind of the western sea,"' he crooned in a gravelly baritone.

'Thank you, Luciano!' Janet raised a hand, cutting her husband off before he could reach the second stanza. 'I never heard the lullaby myself, regrettably, but soon enough, other weird things began to happen. Victoria's cuddly lamb would end up in Samantha's cot, and Sam's cuddly bear would be in Vicky's. I thought I was losing my mind. One day when I put the girls down for their nap, it was a little warm in the nursery, so I didn't swaddle them in blankets like I usually did. When I came back to check up on them, though, both the girls were tucked in. Alan was always so good with the girls that I accused him of doing it.'

Alan raised an honest-injun hand. 'Not I.'

'He didn't believe me at first.'

'Quite true. I'd read about post-partum depression and, just between us, I thought the old girl was losing her grip.'

Jon swiped at the strand of corn silk that insisted on flopping over his left eye no matter how many haircare products he used. 'Post-partum depression has been known to cause hallucinations and delusions.'

'Perfectly true,' Alan agreed. 'So I arranged some little experiments. I'd leave their booties untied; they'd somehow get tied.'

'One day I left Vicky's dummy on the dresser, and when I came back half an hour later, I found Vicky happily sucking on it,' Janet added.

'And every once in a while, late at night, I'd hear someone singing that lullaby again.' Alan picked up a bowl of oven-roasted potatoes, spooned a couple on to his plate, then passed the bowl to me. 'We came to the conclusion that our house was haunted, but it was such a gentle spirit that we started calling her the Child Minder.'

'Runner beans?' Janet asked, sending the vegetable bowl on a circuit around the table. 'One afternoon I mentioned the Child Minder to a friend at St Saviour's Church and right away, she introduced me to Susan.'

'I was new to the community, then,' Susan said, flushing modestly. 'Word hadn't gotten around about my special gift. Believe it or not, I'm really rather shy!'

'No walking up to strangers in the street?' I teased.

'Exactly. That came later.'

'Anyway,' Janet continued, 'this friend suggested that Susan might be able to communicate with our spirit, find out why she was hanging around the house. Our dream was to open a bed and breakfast, but we didn't think a resident ghost would appeal to the kind of clientele we hoped to attract.'

'I'm not so sure about that,' Paul commented. 'Horn Hill House could be a stop on the Haunted Dartmouth Tour.'

Alan frowned, Paul's lame joke falling flat. 'We really didn't think it would be good for business.'

At the other end of the table, Janet's head bobbed emphatically. 'So, to make a long story short, we invited Susan for tea without telling her anything about our "little problem".' She drew quote marks in the air. 'We walked her all around the house. Ground floor, nothing. First floor – that's where Alan and I had our bedroom at the time – nothing. But when she got to the nursery!' Janet pressed a hand to her mouth, overcome with emotion, as if the day were happening all over again.

Susan laid a comforting hand on Janet's shoulder. 'I'll take the story from here if you like.'

Janet nodded. I thought she was about to cry.

'Almost immediately,' Susan began, 'I sensed a strong female presence in the nursery. So I sat down in the rocking chair and waited. Gradually, the presence revealed herself. I got the impression of someone white-haired and fragile. She told me her name was Eleanor, and that she was there to look after the babies.'

'We knew the history of the house,' Alan interrupted, 'so I informed Susan that I was positive that in all its one hundred plus years, nobody by the name of Eleanor had ever lived here.'

Susan leaned forward. 'And Eleanor must have been listening, because she spoke right up to explain. She told me that she came home from the hospital with the babies.'

Alison's eyes sparkled in the candlelight. 'How spooky!'

'When I asked her why she wanted to stay with the babies,' Susan continued, 'Eleanor told me that she was a widow. Her only daughter had died childless so she never had any grandbabies. When Samantha and Victoria were born, she simply decided to go home with them.'

'But this is fascinating, Janet,' I said, turning to face our hostess. 'Why didn't you tell me about Eleanor the other day when I told you about meeting Susan in Foss Street?'

Janet flushed. 'I didn't want to frighten you away, Hannah.'

'Why would I have been frightened away?'

Janet stole a quick glance at her husband, then looked back to me. 'Because the room that you and Paul are staying in used to be the nursery.'

I have to admit that I felt a shiver begin at the base of my spine, but another fortifying sip of wine kept it at bay. 'Is she still there?' I whispered.

'Eleanor? No,' Susan answered. 'Eleanor explained that she worried when the mother – that would be you, Janet – let the poor babes go on crying for hours and hours.'

'Two minutes!' Janet sputtered. 'Imagine being criticized by a ghost.'

Susan chuckled. 'Spirits have their own timetables, dear. Anyway, after I explained that Janet was a good mother, and that recommended child-rearing techniques had changed a lot since her day, Eleanor agreed to go.'

'Then Susan lit a candle, waved some rosemary about, and that was that,' Alan added.

'Woo-woo.' Jon waggled his fingers.

Rather than take offense, Susan shot a benevolent smile in Jon's direction. 'I probably shouldn't admit this, but I feel I'm in safe company. Lighting an aromatic candle and waving a bundle of herbs through the smoke doesn't actually *do* anything, Jon, but it makes the client feel good because it's something they can *see*. Mostly I simply reassure the spirit that all is well, pass on any messages the spirit may have for the living, and make sure they can both rest easy. Laying spirits to rest is one of the most popular segments of my television show.'

'I just *love* your show,' Alison gushed. 'I'd *love* to attend some time.'

'As a matter of fact,' Susan said, reaching down for her handbag, 'I'll be taping a live broadcast at the Palace Theatre in Paignton on Wednesday night.'

'Paignton! That's just twenty miles from here!'

'It's sold out, I'm afraid, but if you call this number . . .' She located her business cards and handed one across the table to Alison. 'There's always the possibility of a cancellation. Here's a card for you, too, Hannah,' Susan said, peeling another one from the pack.

The card was elegantly simple, printed on cream-colored stock: *Dead Reckoning*, website URL and telephone number, that's all. No crystal ball graphics, no freephone numbers to psychic hotlines.

'I'll call first thing in the morning!' Alison tucked the card into her pocket and patted it for security.

Paul leaned across the table. 'Susan, I hope you don't think I'm being impertinent, but do you mind if I ask you a question? Do you have a code word?'

Susan paused in the act of returning her business cards to her handbag. 'Code word?'

'Like Houdini. He promised his friends that when he died, he would try to communicate with them from the other side. I understand they had a prearranged code so that if a message came to them from the Great Beyond, they would know it was really Houdini speaking.'

Susan's smiled seemed a tad forced. 'The spirits I talk to don't speak in code, Paul, but if I had to pick a word, it would be Basingstoke.'

'Basingstoke!' Alison clapped her hands. 'How delightful!'

Jon was the only one around the table who looked confused.

'It's a town in Hampshire, darling. But that's not the delightful part. Tell him, Susan.'

'It's from Gilbert and Sullivan's operetta, *Ruddigore*,' Susan explained. 'Mad Margaret keeps lapsing into hysteria, so she and Sir Despard Murgatroyd hit upon using the word Basingstoke to calm her down whenever she goes off on a wild tangent.'

'*Poor child, she wanders*,' Paul quoted airily, having seen the production half a dozen times. '*Margaret, if you don't Basingstoke at once, I shall be seriously angry.*'

I looked at my husband and grinned. 'Basingstoke it is.'

'How do you know Susan's not making it all up?' Paul asked Alan in an aside after Susan trailed off into the kitchen after Janet to help her get the dessert together – summer pudding with red fruits, as it would turn out. Paul wore skepticism on his face like a badge, but what Alan said next shut my husband's I-told-you-so mouth right up.

'That's the astonishing part,' Alan whispered. 'Susan could have had no idea on what day our girls were born, yet when I had a friend check the death census at Torbay Hospital for January the third, there were only two names on it. A Henry Thomas, twenty-seven, who died in a road accident, and Eleanor Swindon, widow, age eighty-two.'

SIX

'We went into the field and walked some 60 to 80 yards. Then he said beneath where we were standing there were two brick and concrete air-raid shelters with steps leading down to them. The bodies were in those shelters and the steps had been blown up to seal them off.'

Ken Small, *The Forgotten Dead*,
Bloomsbury, 1989, p. 209

Eleanor Swindon's ghost may have moved on to a happier afterlife, but Cathy Yates clung like my shadow, dogging my trail all day Friday, the day Paul and Alan had set aside for a bike ride to Kingsbridge along the coastal road. With the guys out of my hair, I'd planned a solitary pilgrimage to Greenway House, Agatha Christie's home, recently opened to the public by the National Trust following a multi-million-pound renovation.

I slipped away from Horn Hill House shortly after breakfast and was standing in a short queue at the Greenway Ferry kiosk at the Dartmouth boat float pawing through my change purse muttering *I know I have something smaller than a twenty*, when Cathy materialized at my elbow, waving a ten-pound note and asking, 'Do you mind if I tag along?'

I did, but Britain, like America, was a free country, and even though it was the height of tourist season, there turned out to be plenty of room aboard the *Dartmouth Belle*.

The *Belle*, I noticed immediately upon stepping aboard, was my kind of boat. It boasted a full-service bar, with bottles of booze suspended upside down in some sort of rack-and-pour dispensing system. Alas, the bar was closed, or I might have ordered a G&T. Cathy had scheduled an appointment with Stephen Bailey at his daughter's house on the following day, so she was in high gear, chattering away in anticipation of the meeting like a sewing machine gone berserk. A G&T would have helped, especially if I poured it down *her* throat.

After a leisurely cruise up the River Dart, Cathy and I disembarked, then wound our way together up a sun-dappled forest trail to the estate proper. While we waited for the clock to tick over to the time stamped on our admission tickets, I showed her around Agatha's garden, the same garden where Amyas Crayle drank a fatal glass of beer in *Five Little Pigs*. Then we wandered down to the pictur- esque Victorian boathouse where poor Marlene Tucker was strangled in *Dead Man's Folly*. Cathy confessed to having seen the DVD of *Murder on the Orient Express*, but had never found the novelist's books 'engrossing'. When she told me she was partial to Patricia Cornwell and Danielle Steele, I bit my tongue and reserved comment.

The highlight of the garden tour for Cathy was a cluster of small gravestones in a fern-shaded rockery, the ceme- tery where the family pets had been buried. 'H, E double toothpicks,' she murmured. 'Even the pets have graves.'

I didn't need Susan Parker at my side to tell me what Cathy was thinking.

Christie's house itself is Georgian, the color of clotted cream, set on several hundred acres of lawns and gardens that sweep down to the river. It was the 'perfect house' where Christie spent every summer from the time she bought it in 1938 until her death in 1976. Due to the generosity of Christie's grandson, Matthew, we found the house just the way the family left it – hats, canes and umbrellas stacked on a table in the hallway, Agatha's favorite serving dishes laid out on the dining-room sideboard, a book resting on a table in the library, bookmarked by reading glasses.

Thankfully, no docents dressed as Miss Marple or Hercule Poirot were hovering in the doorways to spin implausible tales for the curious visitor about bodies in the library or corpses in the studded leather Baghdad chest, just there, in the hall! No velvet ropes kept us back. We were able to wander the house freely, as if we were Agatha's guests and she'd just stepped out to the shops for a moment. I wanted to leave Cathy to poke around by herself in the gift shop, park myself in the wingback chair by the window and re-read each of Dame Agatha's novels in chronological order, calling on the butler at regular intervals to fetch me sustaining cups of tea.

The following day, 'The Hannah and Cathy Show' continued with Cathy's planned interview with Stephen Bailey at his daughter's home on Waterpool Road, a short uphill walk from our B&B.

Alison answered our knock. 'Dad's in the conservatory, but I should warn you that he's in a bit of a snit. Some American just made a cheeky offer for the farm. He's rejected it out of hand, of course,' she said, leading us down a long hall toward the back of the house. 'Since the evacuation, Dad doesn't think very highly of Yanks, Cathy, so you've been warned.'

The hallway opened into a bright conservatory. At the far end, a pair of glass doors stood open, admitting a delightful morning breeze. The doors led to a manicured rose garden, my friend Alison's pride and joy. Just beyond the roses, tiered planters held neat rows of rocket – arugula to us Yanks – and other lettuces. Tomato plants thrived on trellises ranged along the north wall.

Stephen Bailey, dressed in khakis and a light blue, open-necked shirt, was holding court in an elaborate rattan chair, like the Raj. Cathy and I sat on the flowered chintz sofa opposite him while Alison, at her father's request, went to check on the tea.

Cathy got right to the point. 'Thank you for seeing me, Mr Bailey. I really appreciate it. Did your daughter tell you that I'm trying to locate my father?'

Bailey nodded. 'She did. Don't know if I'll be able to help you or not, Miss Yates.'

'It's actually Hannah's idea. She suggested that you might be able to tell me the real story of Slapton Sands.'

'Don't know as anyone's got the whole story.' Bailey

clicked his tongue. 'All I can tell you is that it isn't in any book *I've* ever read. Take that Sherman tank you saw the other day, for example. A fine memorial to some fine young men, to be sure, but it wasn't lost during Operation Tiger like everyone thinks.'

Cathy's eyebrows disappeared under her bangs. 'It wasn't?'

That was news to me, too.

The hint of a smile transformed Bailey's face. 'I know this chap, a senior guide at the Brixton Battery. Gives lectures from time to time. The way he tells it, on the sixtieth anniversary of D-Day, he went down to the tank for the big celebration and ran into a group of four Yanks – uh, beg your pardon, US soldiers. Old blokes, they were, wearing hats and medals.' He leaned forward, forearms resting on his knees. 'Do you know what connected them?'

Cathy shook her head, lips compressed into a thin line.

'Believe it or not, they were the survivors of that very tank's crew!'

'Well, God Bless America!' Cathy exclaimed.

If Bailey was perturbed by this outburst, he was careful to hide it. 'So my friend from Brixton, he asks 'em, "How did you lose this tank, anyway?" And do you know what they said?'

Cathy and I shook our heads.

'"Driver error," they say! Hah!' He slapped his knee, enjoying the joke. 'Apparently they were transferring the tank from an LST to a barge. *Backing* it on to the barge, if you please. One of the tracks ran off the edge of the ramp and the tank simply toppled into the sea. Sank like a stone, it did, but the driver managed to escape.'

Cathy frowned. 'Didn't I read that the tank at Slapton Sands was one of those swimming tanks? You can still see the gear boxes and the propellers. Wouldn't it float?'

'Not with the hatches wide open, it couldn't. Hah!'

'That's interesting, sir, and I'm glad the crew survived and all, but I'm wondering if you can tell me a bit more about the bodies?'

'I'd be lying to you if I said nobody was killed at Slapton

Sands, Miss Yates, but that was a day earlier, before the
sub attacks, when the operation began and soldiers stormed
the beach. They were using live ammunition, don't forget.
Some of the soldiers . . . well, I guess they forgot to duck.'
    'Cathy's father was aboard one of the doomed LSTs,' I
told him.
    'Hannah's right, sir. Number five three one.'
    Bailey nodded sagely. 'Well, then. His body would never
have washed ashore at Slapton Sands. None of 'em did.'
    'What?' Cathy and I said in unison.
    'God's truth, ladies. When it was attacked by the German
E-boats, that convoy was in Lyme Bay, twelve miles west-
southwest of Portland. It was a major disaster, all right, but
when those LSTs went down and the bodies floated ashore,
they floated ashore at Chesil Beach in Dorset.
    'Some never came ashore, I'm sorry to say. The current's
strong in the bay. Carried many of 'em up the English
Channel where they were never seen again.'
    'But what about the bodies that *did* float ashore? What
happened to them?'
    'It took the Yanks eight days, but I can tell you on good
authority that every body that washed ashore was accounted
for. *Had* to be. Do you want to know why?' His eyes twinkled mischievously.
    Cathy nodded like a five-year-old at story hour, enrapt.
    'Ten of the missing men carried top-secret maps with
details of the invasion. Until those maps were recovered,
D-Day would be off.'
    Cathy took a deep breath. 'Since the invasion went
forward, they must have . . .'
    Bailey leaned forward, cutting her off. 'All present and
accounted for. The Americans had this burial regiment, you
see. Efficient blokes. They loaded all the bodies into lorries
and carried them to a cemetery in West London. Later, the
bodies were moved to Cambridge.'
    Tears filled Cathy's eyes. 'Were there any survivors, Mr
Bailey?'
    'More than three hundred, I'd say. Every available boat
in Portland, Weymouth and West Bay went out to help pick

up survivors. Horribly burned they were, suffering from hypothermia, too.'

I shivered. 'What happened to them?'

'They were taken to hospitals all over the United Kingdom. Split up, kept out of contact with their families and with each other for more than five weeks. Locked up, some of them. Guarded twenty-four-seven. You know why, don't you?'

Cathy was a quick study. 'They had to protect the secret of the D-Day invasion.'

Bailey leaned back, folded his arms across his chest. 'Exactly.'

'I have this fantasy that my father survived,' Cathy said, clearly grasping at straws. 'Maybe he lost his dog tags when he jumped overboard. Maybe he was injured, suffering from amnesia.'

'Frankly, Miss Yates, if your father was not accounted for at Chesil Beach, or listed among the survivors, most likely he floated out to sea. I'm sorry, but that's the way it was.'

'Missing in action. I know.' Cathy sat silently for a moment, staring out the window where a sparrow was busily scattering seeds about the base of a feeder. 'But you can't be sure, can you? You didn't actually *see* it.'

'No. At the time, I was only seventeen. My family had been evacuated to a farm near Dittisham.'

'Weren't you ever curious what was happening to your farm, Mr Bailey? Didn't you sneak back just to have a look?'

'Dad and I wanted to, but American security was too tight. Even the Home Guard weren't allowed into the American Zone, although they patrolled the roads that led up to it.'

Cathy puffed air out through her lips. 'And we should believe what the government tells us – why?'

'There's no denying that there was a cover-up, but surely you can understand why.'

'Then? Sure. But now? So long after D-Day? There can't be any good reason to keep the details secret now!' Cathy closed her eyes, massaged the bridge of her nose with two fingers. 'Some of those soldiers and sailors are shriveled up old men now, dying of emphysema in VA hospitals,' she said at last. 'Death's knocking at the door and they're *still* covering their patooties.'

Somewhere deep within the house, a telephone rang, filling a sudden silence. We hadn't laid eyes on Jon as yet, but he must have answered the call because he appeared at the door of the conservatory after a few minutes, waving a portable handset and asking, 'Hannah, can you spare Paul for a few days?'

'The last time you asked me that question, Jon, Paul ended up helping you build the very conservatory in which we are presently sitting.'

Jon beamed. 'And a fine job it was, too. No, I entered my boat in the races at Cowes, and I need a grinder. I have a six-man crew, but one chap just dropped out.'

Grinders, I knew, worked in pairs, cranking sheets – ropes to you landlubbers – on a variety of winches to help shape the sails in coordination with other guys called trimmers. Grinding was not for the flabby, and Paul, still lean and mean at the ripe old age of . . . well, never mind . . . would be good at it.

'Unless I miss my guess, Captain, Cowes Race Week begins this Saturday, as in just a week from today.'

'Short notice, I know.' He flashed a toothy, apologetic grin.

I gave Jon Paul's cell phone number and resigned myself to a week of temporary widowhood. Cowes Race Week – unfolding on the waters of the Solent between the south coast of England and the Isle of Wight – was huge in sailing circles, and because of the area's strong double tides, exciting. There was no way Paul, an experienced sailor, was going to say no to the opportunity of joining a team, even if he had to be a lowly grinder rather than, say, a navigator or tactician.

'What boat are you racing, Jon?'

'You know the boat, Hannah. *Biding Thyme*. A Contessa Thirty-Two.'

Egad! *Biding Thyme* was the same Contessa 32 that Beth
Hamilton had been last seen sailing. If Paul had died aboard
that stupid boat I'd have put it on the market so fast it
would have made his head spin. In the afterlife, of course.
'Alison!' Stephen Bailey bellowed after Jon had disappeared, presumably to telephone Paul. 'What's happened
to my tea, girl?'

Cathy took this as a sign that her interview with Stephen
Bailey was over. 'Well, I have to be going,' she said, gathering up her sweater and handbag. 'Thanks so much for
your help, Mr Bailey. I really, really appreciate it.'

Before her father could answer, Alison interrupted,
breezing into the room carrying a tray laden with the where-
withal for tea. 'Won't you stay for tea, Cathy?'

'Thank you, but no, Mrs Hamilton, I've got to be going.
I have an appointment with a woman from BASH and if I
don't hurry, I'll be late. Do you know her? Lilith Price?'

Stephen Bailey grunted, which Cathy took for a no. 'She
was twelve years old during the American occupation of
South Hams,' Cathy explained, 'so I'm going to talk to her
about what it was like when the Americans were billeted
here.'

BASH I knew, was the Blackawton and Strete History
Group. They'd published several illustrated booklets that
made interesting reading even if you weren't a World War
Two history buff.

Stephen Bailey struggled to his feet, reached into his
breast pocket and drew out a folded piece of paper. 'Here's
the number of that fellow in Brixton. Perhaps he'll be of
some use to you.'

Cathy accepted the paper and tucked it into her handbag.
'Thanks ever so.'

While Alison busied herself with the tea, I walked Cathy
to the door. 'See you back at the B&B?'

She tapped her temple in salute. 'You betcha!'

'And good hunting with BASH,' I called after her has
she headed down the walk.

Cathy smiled and waved. 'Your mouth to God's ears.'

SEVEN

'Having left the mess room I called into the "ladies room" in the main corridor opposite the main entrance to the college. On my way out I passed the time of day to a Petty Officer Wren. The first bomb dropped . . . on B block and the quarter deck . . . and [I learned that] the Wren that I had just spoken to had been killed. This greatly upset and distressed me, but in wartime all we kept saying and singing was, "There'll always be an England."'
Joyce Corder, *Memories of War by Local People at Home and Abroad, 1939–1946,* Dartmouth History Research Group, Paper 16, 1995, pp. 5–6

'**G**ood. You're back. Tea's getting cold.' Alison indicated a cup of milky brew, clearly intended for me, quietly steaming on the coffee table in front of the chair I'd recently vacated.

Adding milk to tea was practically automatic, as English as fish and chips or bangers and mash. I was a little surprised that Alison hadn't remembered that I drank my tea black, but decided what the hell, I'd drink it anyway. I sipped and swallowed, trying not to make a face. 'Where's your dad?'

'Jon's driving him to the garage to pick up his car. It's having a dent in the bonnet repaired. Wasn't paying attention and drove right under a turnstile without waiting for the arm to go up. Brand new car, too.' She sighed. 'One of these days, Hannah, we're going to have to take away Dad's car keys. I don't want to think about it.

'I thought this would be a good time to show you that video of *Dead Reckoning,*' she continued, promptly changing the subject. 'Dad wasn't keen to stick around for that, anyway. The way he scarpered out of here you'd think

I was going to handcuff him to the chair and force him to watch home movies of the Big Switch On at Blackpool.'
'A million bulbs? Six miles of the Promenade lit up like Las Vegas on steroids?' I grinned. 'Frankly, I'd find that irresistible.'

Carrying our cups, we moved to the lounge and settled down in comfortable chairs arranged in front of Alison's flat-screen television. Floor-to-ceiling bookshelves flanked the screen. One held an impressive array of electronics – a DVD player, a Sky+ box, even a hunk of metal and plastic that I recognized as an obsolete Betamax machine. The other held what must have been the world's largest collection of DVDs, including boxed sets of several long-running television series.

Alison aimed the controller at the Sky+, pressed play, and fast-forwarded through the advertisements to get to the opening of Susan's show.

'What made Susan decide to take her show to Britannia Royal Naval College?' I asked as a man and a woman raced down a beach in fast-forward, whatever romantic issues they had been having completely resolved by some product in a green box that flashed briefly on the screen.

'One of her producers has a son who attended the college. Apparently the young man found the place a bit creepy at times. He mentioned this to his father, who suggested to Susan that she have a look see.'

'How on earth did Susan get permission to film there?' I eased off my shoes and got comfortable on the sofa, tucking my feet underneath me. 'During our time in Dartmouth, even major movie companies were routinely turned down.'

Alison grinned. 'Not turned down, exactly. The Navy charges a hefty fee for permission to film at the college. Or so Jon says. Obviously Susan has deep pockets.' She stabbed a button on the controller, freezing the program at the opening credits, plump text morphing into clouds that flitted in Casper the Friendly Ghost-like fashion across the screen.

'They probably made arrangements through the public

affairs officer in Portsmouth. He showed up, anyway. You'll
see him among the official party, along with Richard Porter.
You remember Richard?'

'I do. The college historian. When we first came to
Dartmouth, he was kind enough to give Paul and me a
private tour.'

I remembered the tour well. I'd been stunned by the
beauty of the campus, sprawled across a hill overlooking
the Dart, dominating the town. Both BRNC and the US
Naval Academy had been designed by prominent architects.
Both had been built in the first decade of the twentieth
century, with careful attention to form and function. BRNC
was smaller in scale than USNA, of course, reflecting the
size of their respective Navies, but I'd felt instantly at home.

On the TV screen, Susan Parker – dressed in a gray skirt,
white shirt and pale pink jacket – stood chatting in front of
the main gate of the college with a man I recognized as
Richard Porter, chestnut hair neatly combed, handsomely
turned out in a dark blue pinstripe suit. A scarlet tie was
knotted around his neck. 'Thank you for inviting me, Richard,'
Susan was saying. 'I appreciate how tight security can be.'

The camera followed the two as they strolled up the drive
to the gatehouse where a man in civilian clothes stepped
out to greet them. 'That's the chap from Portsmouth,' Alison
whispered, almost as if she were afraid he'd overhear her.

Even in pre-9/11 days, security had been tight at British
military installations, the college included, because of the
Irish Republican Army. Afterwards . . . well, it took a written
invitation, several forms of identification, and an official
escort before they issued you a visitor's badge and let you
past security at the gates.

On the screen, the man Alison had identified as the PAO
handed Susan a plastic badge, waited while she clipped it
to her lapel, then the three walked through the gates together.
A uniformed sentry stood at stiff attention in the doorway
of the gatehouse as they passed.

The cameraman panned from the rigid form of the sentry
down to the bottom of Prince of Wales Drive. Four individuals stood where it intersected with College Way, just

as rigid and silent as the sentry, holding signs. I leaned
forward and squinted at the screen, but the camera panned
by the demonstrators so quickly that I couldn't read what
the signs said. 'Who are those people?'

Alison hit pause, freezing the frame on one of the individuals in question. She clicked forward frame by frame
until the sign the guy was holding came into focus: *The
Bible. The Real Message from Beyond.*

'Protestors,' Alison said. 'In a minute Susan will mention
them.' She clicked play, and Richard Porter promptly
complied by asking the medium, 'What can you tell me
about the demonstrators, Susan?'

The medium waved a dismissive hand. 'They seem to
follow me wherever I go, Richard. Comes with the terri-
tory, I guess. I suppose I should be flattered that I have
groupies, like the Rolling Stones.'

'Or the Grateful Dead?' I quipped, causing Alison to
nearly fall out of her chair laughing at my stupid joke.

When we returned our attention to the program, Richard
was saying, 'Security is tight at the college, as you can
imagine. We've tried to keep your visit with us today very
low key. How did the demonstrators know you'd be here?'

'If I didn't know any better, I'd say that at least one of
them is psychic, except they don't believe in that, do they?'
The camera moved in for a close-up which showed only
wry amusement rather than concern on Susan's face.
'There's a mole among my production staff in London, I'm
afraid. But I've had occasion to talk with these people, and
although we obviously don't see eye-to-eye, they appear to
be harmless. Frankly,' she went on, moving forward again,
eyes on her feet, 'I have an ex-husband in California suing
for half of my assets, so a few . . . how shall I say . . .?'

'Crackpots?' Richard suggested, brown eyes twinkling
behind the glasses.

'Um, yes. Anyway, in the vast scheme of things, I think
these demonstrators are the least of my worries.'

Susan certainly knew how to work the camera. She
stared straight into the lens and winked out at the television audience. 'Besides, if anything ever happened to

me, I'd come back and whisper in your ear, "If yer lookin'
fer the bloke what done me in, his name is Greg Parker."'

After a beat, the camera focused on Richard's astonished
face, then panned out, located another one of the demonstrators, steadied and zoomed in on the sign she was
carrying: *There shall not be found among you a consulter
with familiar spirits for all that do these things are an
abomination unto the Lord. Deut. 18:10–12.*

And the program cut to an ad.

'Abomination? Doesn't sound harmless to me,' Alison
remarked, fast-forwarding through the ad. When the program
resumed, Susan and Richard were seated in an officers'
lounge in comfortable club chairs arranged in a conversa-
tional group in front of a long bar. Richard was pointing
out the saucer-sized circles on the ceiling where celebrating
cadets at various times had hoisted Prince Charles, his
brother Andrew, and Charles's son William up on their
shoulders to autograph the ceiling.

When they got up to leave, I imagined the cameraman
scuttling backwards as he preceded Susan and Richard into
the Senior Gunroom. 'Gunroom?' Susan's eyes darted from
one wonder in the room to another. 'Who knew?'

I could understand her confusion. The gunroom is actually an elegant dining room – mess hall, to be precise – with
a vaulted ceiling decorated with beautifully painted and gilded
bosses. Portraits of famous naval officers lined the richly
paneled walls. None of the officers appeared troubled,
however, or making any effort to contact the living, so the
party moved on, pausing at the dress uniform of King George
VI, dripping with medals, in a glass case. King George didn't
appear restless or eager to communicate either, so they set
off again, walking briskly down the highly polished floors
of a long narrow corridor, anchored on one end by the
gunroom and on the other by the chapel.

Halfway along, the corridor opened into a vast entrance
hall. On Susan's right, huge double doors opened out, I knew,
on to a marble staircase that led down to the parade ground
overlooking the town and beyond it, the sea. On her left lay
the heart of Aston Webb's design for the college, the

Quarterdeck, its entrance flanked by larger-than-life-sized portraits of Prince Philip and Queen Elizabeth, respectively. When Susan commented on the portraits, Richard said, 'Young Philip was a cadet here in 1939 when King George VI and the Queen arrived on the royal yacht with their daughters, the Princesses Elizabeth and Margaret. Elizabeth was then thirteen. He escorted them round.' The camera caught Richard smiling. 'We have photographs of them playing croquet.'

The focus then shifted to Susan, hands clasped behind her back, studying Prince Philip's portrait. Suddenly she raised a hand. Sniffed. 'I smell smoke.' She waved in the direction of the Quarterdeck. 'What's behind those doors?'

Rather than answer, Richard smiled enigmatically and held the door open for her. She hustled through, trailed by the cameraman and the soundman, his boom making a cameo appearance in one of the shots. As Susan moved to the center of the great hall, the camera took full advantage of the opportunity, zeroed in on her face, creased with concern, then arched up to take in the dark-timbered vaulted ceiling. It swept around the gallery, known as the poop deck, that surrounding the Quarterdeck on three sides, and would likely have examined the intricate wrought ironwork of the balustrades in more detail had not Susan pressed a hand to her throat, and said, 'The smoke is really intense in here.'

The cameraman was on the case. He followed the medium to the far end of the room where a statue of His Majesty King George V stood wearing a heavy overcoat of marble. She stroked the marble, gazed thoughtfully into the old king's face as if listening to what he had to say, then turned to Richard who waited silently, hands clasped in front of him. 'This area was bombed, wasn't it? A direct hit?'

'Yes.'

'Is that when this happened?' she asked, touching the hem of the king's coat where a triangular piece of marble appeared to be missing.

Richard nodded, then, as if remembering that there was a camera in the room, said, 'Yes.'

'I'm thinking the college was very lucky,' Susan continued,

her hand still resting lightly on King George's overcoat. 'I don't feel death here.'

'Fortunately, the bomb fell on a day when the cadets were not in residence. Otherwise . . .' Richard shuddered. 'It could have been a lot worse.'

Susan bowed slightly at the waist. 'Thank God.' After a respectful moment of silence, she led the little group back the way they had come.

'They're heading for the chapel,' Alison whispered, freezing the action on a frame of Susan with her mouth forming an O. 'Watch this.'

I would like to have seen what Susan 'saw' in the chapel, containing as it did many historical objects, including an altar cloth made from the same bolt of cloth as Queen Victoria's wedding gown. But before she got anywhere near the chapel, however, Susan stopped dead in her tracks. She pressed a hand to her chest, breathed heavily. 'Oh, my goodness!'

Nobody said anything. A jet plane roared overhead, stealing the silence, but for some reason, the post-production people hadn't edited the noise out.

'There's a woman here,' Susan said after the noise of the jet had faded away. 'She's wearing a uniform.'

Considering they were standing in a Navy school, that was a safe bet.

'I'm getting an H. Helen?' Susan squinted thoughtfully into the camera. 'No, not Helen. It's Ellen!'

The camera swung quickly from Susan back to Richard in order to catch his reaction. Viewers were not disappointed. Richard's eyebrows shot upwards, then returned to a neutral position. He said nothing.

The camera swung back to Susan whose head was cocked at that angle I now recognized, when she seemed to be taking counsel from spirits in the great beyond. 'Ellen says she's dying of embarrassment. Does that mean anything to you?'

The camera swung back in time to catch the corners of Richard's mouth twitching upwards in what might pass for a smile. Still, he said nothing.

'It means something to me!' I yelled at the television screen.

Alison glared at me. 'Shhhh!'

'The plaque is right behind her, Alison. She can't help but notice it.'

'They covered it up, silly. You'll see in a minute.'

Sure enough, when the camera panned back, the bronze plaque that commemorated the event that cost Ellen Whittall her life had been covered with a dark cloth, taped to the wall with duct tape. Crafty Richard! He might agree to let a medium troop around the college with her entourage, but he had been careful to even up the odds. Susan had many talents, but I didn't think X-ray vision was among them. 'She's doing this.' Susan traced a circle in the air. 'She wants me to turn around.'

I have observed that in buildings designed exclusively to accommodate men, women's restrooms are often tucked away in odd, out-of-the-way places, in closets, for example, or under staircases. When Susan did as the spirit instructed, she found herself facing the ladies' restroom, squirreled away in a corner just off the elegant entrance hall. The camera caught her smiling in amusement, then her face grew serious. 'You poor thing!' she soothed. Susan glanced over her shoulder and out into our sitting room. 'Ellen's telling me she was in the loo when the bomb exploded. She's saying she had higher aspirations when she joined the military than dying with her knickers around her knees.'

'So!' said Alison, pausing the program at the point where Richard's bemused face filled the screen. 'What do you think about *that*?'

'I think it makes for interesting television,' I answered, channeling Paul, 'but the fact that a Wren was the only casualty of the bombing is common knowledge. I think it's even mentioned in the BRNC brochure.'

Alison pouted like a three-year-old. 'But everybody doesn't know about the loo.'

'*I* know about it.'

'Yes, but you've spent time at the college. Susan's never been.' Alison waved the remote. 'Until now.'

'Point taken, but . . .' I thought the show we'd just seen was one of the least convincing demonstrations of Susan

Parker's talents as a medium. However, watching Susan communicate with the restless spirit of a victim of World War Two (or not!) had given me an idea. 'Does Susan do a walkabout like this on every show?'

'Oh, yes,' Alison said. 'You'd be amazed how many haunted places there are in Britain.'

Considering that the history of the country went back to before the Stone Age, I could believe it. One Celt runs an iron sword through another and a restless spirit is born. 'If she's open to suggestions, I think I have an idea for her show.'

Alison was sorting through some DVDs on the end table. She looked up. 'Oh? What's that?'

'What if she were to go to Torcross? She could stroll along the beach at Slapton Sands and see if she encounters any of the soldiers or sailors who died there. If *any* spirit is restless, it ought to be one of those poor guys. Dark, cold, wet, severely burned. They were a long, long way from home when the end came.'

Alison pressed her hands together and clapped silently. 'Brilliant!'

I bowed my head in mock modesty. 'Thank you.' I didn't know how Cathy Yates felt about medium-slash-clairvoyants, but if the idea captured Susan Parker's imagination, and the people on the London end of *Dead Reckoning* agreed, I'd have something positive to tell the American.

Or maybe Cathy would think I was as nutty as a fruit-cake.

I hadn't known Cathy very long, but when it came to uncovering information about her father, I figured Cathy would leave no stone unturned, no matter how unconventional.

And I was betting that Susan would go for it, too.

EIGHT

*'Well, maybe you're right. I don't like being wrong
one bit. But, maybe this once I might be a little wrong.'*
Lady Elaine Fairchilde,
Mister Rogers' Neighborhood

Early the following morning, I was awakened in our
room at Horn Hill House by my iPhone vibrating like
a dentist's drill on the bedside table. I fumbled for it,
thumbed the screen on.

'Mumpf.'

'It's Alison, Hannah. I was able to bag three tickets to
Susan's live show in Paignton on Wednesday night!' she
bubbled. 'Do you and Paul want to go?'

'Let me check.' I touched mute, then nudged my husband
awake. When I asked him the question, he groaned, covered
his eyes with his hand and said, 'I'd rather crawl naked
through a nest of fire ants.'

'I'll take that as a no, then.'

Paul raised himself up on one elbow. 'Besides, I'm sailing
Biding Thyme to Cowes with Jon, remember?'

Back on the phone, I skipped the part about the fire ants
and reminded Alison that Susan's show would conflict with
my husband's plans to help her husband sail *Biding Thyme*
to victory at Cowes.

'Blimey! I was so excited, I completely forgot! Well,
never mind. I'll figure something out.'

'Do you want me to ask Janet Brelsford if she'd like to
join us?'

'Uh, no. I've just had a radical idea, Hannah. I'm going
to ask my dad!'

If you'd asked my opinion, I'd have said that Stephen
Bailey would be down on the ground along with Paul,

crawling through that nest of fire ants, but it was Alison's ticket, so I kept my opinion to myself. Besides, Alison was volunteering to drive. 'The show starts at seven, Hannah, so we'll pick you up at half five.'

Alison and her father were waiting at the foot of Horn Hill in a sleek blue Prius pulled to the curb in the little lay-by directly opposite Khrua Thai Restaurant. I didn't recognize them until Alison gave a light tap on the horn, then waved at me from the window.

'What happened to your Micra?' I asked as I climbed into the back seat of the Prius.

'It began begging for a new transmission,' Alison explained, checking the wing mirror and letting a minibus pass before pulling out into Higher Street. 'Jon said no way were we going to throw more money at it. This is Dad's car.' She smiled at her father who was belted so securely into the front passenger seat that I thought he was in danger of getting gangrene from the waist down. White hair tamed and slicked back, he wore a striped shirt and a checked sports coat, both patterns at war with a yellow paisley tie. 'Dad's letting me drive for a change.'

'I have to confess I'm surprised to see you, Mr Bailey. You seemed like such a skeptic the other day.'

'Ulterior motives,' Bailey mumbled. 'Haven't seen the Palace since they finished the renovations back in oh-seven. Hear they did a smashing job.'

Alison grunted. 'Dad thinks I need a chaperone.'

Ably chaperoned by the two of us, Alison drove in a clockwise direction through town, taking the long way around to the foot of Coombe Road where we waited at the Floating Bridge Inn, engine idling, for the Higher Ferry, a newly commissioned, state-of-the-art vessel that had been in service only a couple of months. During the short three-minute ride across the Dart, I stepped out of the car briefly to watch in fascination as the ferry was pulled across the river on stout steel cables. Once we reached the Kingswear side and were on our way again, I loosened my seat belt and leaned over the back of Alison's seat, speaking into her left ear. 'Do you think they'll be taping Susan's show for television?'

'They usually do, but only the best bits will make it to the telly.'

'What do you expect, Alison?' grumped her father from the passenger seat. 'They're not going to show her being wrong on the telly, now, are they?'

'True enough,' I said. 'That's why I think it will be interesting to see what she does in front of a live audience. She'll be on stage for two hours, performing without a net, as it were.'

'Complete and unexpurgated,' Alison added.

'There will be shills,' her father proclaimed in the same confident tone of voice that God must have used when he said, 'Let there be light.'

'I've seen only a bit of that one show you captured on video, Alison. What are they generally like?'

'It's an hour long, and they're usually in three parts. First, there's a pre-arranged reading. I remember one . . .' She paused, lightly braking to take a curve at a more prudent speed. 'Susan didn't know anything about the woman, had never met her, but she brought a message from the woman's husband, a soldier who'd been killed in Afghanistan. It was a private detail about a silver bracelet he'd given her on the last night they'd spent together before he was deployed. The woman was in tears, and so was I.'

Bailey exploded. 'Bollocks!'

'You didn't *see* it, Dad. Susan was amazing.'

'You said three segments?' I asked, trying to keep the conversation on track.

'Right. There's the part where she walks up to strangers in shops or on the street – like what happened to you, Hannah, but with cameras. Then she'll go somewhere that's haunted, and my God, we do have a lot of places like that in England, don't we, Dad?'

'Henges, circles and barrows. England's got more haunted places than dogs have fleas.'

'And they're not all crumbling ruins, either, with wailing damsels or ghostly knights in armor clattering around the

courtyards on horseback,' Alison continued. 'This couple in
a semi-detatched in St Albans complained to Susan about
objects constantly being moved. One photograph, in particular, kept ending up face down on the mantel. Susan said it
was their dead son trying to get their attention. He'd committed
suicide. Or so they thought,' she added mysteriously.

'And?' I prodded.

Alison shot a quick glance over her shoulder. 'Turns out
he wasn't alone when he passed.'

'So that Parker woman said,' muttered Alison's father.

'So she said.'

Stephen Bailey loosened his seatbelt and swiveled in his
seat so he could face me. 'You can see why I'm coming
along on this little excursion, can't you? Jon aids and abets
her in all this nonsense. Someone has to grab Alison's ankles
and pull her back down to earth when she goes off like
this.'

Alison's eyes caught mine in the rear-view mirror. 'How
sweet to see he's still looking after me.'

'Devon might be starring in another segment of *Dead
Reckoning*, Mr Bailey, if Cathy Yates has her way.'

'That American?' Bailey snorted, apparently forgetting
that I was an American too.

'As you know from when you talked to her, Mr Bailey,
Ken Small's book got Cathy all fired up. So she delivered
a copy to Susan's flat the other day, with Post-it notes stuck
in all the relevant places. Cathy hopes Susan will be able
to locate that farmer's field where Small said the bodies
had been buried in a ruined air-raid shelter.'

'Good luck to them, then,' grumbled Alison's father.
'There were thirty thousand acres of farmland in the area
that was evacuated in 'forty-four. She can't tramp over all
thirty thousand with that daft cow and her camera crew.'

'I imagine she'll start at the Sherman tank and seek direction from any spirits she finds hanging around there,' I said
sweetly.

Bailey turned to face me, nose twitching. 'Not you, too!'

'The jury's still out, Mr Bailey. I like to keep an open
mind.'

'Drop me off at the nearest pub,' he harrumphed. 'That's where they've got spirits I can relate to.'

When we reached Paignton, we tucked the Prius snugly away in Artillery Lane, had a quick bite at a little Chinese restaurant, then walked back to the Palace Theatre, a lovingly restored red and white brick structure overlooking an elliptical park.

'And here I thought we were so early,' Alison observed as we trudged up the hill. 'People are already queuing!'

'I think they're Susan's groupies,' I said when we got a little closer.

And so they were. A man dressed like a missionary in dark pants and a white short-sleeved shirt stood on an upturned milk crate next to a red pillarbox, holding a Bible out in front of him. Sparse strands of yellowish-gray hair were combed over his pink skull, and sideburns crawled along his cheeks. His eyes flashed with the zeal of the book of Revelation, from which he appeared to be reading, raining fire and brimstone down on all who dared enter the theater doors.

The other members of his team carried picket signs that, on closer inspection, proved to be constructed of two pieces of foam board taped around a dowel. One was the quote from Deuteronomy I recognized from Alison's video, carried by a young man this time, while *False Prophets Shall Bring in Damnable Heresies. Peter 2:1* was being waved back and forth like a windshield wiper by a woman who was probably the young man's mother, considering the similarity of their profiles.

Next to her, a dark-haired young woman wearing a red headband and an ankle-length flowered dress held aloft a sign that said *Exodus 22:18* in black gothic letters.

'Are we supposed to know what that means?' Alison wondered. 'John three:sixteen I know. The twenty-third Psalm, ditto. Exodus twenty-two:eighteen doesn't exactly roll trippingly off the tongue.'

'I'm usually good with chapter and verse, but I'm not familiar with that one,' I confessed. 'Hold on.' I whipped out my iPhone, touched the Google icon and began tapping letters. After a few moments, I had the results. 'Jeesh.'

'What's it say?'

I showed Alison the screen: *Thou shalt not suffer a witch to live.*

I'd rarely seen rage bubble up so quickly. It started in Alison's shoulders, stiffened the tendons in her neck, reddened her cheeks and the tips of her ears then exploded from her lips. 'What's the matter with you people?' she shouted at the Stepford Wife who was holding the offending sign. 'Don't have the *balls* to say it out loud? That is a *threat*! Someone ought to report you to the police!'

Bailey grabbed his daughter's arm and pulled. 'Come on, girl.'

I lagged behind, staring at the object of Alison's anger, the woman with the headband, who stared back with about as much emotion as a mannequin in a shop window. 'I honestly can't see your objection,' I told her. 'As a Christian, don't you believe in life after death?'

The woman didn't say anything at first, and I wondered if the guy standing on the milk crate had trained his minions to keep their mouths shut, no matter what the provocation, like the guards at Buckingham Palace. 'Alf!' she shouted, to my utter astonishment. 'You got any brochures left in the boot?'

'Who is worthy to open the book and loose the seals thereof,' Alf proclaimed breathlessly from atop the milk crate. 'Two boxes of 'em, girl . . . and no one in the heaven, or on the earth . . .'

'Come with me,' the young woman said. She propped the offending sign against the wall and led me around the corner to a car park and a dark blue vehicle so covered with window decals and bumper stickers that I would have been hard pressed to come up with its make and model.

TGIF – THANK GOD I'M FORGIVEN
ABORTION: 1 DEAD, 1 WOUNDED
I SAID, THOU SHALT NOT KILL. GO
VEGETARIAN.

THE ROAD TO HEAVEN IS A ONE-WAY
   STREET
TEN COMMANDMANTS, NOT SUGGESTIONS

'This your car?' I asked.

'Nah. It's Alf's.' She balled her hand into a fist and gave
the lid of the boot a solid thwack. It popped open obediently, revealing a jumble of boxes, oily rags, jumper cables
and empty one-liter beverage containers. She stripped the
packing tape off one of the boxes, pried up the lid, and
peered into its depths. 'Keep it,' she said, and handed me
a glossy brochure entitled *WTL Guardians*. The group was
represented by a logo that superimposed images of a cross
and a book over the rising (or it could have been setting)
sun.

'What are you guardians of?' I asked, tucking the brochure
into my handbag to read later.

'Way, Truth and Life,' she replied. 'WTL. Get it?'

I got it. 'What's WTL's problem with Susan Parker, then?'
I asked.

'S'plains in the brochure,' she said, slamming the lid of
the trunk closed. 'My name's Olivia Sandman, by the way.
What's yours?'

'I'm Hannah.'

'You from Canada?'

'Vancouver,' I lied. 'Well, thanks for the brochure,' I said,
patting the side pocket of my handbag. 'I'll give it all the
attention it deserves. Right now, though, I'd better hurry to
catch up with my friends.'

I hustled back up the hill, passed Olivia's colleagues,
keeping my eyes down, and joined Alison and her father
in the queue of early arrivals, snaking up the handicapped
ramp toward the entrance doors. Eventually we were
allowed into the lobby where we joined still another line
waiting to be let into the theater proper.

To our right, groups of theater-goers clustered around
long, cloth-covered tables selling *Dead Reckoning: Season
One* DVDs, copies of Susan's autobiography, *I'm Not Dead
Yet*, and souvenir T-shirts in a variety of pastel shades. While

Stephen Bailey held our places in line, Alison and I joined a clot of fans milling around the T-shirt table.

After carefully considering how it would go with my sister's prematurely white hair, I bought a blue 'I'm Not Dead Yet' T-shirt for Ruth. I thought she might enjoy reading Susan's book, too, but decided to buy it from my friendly, neighborhood independent bookseller once I got home to Maryland. I was ounces away from the weight limit already. No way I was going to pay British Airways an additional £30 for an overweight bag.

'Watch me rattle his cage.' Alison positively twinkled as she held up a green T-shirt for her father's inspection. 'Want one, Dad? Birthday coming up.'

Bailey folded his arms across his chest and scowled.

Alison selected a yellow T-shirt for herself, paid for it with cash, then joined me back in line. We moved along slowly, amusing ourselves by listening to the conversations going on in the line around us:

– *This is the third of her live shows I've been to. I'm hoping Lucy will come through.*

– *Can't afford two hundred pounds for a private reading, can I?*

– *She told Sandra that her mother's ring was just gathering dust and that she should get it sized and wear it!*

– *Why don't they ever say, 'I forgot to tell you about the bank account I have in Switzerland. The number is CH10 0023 blah blah blah'?*

I wondered about that last one myself.

Our seats, when we found them, were primo, on the aisle and only four rows back from the stage. 'I need the seat on the aisle,' Stephen Bailey insisted, standing to one side as we passed by him into the row. 'Might have to leave in a hurry.'

'Bladder,' Alison whispered as we eased into the plush velvet seats, the red upholstery as yet unbaptized by food spots, bubblegum, or hair oil.

'How did you get these seats?' I was impressed. 'Susan told us the show has been sold out for weeks!'

'I called the number on Susan's card,' Alison said as she

sat down. 'But the waiting list was a mile long, so I went to Plan B.'

'Which was?'

'Jon has friends in high places.' Alison smiled enigmatically.

'Old school tie?' I asked.

'More like *those who sail together* . . .' she giggled. 'He and this chap share a London club. Apparently ITV hold back a certain number of tickets for emergencies.'

'Like if Charles and Camilla take a notion to attend?'

'Exactly. Jon's mate calls them "Ooops tickets".'

Feeling grateful that the Prince of Wales and the Duchess of Cornwall were otherwise engaged, I settled into my seat and admired the set. Bathed in soft lavender light, it looked for all the world like my late grandmother's living room in Cleveland, Ohio. A round table covered with a lace cloth and an upholstered wingback chair were tastefully positioned on a scrap of oriental carpet. An enormous arrangement of golden daylilies sat in a vase in the center of the table. Giant closed-circuit television screens were mounted overhead on each side of the proscenium which showed the set from different angles. To our right, a long-necked boom camera bobbed and weaved. Nearer the stage, a technician wearing earphones fiddled with a black control box and communicated with someone high at the back of the steeply raked auditorium who appeared to be adjusting the controls at a similar workstation. A second cameraman shouldered his Steadicam, shrugged it into position, and faced the stage. Everything seemed to be ready, but as yet, there was no sign of Susan.

At 8:02 precisely – by the light of my iPhone – a spotlight lit the stage and Susan walked on to it, smiling broadly and waving, wearing a long, dove-gray skirt and matching sweater-coat. A scarf of many colors was twisted into an elaborate knot at her throat.

The applause that greeted the medium's arrival could have drowned out a launch of the space shuttle.

From a position in front of the armchair, Susan bowed slightly to right, left and center, accepting the accolades,

then raised both hands for silence. 'Good evening!' she
began, but whatever else she had planned to say was
drowned out by a renewed round of applause.

Susan laughed, eyes flashing in the theater lighting.
'Welcome! It's good to see so many of you here tonight,
both new friends and old!' With a sweep of her arm, she
appeared to be acknowledging a rowdy group of individuals in a block of seats to our left who were whooping it
up like die-hard Manchester football fans. 'As you know,
I am totally governed by spirits, so I have no idea what's
going to come through tonight. My job is to convey
messages, so if a message seems to be for you, if you can
relate to it, don't be shy. Stand up!

'And here's the first important message. Do you have a
mobile phone?' She waited a beat, surveying the audience,
then continued. 'Of course you have a mobile phone! I want
you to reach into your pocket, or into your bag, and turn
that phone off. *I'm* the only one getting messages here
tonight!'

Ripples of laughter accompanied a chorus of chimes,
beeps and tweets as those who had forgotten to silence their
phones before coming into the theater finally did so.

Including me.

'Thank you!' Susan said after the commotion died down.
'Now, some of you out there are skeptics.' She pointed a
finger, panned the audience. 'You know who you are. And
right now you're thinking *I'll bet she Googles everyone.*'
The boom camera zoomed in for a close-up, and on the
screen to our right, Susan rolled her eyes. 'Like who has
time? I barely have time to blog let alone Twitter!

'And I'm the first to admit to you that I'm not always
right.' Susan paused, cocked her head. 'Wait a minute.
John's here. Couldn't wait, could you, John?' she chuckled.

At the mention of the name John, hands shot up all around
the auditorium.

'Lights on in the house, please,' Susan said. 'This John
is around fifty, and he has brown hair going just a bit gray,
here.' She flicked her temple with her fingertips.

Among the early arm wavers, only four individuals

remained standing. From the stage Susan shielded her eyes with her hand and surveyed the audience, like a Cheyenne Indian scout on the lookout for General Custer. 'He's kind of a nervous guy, our John,' she continued. 'He's doing this.' She pumped her shoulders up and down.

Behind us, somebody screamed, 'That's my Jack!'

The boom camera swung around like a giraffe grazing for leaves in a fresh treetop. On the overhead screens, a woman wearing a flowered sundress and a strand of red and green glass beads began to bounce up and down on her toes.

'This message is probably for you, then,' Susan said from the stage. 'What's your name?'

'Grace.'

'Jack passed away recently, didn't he, Grace?'

Grace sucked in her lips, nodded. 'Last year, about this time.'

'He's saying, "I like what you've done with the lounge."'

On the overhead screens, a fat tear glistened and began to slide down Grace's cheek. 'I took down the wallpaper and painted it yellow. It looks ever so fresh and bright!'

'He's smiling, Grace. He says he always *hated* that wallpaper.' Susan wagged a finger. 'But he's also saying, "Don't you dare touch my workshop!"'

Grace's hands shot to cover her mouth, then parted slightly to let out a little-girl giggle. 'He was a keen woodcarver, my Jack. Carved the most comical ducks out of pine. Sold them at the village market on Tuesdays.' Her voice shot up an octave. 'I'm keeping yer ducks, luv!'

'He wants you to know that he's fine, and that he loves you.' Susan was summing up, preparing to move on. On the screen, Grace swiped at her eyes with a tissue produced from a handbag somewhere off camera. Susan stepped back, paused, cocked her head then suddenly returned her attention again to Grace. 'Does the name Leo have any significance, Grace?'

Eyes wide, Grace nodded silently.

'Jack wants you to know . . . wait a minute. Yes, OK. He's telling me it's fine with him about Leo. Can you relate to that?'

'Leo's Jack's best friend. He's been asking me to step out with him, but . . .' She heaved a great sigh. 'Thank you!' Her face relaxed, the deep lines on her forehead disappeared, and she suddenly looked ten years younger. Leo would be pleased.

The applause began to our left, one person, then another, and suddenly the entire auditorium was putting their hands together. Susan Parker took the opportunity to sit down in the chair.

Stephen Bailey, on the other hand, took the opportunity to mutter, 'Bollocks!' under his breath, just loud enough for Alison and me to hear. He jerked his head toward the stage. 'I'll wager that Parker woman has spies out in line while we're waiting to get in. Silly cow was probably rabbiting on about her poor dead Jack out there, and how she's having a bit of how's your father with Leo.'

Alison's elbow scored a direct hit where she shared an armrest with her father. 'Shhhh.'

From the chair on stage, Susan raised a hand. 'I'm looking for someone named Lisa.'

From a row in front of us and to the left, someone shrieked, and three young women leapt to their feet. 'I'm Lisa!' one of them squealed, then pressed both hands to her mouth and continued to squeal.

'Are you sisters?' Susan asked.

Well, that was obvious, even to me. Same height, same build, same chestnut-colored hair. The way they giggled in unison at the same decibel level, pummeling each other with their elbows.

'I have a father figure here,' Susan continued.

A fresh chorus of eee-eee-eees erupted from the sisters.

'He wants to apologize.'

The girls' heads bobbed in unison.

'This is difficult.' Susan stood up and walked to the edge of the stage so she could face the three women directly. 'Did he end his own life?'

On the overhead screen, the girls stood silent and grim, like the See No Evil, Hear No Evil, Speak No Evil monkeys. The girl named Lisa, hand still pressed to her mouth, nodded silently.

'He wants me to tell you that he'll be there on the aisle. Do you understand that?'

A sister who wasn't Lisa spoke up. 'Yes! I'm getting married next week!'

Susan said, 'He's going, "Uh, uh, uh . . ."'

'Oh. My. God! That's what Dad does when he's thinking!' the third sister screeched.

'Do you ever lose your car keys, Lisa?' When Lisa nodded, Susan said, 'Your father says to tell you that *he* steals the keys. So when they go missing, it's just a reminder that he's watching over you.' Susan raised a hand. 'Hold that thought, Lisa. Somebody else is coming through.' A pause, listening. 'I have a message for Brenda. Brenda? Where's Brenda?'

A spotlight began sweeping the audience, looking for Brenda, too. It settled on a woman in the back row who seemed to be struggling to her feet with the help of a younger companion. When she was finally upright, gripping the back of the seat in front of her, Susan said, 'This must be a night for sisters because I have a woman here who says she's like a sister to you.'

'Oooh!' On the overhead screens, Brenda's eyelids fluttered and her eyes rolled back. I thought she was going to pass out.

'Why is she doing this?' Susan pressed her hands together palm to palm, like a supplicant angel in a Renaissance painting.

'Oooh, oooh, oooh,' Brenda managed, swaying dangerously.

If Susan was cold reading, relying on verbal clues from this woman, she was out of luck. 'She loves you, Brenda. And she's reminding you to take your meds!'

Brenda steadied herself as if preparing to hear more, but Susan waved a buh-bye hand. 'That's all, I'm afraid. The spirit was willing, but the signal was weak. She's gone.'

The sisters in the front row were still hugging each other and dithering when Susan turned her attention back to them. 'Lisa! One more thing. Your father says he's not particularly happy about the tattoo, but he's glad you got it in a place where it won't show.'

'It's on her bum,' one of the sisters volunteered, bouncing up and down on her toes. Lisa began tugging at the waistband of her jeans and I feared she was going to moon the audience in order to prove that, once again, Susan Parker, Medium and Clairvoyant, was right on the money. Fortunately, two clearer heads and two pairs of hands prevailed and the three sisters sat down.

Back on stage, Susan Parker was taking a break. She twisted the cap off a bottle of water, poured half of it into a glass and drank deeply. After setting the glass down on the table, she paced, studying her shoes. Suddenly she snapped to attention, held up a hand. 'Someone else is coming through. Yes, yes, I hear you.' Susan turned to face the audience. 'It's a woman, and she's showing me a flower. What kind of flower?' She closed her eyes for a moment. 'Is it a lily? A pansy? Wait a minute.' Her eyes flew open. 'Thank you! No, it's a rose.'

The guy carrying the Steadicam rushed up the aisle near us, and pointed his lens at the stage. The boom camera, its red eye blinking, began to scan the audience, a brontosaurus, looking for fresh meat.

'You, sir,' Susan said, pointing in our direction. 'You in the yellow tie.'

As the guy with the Steadicam closed in, Stephen Bailey pressed his hand to his chest in a classic *who-me?* gesture.

'Dad! She's talking to you,' Alison hissed, elbow working overtime. 'Stand up!'

Bailey unfolded slowly, rising to his feet by degrees, eyes wide, like a deer caught in the headlights.

'She says her name is Rose. Who might this refer to?'

Bailey looked blank. 'Nobody I know that's passed on. There's a Rose who cuts my hair.'

Susan stared thoughtfully at the ceiling, fingers tapping her lips. 'She's saying that she's sorry she broke your heart. Do you know what she's talking about?'

Bailey shrugged.

'Now she's showing me an engagement ring. No, wait a minute. Not an engagement ring. It's a signet ring of some sort, with a red stone.'

'Never been engaged to anyone but my Doris, miss, and Doris, she's been gone these six years.' Alison squeezed her father's arm reassuringly as he continued, 'If you can bring me a message from my Doris, then I'll give you a listen.'

Susan faced the Steadicam and smiled brightly into it. 'Rose's message must be intended for someone else, then.' As the camera followed her closely, Susan once again addressed the audience. 'I have a message from Rose.'

The spotlight swooped over our heads and settled on a man at the far end of our row. 'Had a girlfriend once named Rosie,' he volunteered. 'Wore a ruby ring, too, Rosie did.'

'Stand up!' Susan said. 'Don't be shy!'

'Told you!' Stephen Bailey crowed, collapsing into his seat. 'It's a load of codswallop.'

Alison patted his knee. 'Never mind, Daddy.'

'You were right about one thing, Mr Bailey,' I whispered as the audience learned of the tragic break-up of Rosie and James back in 1963.

'What's that?'

'That bit of tape with you on it?' I made a snipping motion with my fingers. 'Cutting-room floor.'

NINE

'Dubois has responded by calling Randi "senile" and "unintelligent", and stating that she has "nothing to prove" to him, remarking that whereas believers such as herself live in the afterlife after they die, skeptics will "look around and go, 'oops!'"'
Allison Dubois, quoted at *www.allexperts.com*

Early the next morning, I drove Cathy Yates to catch the eight-fifteen from Totnes so she could connect through Paddington to her mid-afternoon flight out of Heathrow. She still refused to drive the rental car.

On the way to the train station, Cathy told me that she planned to contact her Congresswoman, Karen Tuckerman-Webb, a pitbull of a woman who had made her mark in politics by standing up to Nancy Pelosi on the issue of universal health care. I pitied anybody who got in the way of either Cathy Yates or Ms Tuckerman-Webb. It could get ugly.

We arrived in good time, so I parked the car and joined Cathy for a farewell cup of coffee in the station cafe.

'I may be back,' she said mysteriously, as we sat down opposite one another at a little table overlooking the tracks. 'I'm thinking about buying a place over here. If I'm going to be travelling back and forth, back and forth . . . it tires me out just thinking about it. And Heathrow? Son of a bishop, don't get me started!'

I smiled over the rim of my cup. I'd always thought that Miami International was the devil's brainchild, until I touched down at Heathrow Airport for the first time, and that had been *before* the recent Terminal 5 expansion where a glitch in the automated baggage system sent 28,000 bags into luggage hell. 'Do you have any place in mind, Cathy?'

She leaned across the table, speaking in a husky whisper. 'Now I'm going to surprise you!'

'Please do!'

'When I took that book over to Susan Parker's that day? She was out in the cemetery with her dog, pulling weeds. I told her about my idea, about visiting Slapton Sands and all, and I'm here to tell you, Hannah, she was on board with it one hundred per cent.'

Funny, I thought it was *my* idea, but I kept my mouth shut and nodded.

'Then . . .' Cathy paused, making me wait for it. 'Then, she gave me a private reading! What do you think about that?'

'That depends on what Susan told you, I guess.'

'Knocked my socks off, Hannah. Blew me away.'

'Susan has a tendency to do that,' I said, remembering my experience in Foss Street not so very long ago.

'After the reading, I marched myself down to that estate agent in Hauley Street, the one near the beauty parlor, you know? Looked through a bunch of listings, then bingo! I think I've found the place, but I have to go home and get the financing together.'

'Where is the place?'

Again the mysterious smile. 'Can't tell you yet. I don't want to jinx the deal.'

'Paul and I have talked about buying a holiday cottage in the UK, but even with the downturn in the market, everything's still so expensive!'

'Confession time?' She raised a neatly drawn eyebrow.

'Uh, sure.'

'I may look like a hick from the sticks to you, Hannah,' she said, pegging me for the snob that I was, 'but my stepfather owned a small chain of motels that sold out to Motel 6 just before he died. What I'm saying? Money is no object.'

When I got back to Dartmouth, I left the rental in the car park near the Visitors' Center and tucked the keys under the rear floor mat, to be collected by the rental company later in the week. I'd miss having the little Corsa at my disposal, but with Paul away sailing at Cowes for the next several days, I wasn't planning on driving anywhere anyway.

I was window shopping my way back to the B&B and had just made the turn on to Duke Street at the Butterwalk when my cell phone rang. Unknown caller. I usually ignore incoming unknowns, but I had time on my hands that morning, so I thumbed the iPhone on. To my astonishment, the caller was Susan Parker.

'Hannah? I hope you don't mind. Janet gave me your number.'

'I don't mind at all! How nice to hear from you. It gives me an opportunity to tell you how much I enjoyed seeing your show in Paignton last night.'

'You were there? I'm so pleased you were able to get tickets.'

'I'm surprised you didn't see me. Do you remember an elderly gentleman, around eighty, sitting on the aisle? You called on him.'

After a slight pause, Susan made an ah-ha sound, as if a light bulb had flashed on over her head. 'The fellow in the yellow tie?'

'You got it. That was Alison Hamilton's father. You met Alison at dinner the other night.'

'Alison's father, huh? Well, I'll be damned. What a small world we live in.'

'You didn't see us?'

'The spotlights can be blinding, and . . . well, when I'm working, I tend to be rather focused.'

'I can imagine.' Just as I was wondering why on earth Susan Parker would be calling me, she apparently read my mind.

'Hannah, there is a reason for my call. Last night, just before I went to sleep, I had another message from your mother.'

I stopped dead in my tracks, cell phone glued to my ear. Somewhere in the back of my brain, a bell started clanging, rung by my conveniently absent husband. 'Here it comes, Hannah,' he was saying. 'The pitch. She's gonna ask you for money. Didn't I tell ya so?'

'I'm sorry she disturbed your sleep,' I said cautiously.

'The spirits, I'm afraid, are no respecters of time or place.' Susan was silent for a moment, the empty air on her end of the line filled by music playing softly. A Mozart string quartet, unless I missed my guess. 'Your father must have been quite a handful,' she said.

'*What??!*' I said it aloud, just like that, with two question marks and an exclamation point. After Mom died, my father had crawled inside a bottle. He'd been sober for years now, thank goodness, but back then, being 'quite a handful' was putting it mildly.

'She's OK with it now,' Susan was saying when I tuned in again. 'Actually, I think the message is meant for your father. Is there another woman in his life?'

The day had turned surreal. There I was, staring through the window of Mullin's Bakery at a tray of plain, ordinary, everyday pork pasties while getting messages from my dead mother concerning my father's sex life.

'Yes,' I admitted. 'He's got a steady girlfriend.' Her name was Cornelia, but I decided to keep that fact to myself in case Susan was able to pluck her name, like a rabbit, out of her hat.

'Look, Hannah, I really feel the need to talk to you privately. Today's insane, but I'm wondering if you could come for a private reading, say eight o'clock tomorrow morning? My place?'

'I appreciate the offer, Susan, but . . .' I paused for a moment, trying to organize my thoughts. What did that guy say at the theater last night? *No way I could afford two hundred dollars* (or was it pounds?) *for a private reading.* As intrigued as I was with the idea of a private session with a world-famous medium who was calling me (little ole me!) on my mobile phone, talking to me like she was my new best friend, I knew that neither my American Express nor my Visa card could take such a hit. 'Susan, I have to be up front with you. I really can't afford a private session.'

Susan laughed, sounding genuinely surprised. 'Oh, Hannah! I didn't invite you over to ask you for money! I just want to talk, I promise. Say you will.'

I must have hesitated a moment too long because she quickly upped the ante. 'I'll brew up a pot of one-hundred per cent American coffee. And if that's not incentive enough, I've got bagels. And cream cheese.'

Then it was my turn to laugh. 'Consider my arm twisted. Eight o'clock then?'

'Eight o'clock. Janet will tell you how to get here.'

As I slipped my cell phone back into my handbag, I found myself genuinely looking forward to the visit. The way I figured it, either Susan Parker was the real deal, or she wasn't. If she was, she might open the door to communication with my late mother. If she wasn't? Well, I hadn't had a decent bagel in a long, long time.

The next morning I was up, dressed and had eaten a small dish of fruit at the table by myself when my cell phone beeped. Susan was texting me. 'Running L8. 8:30?'

'OK,' I texted back. A woman of many words, that's me. My daughter, Emily, would have texted 'K', but I felt that as a celebrity, Susan deserved the bonus 'O'.

I was already halfway out the door, so I decided to kill some time by walking the long way around by Bayards Cove – where the *Mayflower* pilgrims first set off for America in 1620 – and watch the Lower Ferry come in. Afterwards, I wandered along the Embankment to the Station Cafe. From 1889 to 1972 or thereabouts, the cafe had actually served as Dartmouth's train station, selling tickets, although there'd never been any platform, tracks or trains. Now it was a restaurant, primarily providing hot beverages and snacks to the tourists who lined up to catch buses or passenger ferries at various locations along the Embankment.

With my hands wrapped around a cup of hot tea, warming them in the cool morning air, I leaned my arms against the railing and watched the passenger ferries come and go, carrying visitors up and down the River Dart to Totnes, Dittisham, Greenway and the Castle, reinforcing the fact that Dartmouth had always been a seafaring town.

With ten minutes to spare and excitement growing, I

tossed my empty cup into a rubbish bin, then headed north along the Embankment to keep my date with Susan.

One might think that after watching Susan strike out completely with Alison's dad, I'd not put much stock in my upcoming reading. Yet Susan had been the first to admit that she didn't always get it right. And for me, it all came down to one word: *refrigerator.*

At one of the many blue and white ticket kiosks that lined the Embankment, just opposite the public restrooms, I was amused to see a border terrier snuffling at the crumbs remaining in a Walkers roast chicken crisps packet, pushing the distinctive gold packet along the pavement with his nose, dragging his leash behind him. When he lost interest in the packet and made a move to lift his leg against the side of the kiosk, the ticket agent shook off his lethargy, stepped out of the kiosk and brandished a fist. 'Here, you! Get along, then!'

It was a busy summer day on the Embankment. Too many cars, buses and pedestrians made it a hazardous place for a little dog out on a stroll by itself. Even then, I was hearing honking horns and sirens. I knelt down, patted the ground in front of me. 'Here, boy. C'mon.'

The terrier cocked his head, considered my offer, then decided that a Cadbury Dairy Milk wrapper had a lot more going for it.

'That your dog?' the ticket agent wanted to know.

'I don't know who he belongs to.' I stood up and moved in. 'Hey, fella. You off on a little holiday?'

The dog retreated a step, studying me suspiciously with liquid brown eyes. I took the opportunity to step on his leash, pinning the leather strap to the pavement. 'OK, now. Let's see who you belong to.' I seized the leash and ran my hand cautiously along its length. When the animal didn't seem of a mind to object, I grabbed his collar and turned it until I could reach the tags that hung around its neck. One tag certified that the dog had been vaccinated against rabies at a veterinary clinic in Hollywood, California. The other tag simply said 'Bruce', and listed a telephone with a 323 area code: Los Angeles.

Susan Parker's dog.

'I know his owner,' I told the ticket agent. I tugged on Bruce's leash. 'Come on, you little rascal. I'm taking you home.'

With Bruce trotting along the Embankment beside me, tags jangling, I felt like a proper Brit, out for a morning stroll. I'd owned a cat once, but keeping a dog in downtown Annapolis, particularly when Paul and I were both working, always seemed like it would be too hard, particularly on the dog. But as the fresh air filled my lungs and Bruce's little legs pumped to keep up, I thought maybe it was time to reconsider the No Dog Rule.

As Bruce and I drew near the first bus stop, the crowd grew denser. I was beginning to wonder why everyone was facing in the same direction, actually moving away from the bus stop, when I noticed the flashing blue lights. I'm as curious as the next person, so I followed the crowd as it surged forward. Bruce began straining at the leash, urging me onward. I had thought the fresh air was making my mind sharp, but it took me a while to put it together. Runaway dog, sirens, flashing blue lights. I broke into a run, elbowing my way through the crowd, dragging poor, frantic Bruce, toenails scrabbling on the pavement, behind me.

Through gaps in the crowd, I saw a man kneeling beside a bundle of lavender clothing that I had last seen Susan wearing. 'Let me through!' I screamed, shoving people out of my way. 'She's my friend!'

I rushed to Susan's side and knelt down. I didn't like the way Susan lay, her body twisted at an unnatural angle, like a question mark. But her eyes were open. That was a good sign, wasn't it? I grabbed her hand and rubbed it briskly. 'Susan, Susan, can you hear me?' I looked up, pleaded with the sea of faces. 'Oh, God! Somebody call 999.'

It took me a second to realize that that had already been done. I'd heard the sirens, saw the flashing blue lights. Even now, a PCSO wearing a bright green reflective vest over his uniform was running toward us on foot from the direction of the police station just a few hundred yards away.

The man kneeling opposite me said, 'I'm a doctor. But

I'm afraid there's not a lot I can do for her.' He was dressed in a T-shirt tucked into a pair of loose jogging shorts. Ear buds dangled loosely from an iPod strapped to his upper arm. A small white towel was draped limply around his neck. 'I suspect her neck is broken. If it's any comfort to you, I think she was killed instantly. I don't think she suffered.'

I sat down, hard, on the cold stone pavement. How would *he* know whether or not Susan suffered? Nearby, flowers blazed red and orange and yellow in an immense stone planter; the fronds of a palm tree stirred in a gentle breeze against a clear, blue sky. Something was terribly wrong with this picture. Tears ran hotly down my cheeks. 'What happened?'

A woman in a pink fleece warm-up suit materialized from the crowd. 'A car came out of nowhere, like. Jumped the curb. Ran right into her, poor thing. Then drove off.' She shook her head. 'What sort of person would do that?'

'What kind of car?' the police officer asked as he waved the crowd aside, clearing a path for the paramedics who had just arrived with a gurney.

'Dark blue,' the woman said.

'No, it was gray,' someone else offered. 'Black, maybe.'

'Make?'

'A Vauxhall?'

'No, it was a Ford. Might have been one of those hybrid cars. Whatchacallum? Focus?'

'No, you berk. It was a Fiat. My brother-in-law drives one just like it.'

Forty witnesses and forty stories. Why the police officer even bothered to ask the next question, I couldn't imagine. 'Anyone see the number plate?'

Blank looks and mumbling.

'So, no one saw the registration number, then?'

'Could have begun with a W, or maybe a V. It all happened so fast, you know.'

Darth Vader could have run down my friend, and no one would have been able to describe the fricking Death Star.

'Ma'am? Ma'am?' One of the paramedics knelt beside

me, speaking softly into my ear. 'We need you to move so we can help your friend.' I felt his hand, cool and slightly damp, ease Susan's lifeless hand out of mine. He escorted me to a park bench, and waited until I sat down. 'Are you going to be all right?'

'Shit, no,' my brain screamed, but my vocal chords had shut down. I nodded dumbly.

What had my mother wanted to tell me? Had there been a message for my father, one of my sisters, or for me? With Susan gone, there was no way I'd ever know.

As the paramedics worked to revive Susan, I squeezed my eyelids tightly closed and prayed – *please, oh please, oh please* – even though I knew, deep down where despair was turning my gut into a roiling bag of snakes, that their efforts would be fruitless.

'Make way, make way.' I recognized the voice of the PCSO and my eyelids flew open in time to see the gurney carrying Susan's motionless body being wheeled along the pavement toward a waiting ambulance whose doors yawned wide to receive it.

'Oooh,' I moaned. Bruce climbed into my lap, tail wagging so hard that his whole body quivered. He rested his forepaws on my chest, nosed my chin, then began licking the tears from my face.

I sat on the Embankment on a beautiful summer day clutching Bruce's leash in my hand like a lifeline, and began to bawl.

TEN

'The Ford Fiesta is not just the best-selling car of
December but of the whole year, selling a staggering
117,296 models by the end of 2009 [taking over] the
top UK sales position from the Ford Focus. The pair
retained first and second place in the sales charts
through to the end of the year. After the Focus follows
the Vauxhall Corsa, Vauxhall Astra, Volkswagen Golf,
Peugeot 207, Mini, BMW 3-series, Vauxhall Insignia
and Ford Mondeo.'

Faye Sunderland, 'Green Car Becomes Top-
Selling Model of 2009,' January 7, 2010,
www.TheGreenCarWebsite.co.uk

I don't suppose anyone was happy about Susan's death
except Samantha and Victoria Brelsford who had
inherited, at least for the time being, Susan's dog,
Bruce.

After an early dinner, Janet's daughters retreated to their
bedroom in the owner's apartment where they proceeded
to dress him up in baby clothes and spoil 'Brucie' with
Sizzlers bacon treats.

I had no appetite for dinner. Claiming a headache – not
so far from the truth – I'd gone up to my room early,
changed into my Betty Boop pajamas, and was trying to
read a Christopher Buckley novel, but even Buckley's
offbeat sense of humor wasn't keeping my brain engaged.
My thoughts kept wandering back to that morning, to
Susan's lifeless body, her vacant eyes, and I'd lose my
place. I had read page twenty-three for perhaps the fifth
time when there was a gentle knock on my door. 'Hannah?'

It was Janet.

I checked my watch, surprised to discover that it was

only eight o'clock. I padded to the door in my bare feet to see what she wanted.

'The girls are settled, Alan's down at the Cherub. Would you care to join me in the lounge for a glass of wine?'

I managed to dredge up a smile. 'Thanks for not asking me how I'm doing, Janet.'

'I know how you're feeling, Hannah. Gutted.' She touched my arm lightly. 'Come as you are. By the time you get downstairs, I'll be in my pajamas, too.'

After Janet left, I splashed some water on my face, then wandered over to the wardrobe where I found the fluffy terrycloth robe Janet provided for each of her guests, pulled it off the padded hanger and slipped into it gratefully. I spent several frustrating minutes looking for my slippers before remembering that I hadn't packed any, then padded downstairs wearing a pair of the gray wool socks Paul never travelled anywhere without.

The door to the lounge was propped open with an iron cat sculpture with marbles for eyes. Inside, I found Janet already sitting on the couch, legs stretched out, feet propped up on the coffee table next to a bottle of red wine and two balloon glasses. The television was on, its volume muted.

Janet patted the sofa cushion next to her, indicating I should park myself there. 'Red or red?'

'After carefully considering the options, I'll take red.'

She poured, but when she passed the glass to me, it was so large I had to use both hands.

We sat in companionable silence, slowly sipping, watching the screen numbly as a silent parade of policemen, some apparently wearing cameras affixed to their heads, brought petty criminals to justice on the highways, byways and back gardens of Britain.

'We were just becoming good friends. And the girls adored her!' Janet sobbed for the third or fourth time since I'd returned to Horn Hill House and delivered the bad news. She snatched a tissue from the box that sat on the sofa between us and blew her nose.

I choked up, too, thinking of my mother and missing her terribly. With Susan gone, that door had slammed shut.

It was as if Mother had died all over again. I reached for a fresh tissue.

Janet had inverted the wine bottle over my glass, wringing out the last few drops, when the clock on the mantel chimed ten. Susan switched to the evening news on BBC One, and we sat through stories about the Iraq war, swine flu, rising university tuition fees and how eating fish might protect us from Alzheimers, but surprisingly, there was no mention of Susan Parker's death.

At 10:25, BBC One gave way to Spotlight BBC South-West. Janet aimed the remote, and turned up the sound.

A news reader with perfectly styled, variegated blond hair fixed serious blue eyes on the camera lens and began:

> 'A woman has been killed by a car in Dartmouth, Devon, following a hit and run, say police. They are keen to trace a dark-colored car with front near side damage and a missing wing mirror, possibly a Vauxhall, which failed to stop at the scene. The woman was treated at the roadside and pronounced dead at the scene. Police are appealing for anyone with information to call them on 0800-555-1111, or Crimestoppers, anonymously.'

'That's it? That's all they're going to say about it?'

Janet flapped a hand. 'Shhh. Look! That's Royal Park Garden!'

While I sputtered in outrage, the camera cut to a panorama of the historic park that stood opposite the Embankment near the spot where Susan had died. Viewers were treated to serene close-ups of the Victorian fountain, cheerfully splashing, flower beds in summer profusion, and tourists resting their weary bones on park benches, before coming to rest on a reporter standing in front of the bandstand, the midday sun highlighting his hair like a halo as the wind swirled it around his head.

The woman in the pink warm-ups must have hung around the scene for some time after the ambulance took Susan away, because she loitered at the reporter's right, shifting her weight nervously back and forth from one trainer-clad foot to another, almost as if she were jogging in place. 'I saw the driver's face!' she told the reporter. 'Screwed up like this, it was.' She furrowed her brow until her eyes became slits. Her lips formed a firm straight line. 'Determined, I'd say. Drove that car deliberately over the curb and aimed it straight at that poor woman!'

'Was the driver a man or a woman?' the reporter asked, then thrust the microphone in the direction of her brightly painted mouth.

'I *think* it was a woman, but it could have been a very short man. The driver was looking *through* the steering wheel, like this.' She raised her hands to a ten and two o'clock position and scowled between them in the direction of the camera. 'Whoever it was had white hair, I'm sure of that. Or maybe it was blond.'

I sat up as straight as anyone could while cradling an oversize wine glass in both hands. 'You didn't mention that this morning, you stupid cow!' I shouted at the florid face now filling Janet's television screen. 'Or maybe you did, and I wasn't paying attention.' I collapsed, melting back into the cushions. 'They must still be trying to notify Susan's next of kin, right? Otherwise they'd be reporting her name?'

'That shouldn't take long. Susan's face will be all over the news by morning.' Janet flicked the controls and the television screen went blank. 'We're out of wine,' she announced after a moment in which the only sound was that of a toilet flushing somewhere in the house. 'But the situation is easily remedied.' She winked. 'I know where Alan keeps the key. Back in a tick.'

And she was, too, carrying two bottles of Cotes du Rhone Villages 1996 and a corkscrew. As she held one of the bottles between her knees and worked the cork out, she said, 'I hope this isn't something Alan's saving for a special occasion.'

'You're a clever girl. You'll think of something to tell him.' I held my glass out for a refill.

Janet poured herself a glass, took a sip, smacked her lips. 'It's not exactly cooking wine, is it?'

'Not even close,' I said, feeling mellower by the minute.

We shared another long cry, during the course of which the box of tissues became empty and the second bottle of wine magically opened itself. Janet topped off our glasses, slopping a bit of wine on the oriental carpet. 'Never mind. It's the same color as the rug,' she said, rubbing it into the thick pile with the toe of her shoe.

I don't remember much after that, except declaring emphatically to Alan when he wandered in from the Cherub somewhere around midnight that no matter what the police had to say, I was in complete agreement with the woman in the pink warm-up suit. Susan's death had been no accident.

Janet, bless her, had the presence of mind to stumble to the kitchen and fetch me a tall glass of water and a packet of liver salts. She watched while I dumped the contents of the packet into the water, waited for it to fizz, then drink the mixture down before sending me upstairs to bed, like a good mother.

Janet should have taken some liver salts herself. Although I was in rough shape the following day, I managed to crawl out of bed, shower, and show up for breakfast around nine o'clock, only to find that Janet was so hungover that Alan was manning the kitchen, cooking breakfast for the guests.

I slid into my chair and made it easy for him by ordering hot tea and a slice of wholewheat toast.

While I nibbled on the crust, I could hear Sam and Vicky playing with Bruce in the kitchen. Their delighted squeals made my head hurt. I hoped the girls would get to keep the dog, and that the little fellow didn't get tied up – like Susan's estate was likely to, considering what she'd said about her ex-husband – in a lawsuit.

After breakfast, I decided to take a walk, hoping the fresh morning air would clear my head. I stopped at the boat float, the artificial harbor where several dozen wooden boats bobbed in postcard-perfect perfection, struck by the way the sky and a scattering of clouds were perfectly mirrored by the water on that calm, windless day.

On the off-chance that somebody would tell me something about the investigation into Susan's death, I headed

for the police station on the corner across from the Flavel
Arts Centre. In contrast to the modern, but thoughtfully
designed cinema/theater/art gallery/library, the police station
was part of a relentlessly ugly, glass and concrete, post-
nuclear style building, housed in a corner storefront tacked
on like an afterthought, having all the style of, say, a
Tandoori takeaway. Although a police car was parked in a
reserved spot nearby, I found the door to the station locked.
Shading my eyes, I peered though the window at a short
row of chairs opposite a closed door and a ticket booth-
style window. Nobody was home. When I stepped back, I
noticed a sign on the door that informed me of the number
I should dial in case of an emergency.

'Damn!'

Back home in Maryland, I had an inside track with law
enforcement. Paul's sister, Connie, was married to a
Chesapeake County police lieutenant. In England, though,
I was on my own.

Trusting that all of Dartmouth's Finest were out inves-
tigating Susan Parker's death, I turned my back on the
empty police station and took a stroll through the lush,
sub-tropical beauty of Royal Park Gardens, ending up at
the bandstand. I plopped myself down on the top step and
closed my eyes, turning my face toward the sun. Somewhere
behind me, a busker began playing 'Fly Me To The Moon'
on a harmonica, the instrument making the tune sound so
plaintive and haunting that I fought back a fresh flood of
tears.

As much as I had wanted to cry on his shoulder, I hadn't
called Paul. I knew he'd put on his Supportive Husband
hat and insist on rushing back to Dartmouth, but the last
thing in the world I wanted was for him to abandon his
adventure – man against the sea – to rescue a damsel, no
matter how keen her distress. I must have been sending out
melancholy vibes, however, because my cell phone picked
that moment to ring.

'Hannah! I just heard about Susan Parker. Dreadful news!'

So I got to cry on his shoulder after all, but had the surprisingly great presence of mind not to mention that I'd actually

been at the scene of the accident. That would have brought Paul back to Dartmouth with a rocket tied to his tail.

After we said goodbye, I found myself inexplicably drawn to the Embankment, to the place where it happened. When I got there, barely twenty-four hours after Susan's death, the spot was already covered with mounds of flowers, everything from single buds to elaborate bouquets from Smith Street Flowers, even a wreath which someone had apparently liberated from a local cemetery bearing the inscription 'RIP Mother'. Stuffed animals, photographs of Susan torn from fan magazines, letters of condolence encased in plastic spilled out over the pavement. I flashed back to the floral tributes at Kensington Gardens following the death of Diana, Princess of Wales, then to the impromptu memorial on the banks of the South River at the spot where the body of my friend Melanie Fosher had washed ashore. Overwhelmed with sadness, I made my way to the nearest park bench and sat down on it.

And I watched them come. Middle-aged women, young twenty-somethings, girls in their teens, even the occasional man showed up to pay their respects to the late medium and clairvoyant. As the sun climbed higher in the sky, warming Kingswear across the Dart until its buildings glowed as if lit from within, I sat glued to the bench, watching the pile of floral tributes grow.

Would Susan's murderer return to the scene of the crime?

Spookily, just as that thought entered my head, I noticed someone familiar loitering at the fringes of the crowd. It was the red headband that first caught my eye, the same headband she had been wearing outside the Palace Theatre in Paignton: Olivia Sandman. Today she was dressed in a long-sleeved cotton top, and I could see the shadows of thin legs through the lightweight fabric of a flowered skirt that swished about her ankles.

I remembered the brochure Olivia had given me and fished it out of my handbag. WTL: Way, Truth and Life. I unfolded it for the first time, and scanned the contents.

Like Mikey from the old Life cereal advertising campaign, the WTL Guardians seemed to hate everything. Animal cruelty, abortion, gays, witchcraft, Muslims, wi-fi networks, the rock star Lady Gaga, and the Bishop Administrator of the Anglican Shrine of our Lady of Walsingham in particular. It was a peculiarly comprehensive catalog. As far as I could tell, the only thing WTL loved was Jesus.

Could one of the Guardians have run Susan down? Susan had always blown the group off, and yet fanatics of any religious persuasion could prove dangerous. Perhaps Susan's flippant dismissal of Alf and his band of tiny-minded men (and women) had been misguided. On the BRNC episode of *Dead Reckoning*, she'd seemed more concerned about her ex – what was his name? Greg? – than about the demonstrators.

So how about Greg Parker himself? But he was in California. Or was he?

I decided it wouldn't hurt to talk with Olivia, shake her tree, and see what fell out of it, so I wandered ever-so-casually over to the palm tree planter where the young woman was sitting and plopped myself down on the warm stones next to her. 'Hi, Olivia. I'm Hannah. Remember me from the other night?'

Olivia considered me through the lenses of a pair of rimless eyeglasses. 'In front of the Palace Theatre, right?'

'Uh huh.'

'It's terrible what happened, innit? That accident.' Olivia nodded in the direction of the floral memorial.

'Very upsetting,' I agreed.

'Someone driving drunk, I bet.'

'I'm sure the police want everyone to *think* it was one of your garden-variety hit and runs, but I understand that they're looking into the possibility that someone ran Susan Parker down intentionally.' I was making it up as I went along.

Olivia's eyes widened. 'That's a terrible thing to say!'

'Put yourself in their shoes, Olivia.' I lowered my voice to a whisper. 'Think of all the people who might have wanted Susan Parker dead. The Guardians, for example. You.'

'You're barmy.'

I shrugged. 'How about that sign you were carrying the other night. *Suffer not a witch to live.*'

Color drained from her face. 'Is that what it said? Bloody hell!'

'You didn't know?'

Olivia grimaced, produced an exasperated click of her tongue. 'I don't make the bloody signs, do I? I just carry the signs my uncle tells me to.'

'Your uncle?'

'Yeah. Alf. He's my mother's brother. Took me in an' raised me after me mum died.'

'I take it you're not completely on board with your uncle's mission, then.'

'WTL? Course I am! But look here. Nobody in WTL would have anything to do with running that medium down. That would be *murder!*'

'Well, exactly.'

'And another thing . . . what did you say your name was, again?'

'Hannah.'

'Look, Hannah. It's like this. We don't kill animals, not even for food.' She stuck out a foot. 'See these sandals?'

I nodded. The soles appeared to have been cut out of spare tires and were attached to her feet by six criss-cross straps, a style that had been popular back in my peace-now, flower-power youth.

'They're plastic,' she pointed out. 'You have to kill a cow to get leather.'

I was reminded of Alf, leathery and cadaverous, his white hair streaked with yellow or vice versa. I thought of the description of the driver given to the BBC reporter by the woman in the pink jogging suit. It could fit Alf, or . . . I sighed. It could fit millions of people – my father's girl-friend, Cornelia, for instance.

'Where were you yesterday morning?' I asked, hoping to catch Olivia off-guard.

Next to me, I felt Olivia stiffen. 'Why should I tell you?'

'I don't know, Olivia. Practicing for what you'll say when the police turn up and ask you the same question?'

She took a deep breath, exhaled through her mouth. 'Glastonbury High Street. We want the town to pull down the wi-fi masts. Everybody knows that EMFs are dangerous.'

'EMFs?'

She gave me one of those how-can-you-be-so-stupid looks. 'Electro-magnetic fields. Headaches, dizziness, rashes, respiratory problems.' She took another deep breath. 'Ever wonder why there's so many cases of autism these days?' She nodded sagely. 'EMFs.'

Childhood vaccinations, mercury, paracetamol, frigid moms . . . what *didn't* cause autism? I wondered. As much as I wanted to pin Susan's death on creepy Alf or one of his minions, if the WTL Guardians had been picketing in Glastonbury the previous morning, there was no way one of its members could have been driving a – Ford? Vauxhall? Fiat? – recklessly in Dartmouth.

While Olivia rattled on about the effects of EMFs on the fertility of women in their middle years, I pulled a notebook out of my handbag, tore out a sheet of paper, scribbled down my name and cell phone number and handed it to her. 'Susan Parker was my friend,' I told her. 'If you think of anything, Olivia, please, just call this number.'

Leaving Olivia to perch on the planter like a pigeon with something to think about – or so I hoped – I power-walked my way to the Castle and back, but instead of defogging my brain, the exercise only made me hungry. By the time I reached The Apprentice, the tea I'd had at the Castle had long worn off, so I popped into the restaurant – formerly St Barnabas Church – climbed the stairs to the second level, and sat down by myself at one of the ultra-modern tables next to a stained glass window. At a table nearby, a man had a laptop open and was checking his email. My server – one of a dozen or so apprentices who lived and worked at the converted church, preparing themselves for jobs in the hospitality industry – materialized out of nowhere on little cat feet, took my order for panna cotta and coffee, and disappeared just as quietly.

The best of all worlds, I thought. Christ on His Throne of Glory on my one hand, the Internet on the other, and a cappuccino – the finest Dartmouth has to offer – on the way.

Too bad Susan Parker wasn't there to share it with me.

ELEVEN

'Looking now at the two brass monuments set in the floor, the one nearer to the altar is considered to be the largest and finest church brass in the whole of Devon, being that of John Hawley II and his two wives, the first on his right Joanna, by whom he had a son. Joanna died in 1394 and was buried in the chancel. Later he married Alicia of the famous, very rich, Cornish family of Tresilian, who died in 1403. John Hawley II died on the 30 December 1408 and all are now buried together under the brass. John Hawley II is considered by some to be the model for the 'Shipman' of Chaucer's Canterbury Tales.*'*

St Saviour's Church: an Illustrated Historical Guide, pp. 14, 16

According to the morning news, the police were still appealing to the public for information about the hit-and-run driver who had killed Susan, but otherwise, over the past several days, the airwaves had been strangely quiet on the matter.

I was stretched out on a lounge chair in Janet's garden enjoying the sun and the latest Andrew Taylor novel when the bells of St Saviour's Church began chiming the hour. I checked my watch. It was noon on Tuesday. If I hurried, I could just make the Christian Aid luncheon. Some of the volunteers, I remembered, had been members of St Anthony's Church before it was made redundant, repurposed by a prominent architect, and Susan Parker moved in.

It might be interesting to hear what they had to say.

St Saviour's Church is nestled in the center of town at the crook of the lane where Anzac Street meets Smith Street. The faithful had been praising God on that spot since the early fourteenth century, and for almost all of those years, the first thing worshippers saw upon entering the sanctuary was a magnificent iron door, decorated with two leopards of the Plantagenets, their rear legs forming the hinges, superimposed over the Tree of Life. It was one of the finest church doors in all England, according to the Victoria and Albert Museum, and who was I to argue with that?

According to the clock in St Saviour's gray stone tower, it was only five minutes past noon when I breezed through the south door with a nod of greeting to the two splendid leopards, then climbed the wooden staircase on my left that led up to the gallery.

People were already eating lunch, seated in small groups at folding tables covered with clean, crisp tablecloths in a patchwork of patterns and colors. I was alone, feeling at loose ends. I surveyed the gallery, but didn't see anybody I knew, so I headed straight for the buffet table which was set up on the north end of the gallery under a rose window commissioned in Victorian times by a former governor of Dartmouth in honor of himself.

I selected a variety of crustless sandwiches, a dab of cabbage and carrot slaw, four carrot sticks, a lemon bar and half a slice of chocolate cake, then took my plate to a chest-high window. In the room beyond – a combination parish office and makeshift kitchen – the church ladies were busily keeping the tea coming. I paid for my lunch, chucking an extra pound in the jar for the poor, as was customary, then went in search of a place to sit.

Most of the tables were already occupied by groups of two or three engaged in animated conversation, but one Old Dear seemed to be lunching alone, so I homed in on her. 'Do you mind if I join you?'

She looked up from a bit of bread and cheese held daintily between thumb and forefinger, smiled invitingly and said, 'Please, do.'

'I'm Hannah Ives, visiting from America,' I said as I sat down in the folding chair across the table from her.

'And I'm Liz Talbot. Didn't I see you here last week?'

She polished off the sandwich and considered me with serene gray eyes.

'You did. I was with my friend Alison Hamilton. She couldn't come today.'

In point of fact, Alison had taken to her bed, still so distraught over Susan Parker's death, she'd sobbed over the telephone, that she'd rummaged through her medicine cabinet, found two tablets remaining in a five-year-old prescription bottle of Valium, and – while I was talking to her – took them both. 'She was friends with Susan Parker,' I explained, 'the woman who was killed on the Embankment the other morning. She's taking it a bit hard.'

Liz tut-tutted. 'I heard about the accident on the telly. Terrible business, that. Sometimes I wonder what this old world is coming to.' She picked up a fairy cake, slathered with thick, pink frosting, and pinched off a small piece. 'I chatted with Susan a couple of times when she helped out with the lunches here. She seemed like such a nice, *normal* person, in spite of what *some* said about her.'

'I understand she lived in old St Anthony's Church,' I said, polishing off a carrot stick. 'I gather not everyone at St Anthony's was happy about that.'

Liz shrugged. 'Making flats out of the church was better than pulling it down, I suppose. Not that I'd want to live there, you understand, not with that graveyard in my back garden!'

'Yes, but St Anthony's is a spiritual sort of place, isn't it? I can see why a church, graveyard and all, might appeal to someone like Susan Parker. After all, people have been praying there for over a century.'

Liz had finished her cupcake and leaned back in her chair. In spite of the summer weather, she was dressed in a brown wool suit and an old-fashioned white blouse with a flounce at the neck. If I peeked under the tablecloth, I was sure I'd find stocking feet laced into sensible, brown shoes. 'There's a difference between being spiritual, as in religious or devout, and spiritual, as in ghostly,' she chuckled.

After a moment, I said, 'I read somewhere that around thirty churches close each year in this country. Makes me wonder if England is losing its faith.'

Liz's eyes grew wide. 'Dear me, no. Stay here long enough and you'll learn one simple truth: the Victorians have a lot to answer for. They simply built too many churches! Even in Victorian times, the churches were only half-full, but money was pouring into Britain at the time, and a regular building frenzy was going on.

'St Anthony's came very close to being preserved by the Churches Conservation Trust,' she continued, 'but after a buyer was found – Susan Parker, as it turned out – well, you know what happened after that.'

I swallowed hard, thinking how much I'd looked forward to seeing Susan's flat, particularly the beautiful Byrne-Jones windows Janet Brelsford had told me about. That would never happen now. 'I've walked past St Anthony House,' I told Liz Talbot, 'but I've never been inside. From the outside, you'd hardly know it'd been broken up into flats.'

'There are strict rules about renovating the exteriors, Hannah, but the insides? I heard of one church, St Ann's in Warrington. They converted it to an inside climbing gym.' She clucked her tongue in disapproval.

'Shocking!' a new voice said. It belonged to a woman seated at the adjoining table. She'd finished her lunch and had taken out her knitting, but had clearly been following our conversation.

'Lilith, this is Hannah Ives, visiting from America. Hannah, Lilith Price. We've just been discussing poor Susan Parker.'

I thought I'd heard Lilith's name before, but I seemed to be suffering from noun-deficiency anemia, so I simply nodded and said, 'Pleased to meet you, Lilith,' and continued eating my sandwich.

Lilith adjusted the yarn around her finger and took another stitch. 'Very sad, but I don't believe in any of that talking to the dead nonsense.'

Earlier, I'd gotten such a rise out of Olivia that I thought I might try similar scare tactics on Lilith. Keeping my voice neutral, I said, 'Some are saying that the police think Susan Parker's death might not have been an accident. There were people who were mightily unhappy when she moved into St Anthony's Church, for one thing.'

Lilith had finished a row. Using her free knitting needle, she rapped the table three times, emphasizing each word. 'Stop right there! I don't know who you've been talking to, Hannah, but I won't stand for anyone making it sound like we had picketers pacing the pavement outside St Anthony's carrying signs with "Yankee Go Home" written all over them. Only a handful of us were left at St Anthony's. We objected to the church being made redundant, that's true, but once the PCC decided that selling St Anthony's was the best course of action, and the bish made his decision, there wasn't much any of us could do.'

Lilith stuck the needle back into her project and began working another row. 'Besides,' she said, knitting furiously. 'St Saviour's is a wonderful church home.'

Liz, on the other hand, seemed more inclined to play along with my darker scenario. 'How about that woman who was furious about her husband's memorial, Lilith?'

Lilith squinted at her work, took out a stitch and re-knit it. 'What woman?'

'It was comical.' Liz turned her attention to me. 'One of the construction lorries backed into his tombstone, toppling it like a tree. A preposterous thing, if you ask me, which you aren't, but I'll tell you anyway. It was an obelisk, this high.' She held a hand over her head, which I took to mean about five feet. 'Wreaths and anchors all over, with trumpeting cherubs and suppliant angels running rampant, and a Greek cross on the top.'

Next to me, Lilith snorted. 'I'll have to agree with you there. Very O.T.T. When my time comes, plant me in a plain pine box wearing one of those nametags that says, "Hello. My name was Lilith" written in felt-tipped pen.

Remembering all the adhesive nametags I'd slapped to my chest at social functions, I had to laugh. I hadn't figured Lilith for a sense of humor. 'So, what happened with the tombstone?' I asked Liz.

'The woman threw a wobbly, threatened to take legal action, so the contractor agreed to move the monument to her garden. She had them set it in place next to the tombstone of her dog, Rex, and she's planted flowers all around.

Her husband's body is still in the graveyard at St Andrews, of course, so I don't know what the point of that exercise was.'

I think I knew. 'After the funeral is over, don't we all need a physical *place* where we can go to mourn?' I thought about Cathy Yates, trying to locate her father's body so she could fill not only the empty plot waiting for him back home in Pittsburgh, but the hole in her heart. And what of the Embankment where mourners continued to build a floral tribute to Susan Parker at the very spot where the medium had breathed her last?

Lilith looked up from her knitting. 'I agree completely, Hannah. And in this electronic age, that place can even be an online memorial page on Facebook.'

'Don't I know!' I said. 'I came completely unglued when I got an email from a friend who had recently passed away. It was sent by her daughter, as it happened, but it gave me quite a turn when my friend's name popped up on the "From" line in my mailbox.'

Lilith inclined her head toward mine. 'Answering machine greetings are the worst, you know.' She shuddered. 'They forget to change them, so you get a voice from beyond the grave.'

'Well, on that cheerful note, I have to be off!' Liz fished around under the table for her handbag, then stood up. 'Nice to meet you, Hannah. Will you be here next Tuesday?'

'I'll walk out with you,' I said, picking up my own handbag.

When we got to the bottom of the steps, however, I revised my plan. 'I hope you don't mind, Liz, but I think I'll stay a while and say a little prayer for Susan Parker. Until next week, then?'

I saw Liz out the door, picked up a Book of Common Prayer from the bookshelf, then made my way down the south aisle to the beautiful little Lady Chapel. I sat down in one of the blue-cushioned chairs, opened the prayer book to the section on the burial of the dead, and read: *I am the resurrection and the life, saith the Lord; he that believeth in me, though he were dead, yet shall he live; and whosoever liveth and believeth in me shall never die.*

Life after death; Susan's stock in trade. Was what she did for a living so incompatible with Christianity? I didn't think so. With the book laying open in my hands, I closed my eyes and prayed for Susan's soul, and that whoever was responsible for her death would be brought to justice. When I opened my eyes again, I noticed a Sacrament lamp – a perpetual candle in a brass holder hanging from a chain attached to the wall. I stared at the lamp, opening my mind, embracing the silence, hoping – but not really believing – that Susan might actually reach out from the beyond and speak to me. But my only answer was the volunteers' happy chatter spilling down from the gallery as they did the washing-up after the lunch.

I took the long way round on my way out of St Saviour's, passing through the Ambulatory – past the antique hand pump fire engine and the Armada chest – through to the Chancel where I found myself standing, quite literally, on the splendid Hawley Brass.

Dressed in a full suit of armor, John Hawley the Second lay tall and ramrod straight between his two wives, looking none too happy about it. Each lady was adorned with jewels in her hair, and was accompanied in the afterlife by a pair of toy dogs wearing bells on their collars. But John, I noticed, was holding Joanna, the first wife's, hand. It was a good thing that Alicia, wife number two, had predeceased old John, or she might have had a thing or two to say about that.

Meanwhile, back in the twenty-first century, I thought about Jon Hamilton and *his* two wives, my friend Alison and Wife Number One, who had perished at sea.

How was it, I wondered, that in all the years that we'd known Alison and Jon, the subject of Wife Number One had never come up? We still wouldn't have known about her if Susan Parker hadn't picked up vibes about an earlier marriage at Janet's dinner.

Clearly, I didn't know Alison as well as I thought. Over the years, we'd exchanged frequent emails, annual Christmas cards. Alison emailed my daughter, Emily – who called her Auntie A – and remembered to send cards on my grandchildren's birthdays. How could a relationship be so one-sided? Now I even found myself wondering if their daughter, Kitty, was Alison's, or Jon's by his previous marriage to . . . who was it? . . . Beth?

Alison and I were friends, weren't we? I figured I'd just pop over to her house and see how she was doing. And while I was there, I'd simply ask her to tell me about Beth.

But before I did that, I decided to pay a visit to the Dartmouth Public Library.

TWELVE

'It has long been said that once a year the River Dart demands a human life and when it is ready for "a heart" it will "cry out" and summon its victim. The sound of the river can usually be heard near the "broad stone" or brad stones. An old saying goes: "Dart, Dart, cruel Dart, every year thou claimst a heart."'

www.Legendarydartmoor.co.uk

The Dartmouth Public Library occupies the ground floor of the Flavel Arts Centre, a modern, tastefully designed building with a dramatic zig-zag roof over a glass façade that exposes each of its three floors to public view, like a doll house. I had to pass by the police station to get there, and as usual, I looked in. Although the station was open, the young officer manning the counter would tell me nothing about their progress on Susan Parker's case except to say that the investigation was ongoing.

Damn, I thought, as I crossed the street and headed for the library. I'd learned more than that from the woman reading the news on television that morning. Forensic analysis was being done of the victim's clothing, the reporter had told the viewing public over their Weetabix, toast and orange marmalade. Furthermore, an accident reconstruction expert had been called in from Croydon, and his report was expected shortly.

As I waited for assistance at the library reference desk, I began to case the joint. I was surrounded by shelves crammed with books, magazines, DVDs, and other material, so closely spaced that the effect was almost claustrophobic. If e-books didn't become all the rage, I figured it wouldn't be long before the library ran out of shelf space. Nearby, a rank of computers was provided for public use. I'd come at a good time, apparently, as only one of the machines was occupied.

A librarian materialized from somewhere in the stacks and greeted me with a friendly, 'May I help you?'

I explained that I was looking for old newspaper reports.

'I suggest you start with Newsbank,' the librarian said. 'That's our most comprehensive resource, and it's online.' She pointed to a terminal. 'Click online resources and you'll find Newsbank among those listed.'

I sat down and followed her instructions.

Newsbank came up immediately, filling the screen with a multicolored map of the UK. Because I wanted to see newspapers in the South West, I clicked on the turquoise section of the map. Of twenty-two newspapers in that general region, almost all had come online in 2007.

Rats.

Surprisingly, the *Dartmouth Chronicle* wasn't listed at all, and of the others, the one of most likely interest, the *Western Morning News* out of Plymouth, went back only as far as 1999. I figured Beth Hamilton had gone missing around 1994, so that was no help at all.

'I guess I should have been more specific,' I told the librarian when she reappeared at my elbow to ask how I was getting on. 'The articles I need would have come out in 1994 or 1995.'

A few minutes later, I found myself seated at a microfilm machine, having flashbacks to my college days at Oberlin as I reeled my way through newspapers on film, starting with the paper closest to home, the *Dartmouth Chronicle*.

Elizabeth and Jon Hamilton had been avid sailors, that I knew, but finding numerous references to sailing races in which they had participated brought that fact into sharp focus. Jon's Contessa 32 was a sprightly little craft, I realized as I scanned the results of race after race. When she wasn't winning outright, *Biding Thyme* was consistently placed in the top three. No wonder Jon was loathe to part with her.

Halfway through the *Dartmouth Chronicle* for 1994, I

found what I was looking for: 'Local Woman Presumed Drowned in Solo Sailing Accident'. When I noticed the date on the article, all the breath left my body.

July 30. The date of Janet's dinner party, when Susan Parker had been guest of honor. No wonder Beth's spirit had been sending out vibes that evening. No wonder Jon had freaked.

Beth had been seen by several people, the newspaper reported, sailing out of the marina alone. Several hours later, *Biding Thyme* had been discovered, sails still set, at Stumpy Steps not far from the Castle. There was nothing in the article that I didn't know already, except that Jon and his daughter had been away at the time, visiting his mother in Exeter.

I paged forward to the following week's *Chronicle* to find, as expected, that police were still searching for Beth's body. The shore on both sides of the Dart had been thoroughly combed by police and volunteers, I learned, but to no avail. A tiny spot of blood that proved, upon analysis, to have come from Beth, had been found on the stern of *Biding Thyme*, but there was no way to tell how the blood had got there, or when. 'There is no evidence of foul play,' a police spokesman said.

The week after that, the *Chronicle* reported, an expert on wind and water current patterns had been called in from Oxford University. Cardiff University in Wales sent the top tide man from their Hydro-Environmental Research Center. When the two experts put their heads together, they produced a series of graphs and hydrographic charts with circles and arrows, and the joint opinion that Beth's body had floated out to sea.

The week after that, nothing. Ditto the week after that.

As far as the *Dartmouth Chronicle* was concerned, Beth Hamilton had vanished off the face of the earth.

I sat back and gnawed on my thumbnail. The way I saw it, there were four possible explanations for Beth's disappearance:

Beth had tumbled overboard and drowned. An accident.

She'd jumped overboard and drowned. A suicide.

She'd been boarded, clobbered, and thrown overboard. Murder.

She went sailing, leaped overboard, swam to shore and disappeared. A runaway.

'Beth is a strong swimmer,' Jon had been quoted as saying. *Is*, I noticed, and not *was*. But what could she have been running away from? A bad marriage? From what Alison had told me, their marriage had been perfect, so there was little likelihood of that.

If not running *from* something, was there anything she'd been running *to*? A lover, perhaps?

I wanted to slap myself for thinking such vulgar thoughts, but the idea must have occurred to the police, too. Two weeks after she went missing, the *Chronicle* had published a picture of Beth with the caption, 'Have you seen this woman?'

Only four explanations for Beth's disappearance. I rubbed my tired eyes and went over them again in my head. Accident, suicide, murder or AWOL. No, wait a minute. Five. Beth could have been abducted by aliens.

Maybe I needed a break.

As I was returning the microfilm reels to the reference desk, I remembered something Janet Brelsford had said the night of the party: *each year the Dart takes a heart.*

Back at the computer, with Newsbank on the screen, I put my fingers on the keyboard and typed in 'Dart' and 'Drowning,' then scanned the search results covering the past ten years. One death a year was about right. A tourist falls off a luxury yacht; a widow drowns near her favorite spot; a canoeist is trapped under his overturned canoe; a drunken youth tumbles off the Embankment. In most cases, the body of the victim had been recovered in a few days. In one case, rescue teams used an Air Force search and rescue helicopter equipped with thermal imaging cameras to help find the body.

Alas, no such technology had been called into play when Beth Hamilton went missing. Gradually, everybody seemed to forget about poor Beth, except for Jon Hamilton and his daughter, Kitty, age six.

THIRTEEN

'An elderly driver caused a spectacle when his vehicle crashed into an opticians. The man, aged 89, had only just started his automatic car when it ploughed into the front of Sussex Eyecare in Broad Street, Seaford. Daeron McGee, the owner of the opticians, said: "I was round the corner . . . and came back to see a car in my front window. The driver seems to be OK . . . He said he had a dizzy turn and hit the accelerator instead of the brake. Thankfully there was nobody in his way but I've got an entire range of Oakleys and Ray Bans which have been demolished."'
'Elderly Driver Creates Spectacle At Seaford
Opticians', *Brighton News*, 27 June 2009

Wednesday morning dawned dark and drear, with rain drizzling from a leaden sky. An earlier phone call to Alison had produced nothing but an invitation to leave a message on her call minder, so after a quick breakfast, I zipped myself up in a slicker, grabbed an umbrella and headed up Waterpool Road to her house.

The way Alison had been carrying on the previous day, I expected to find the shades drawn, a black wreath on the door, and have my knock answered by a lugubrious butler droning, 'I'm sorry, Madam, but Madam is indisposed.'

Imagine my surprise, then, when Alison herself opened the door almost immediately, dressed in neat jeans and an Aran pullover, hair brushed until it shone, and make-up so expertly applied that it hardly showed. She held an open lipstick in her hand; I'd apparently interrupted her in the act of applying it while peering into the mirror in the tiny foyer.

'Come in, Hannah! Good to see you.' She stepped aside

so I could get out of the rain. 'I'm just heading out, I'm afraid. Dad called this morning all at sixes and sevens. He's got some Hooray Henries coming all the way from Manchester for a viewing, and the house is a tip.' She opened a handbag that lay on the table under the mirror and tossed her lipstick in. 'But then, what else is new?'

'I just stopped by to see how you're doing. I called first, but got the machine.'

'Sorry! I unplugged the phone yesterday and forgot to plug it back in.' She reached for a raincoat that hung on a hook behind the door. 'Almost wish I hadn't. Dad's call came in so fast after I plugged it back in that he must have had me on speed dial.'

'Want company?'

'That would be super!'

Three pairs of boots were lined up along the wall under the coat rack. Alison reached down and handed me a bright green pair. 'You'll need some wellies,' she said. 'It's been raining since midnight and the lane is going to be a mucky mess.'

I held the bottom of one of the wellies up against my shoe. 'It should fit.'

'They're Kitty's,' she said, referring to her daughter. 'I've been nagging her to come and pick them up, but now I'm glad she didn't.'

I sat down on the third step of the staircase that led up to the first floor, pulled on the wellies, turning my foot this way and that, admiring the fit. 'These will do nicely.'

Alison slipped her feet into her own boots, grabbed an umbrella out of the stand and waved it in the air like a baton. 'Why couldn't those people come on a *sunny* day! Sod's law, I suppose. Ready?'

'As I'll ever be.'

The twenty-minute drive to Three Trees Farm took us nearly forty. Alison had not yet replaced her Micra, so we were riding in Jon's old but still serviceable Peugeot. Even with the windshield wipers set to frantic, visibility was so poor that Alison hunched over the steering wheel, gripping it tightly with both hands, focusing her attention to the road. When we reached the relatively straight stretch on the outskirts of Merrifield and Alison relaxed her grip on the wheel, I figured the time had come. 'Can I ask you something, Alison?'

'What?'

'Kitty. Is she yours, or is she Jon's by his first marriage?'

Alison took her eyes off the road long enough to flash me a wan grin. 'I think you can do the math on that, Hannah.'

'She's twenty-one, and you and Jon have been married for . . . how long? Fifteen years?'

'Bingo.'

'So she's Beth's daughter?'

Alison bit her lower lip, concentrating as she guided the car through a pool of water that had accumulated on the road. 'Yes.'

I've got a fairly tough skin, but the fact that Alison hadn't shared that important part of her personal history with me really stung. But I decided there was no profit in giving Alison a hard time about it. I was sure she had her reasons, and with time and a little gentle prodding, I'd find out what they were.

'It never occurred to me that Kitty wasn't your biological daughter,' I said. 'She looks like you for one thing. Same coppery hair, same green eyes.'

'She favors Beth,' Alison said wistfully. After a beat she added, 'I've always wondered if that wasn't why Jon was attracted to me in the first place.'

Alison had the heater going full blast to keep the windscreen defogged, so I adjusted the dashboard air vent to blow upward and unbuttoned my slicker. 'I don't think I've ever asked you, but where did you and Jon meet?'

Next to me, I saw her smile. 'In a tiny village in Wiltshire. I'd gone there with a friend on bank holiday weekend to attend the Edington Music Festival. I ran into Jon outside the tea hut.'

'I didn't know you and Jon were into classical music.'

She shook her head so emphatically that her teardrop earrings bounced against her neck. 'You're thinking of the

Three Choirs Music Festival. Edington's not a series of classical concerts like that. It's music within the liturgy.' She smiled at me again. 'Basically, you go to church four times a day for a week. Very smells and bells.'

'So, the choir is singing masses? Sounds divine.'

'Not choir. Choirs. It's August and most of the choirs in England are on hiatus, so Edington is able to attract choristers from all over the country. There's a choir of men and boys, a mixed group called the Consort – counter-tenors and all! – and the Schola. They're my favorite.' She was grinning hugely. 'Twelve guys singing Gregorian chant by candlelight. To. Die. For.'

'Sounds like you and Jon hit it off right away.'

'He was so depressed, Hannah. He'd just lost Beth, and Kitty was only six. He told me later that he hoped the music would bring him closer to God, help fill the vast emptiness inside him.' Alison glanced into the rear-view mirror, tapped the brakes, then turned left into a narrow country lane. 'We were both a little surprised at how quickly it seemed to happen. One minute we're drinking instant coffee in a sunny churchyard, the next minute we're tearing at each other's clothes and falling into bed at the Travelodge near the Little Chef at Warminster.'

'How come you never told me about this?'

'I guess we were both a little embarrassed about moving in together so soon after Beth's disappearance.' Alison braked hard as a pheasant flapped its way out of the hedgerow, narrowly missing the windscreen. As the car sat idling on the lane, she faced me and said, 'It sounds ghoulish, I know, but God, I wish they'd found her body!' She shifted the car into park. 'The first year we were together, I lived every day in fear that Beth would come back. Then what would I do? "Hello, Jon, I'm back. You can go away now, Alison."' She made a brushing, run-along-now motion with her hand.

'At dinner that night, when Beth tried to come through? I rejoiced, Hannah! Rejoiced! Because that meant . . .'

'She was really dead.' I finished the sentence for her.

'Yes! God forgive me, but I was happy about that. Jon

was crazy about Beth, Hannah. When we first met, he talked about her constantly. I always felt I could never measure up. You always said that I had impeccable taste in decorating, but it was all Beth. Jon didn't want me to change anything, at least not at first. Kitty's bedroom was a shrine to Beth. Photographs, Beth's hairbrush, her little bottle of Chanel Number Five. Every time I went in to clean . . . well, it broke my heart. All that moved out with Kitty when she married, thank goodness, but I know that Jon kept a picture of Beth in his wallet for the longest time.'

I wondered if that was the same picture of Beth that had been published in all the newspapers. If so, I thought Alison's resemblance to Beth was superficial, more like a second cousin than a sister, but I didn't say so.

Next to me, Alison leaned back against the headrest. 'Maybe if we'd been able to have children of our own . . .' She let the sentence die.

I didn't know what the laws were in Britain, but in the United States, one had to wait seven years before a missing person could be declared officially dead. Unless Jon had divorced Beth for 'desertion,' or petitioned the court to have her declared dead, I imagined he and Alison would have had to wait quite a while before they could legally marry.

'But, after a while, when it must have been clear that Beth was never coming back?'

'Oh, I wanted to marry and have babies of my own, but it wasn't to be. It wasn't Jon's problem, obviously, since he'd already had Kitty.'

'Does the National Health cover fertility treatments?' I asked.

'They do now,' she explained, 'but the waiting list can be very long. Most couples opt for private treatment, but that can be very expensive.' She turned her face toward me and smiled wanly. 'And we could never be one hundred per cent certain about Beth, could we?'

A stray thought wafted into my head, took root, and blossomed. Before Alison could put the car into drive and begin moving forward, I touched her hand where it rested on the gear lever, and said, 'Alison. You and Jon never married, did you?'

I watched as a blush of embarrassment turned Alison's cheeks from white to pink. 'Please, Hannah. Don't tell my father! It would kill him.'

'Now why would I do that?'

'Kitty doesn't know, either.'

'Jeeze, Alison!'

'I know, I know. We've meant to tell her, of course. I've started to many times, but the time just never seemed to be right. We just let everyone assume we'd eloped to Gretna Green or somewhere, like that silly Bennett girl in *Pride and Prejudice*.'

'Seems to me that the right time would be for you to turn this car around, drive back to Dartmouth, brew up some tea and have a little chat with your daughter.'

Alison bit her lower lip, nodded. 'You're right, of course, but it'll have to wait until Jon gets back from Cowes. This is something we need to do together.' As she accelerated down the lane, she added, 'Besides, I have to take care of this business with my father right now.'

'If it isn't one thing, it's another,' I said as the Peugeot slid around a curve.

'Shit!' Alison wrenched the steering wheel right, then left, finally regaining control of the vehicle. 'That low spot is always a bloody mess!'

'Are we there yet?' I sing-songed, channeling my four-year-old grandson.

'Yes, sweetheart. And if you're especially good, Mummy will give you a lolly.'

Alison ducked her head and pointed left through the windscreen. 'See that stone farmhouse at the crest of the hill? That's Dad's. The property starts right . . . about . . . *here*. See where the fence line changes?'

I did. In contrast to barbed wire draped almost casually from wooden post to wooden post, Three Trees Farm was enclosed by a neat stone wall. We followed the wall for about a quarter of a mile, then turned into an even narrower lane, beginning a steep, winding ascent to the farm proper.

I had the farmhouse in view the whole time, first to my left, then to my right. Behind the house was a long, low barn built of the same honey-colored stone as the house and roofed with thatch. Stephen Bailey's Prius was parked next to the barn. I was wondering where the cows were when Alison pointed them out, a patchwork of brown and white, huddled under a tree in the pasture, mud coating their legs up to their hocks. 'Meet Graceless, Aimless, Pointless and Feckless,' Alison said with a grin. 'Daddy named them after the cows in *Cold Comfort Farm*.'

We had passed through a gateway marked by two stone pillars and a hand-painted sign that said Three Trees Farm when Alison muttered, 'What the hell?' She braked suddenly and I instantly wrenched my gaze from the poor, rain-soaked cows to whatever had attracted her attention. 'What is that silly man doing?'

As we watched, Alison's father climbed into the driver's seat of the Prius. After a few seconds, the car began rolling down the hill in our direction. 'Oh, for heaven's sake! Has he forgotten we're coming?' Alison accelerated, causing the Peugeot to fishtail on the muddy track, so she cut back to a crawl.

'Take it easy,' I said reasonably. 'He has to come past us. We can always wave him down.'

The Prius was still more than a quarter of a mile away when it seemed to pick up speed. 'What the bloody hell is he *doing*?' Alison shouted. 'Dad!'

As we watched in horror, her father's vehicle slowed, fishtailed, slowed again, then shot forward like a racehorse out of the gates, barreling down the hill toward us at high speed.

'Jesus, Jesus, Jesus, what do I do?' Alison whimpered, seemingly paralysed at the wheel.

I opened my mouth, but before I could say anything, Stephen Bailey sailed by us, his face set and grim. He slid on to the verge, sideswiped one of the pillars, and in almost balletic slow motion, brought his brand new Prius to a slow, grinding halt against the trunk of a tree that grew out of the hedgerow.

Alison and I were out of the car and at the scene in seconds. 'Dad, Dad!' Alison screamed as she wrenched the driver's side door open.

'I'm fine,' the old man said. 'Don't fuss, Alison.'

He didn't look fine to me. Although the air bags had deployed on impact and now lolled out of the glove box and a flap in the center of the steering wheel like limp tongues, Bailey had a small cut on his chin, and his right thumb was twisted back at an angle Mother Nature never intended. While Alison helped her father out of the car, I fetched the Peugeot and backed it down the road, parking it opposite the damaged Prius. Holding his arm, Alison guided her father to the back seat and forced him to sit down.

Alison smoothed her father's hair back from his forehead so she could examine him for injuries more closely. 'You'll live, but I think that chin will need a couple of stitches.'

Bailey batted his daughter's hand away. 'Don't fuss, daughter.'

Undaunted, Alison reached into her handbag, pulled a clean tissue out of a pack, licked a corner of it and used it to dab some of the blood off her father's forehead. Seemingly satisfied that he was in no imminent danger, her tone changed from solicitation to exasperation. 'Dad, where on earth were you going?'

'I started to do the washing-up, but we were out of Fairy Liquid.'

'Why didn't you call me, then? I could have brought you some.'

'I didn't want to trouble you.'

Alison stared up at the heavens as if praying for patience. I could almost see the wheels turning. *As if asking me to come all the way out here today wasn't already trouble enough?* 'What happened?' she said instead. 'We saw you start down the hill, but all of a sudden you were coming at us like a bat out of hell.'

Cradling his broken thumb in one hand, Bailey winced. 'That damn cat that's been hanging around the barn ran across the lane, and I went to hit the brake, but I think I got the accelerator instead.'

Alison pulled her cell phone out of her handbag. 'I'm going to take you to the hospital, but first, I'm going to call the AA and have them come for the car.'

'No!' Bailey ordered. 'Leave it. Tom'll fetch it with the tractor.'

'You pay for breakdown coverage, you old fool. You should use it.'

'Tom'll haul it up to the barn so I can think about it. Just had some body work done, remember. If I file another claim, I'll have a rise in premium. Can't afford that. Not at my age.'

Alison shrugged, capitulating. 'It's your car, so you can do what you bloody well want with it, you old fool.'

'Who's Tom?' I asked as Alison fastened the seatbelt around her father and prepared for the long drive to Dartmouth Hospital.

'He's one of the lads who helps with the chores. Works part-time at a body shop in Plymouth, so Dad probably figures Tom can pop the airbags back in, pound out the dents, and repaint for pence on the pound.'

'What will I do about the people who are coming to see the house?' Alison's father said wearily.

Alison raised both eyebrows and shot me a pleading look.

I took the hint. 'Don't worry about that, Mr Bailey. I'll stay at the house until you and Alison get back. What time are you expecting the estate agent?'

'Half two.'

'No problem. I'll wait. Is Tom working today?'

'He'll be in the barn.'

'And I'll see to it that Tom takes care of the car, then.'

While Alison and her father were at the hospital, and after speaking with Tom, I moved through the house like a whirlwind. Tossed two sweat-stained T-shirts, a pair of grimy khakis and half a dozen mismatched socks into the washing machine and slammed the door closed. Threw two pairs of shoes and some slippers into the bottom of a wardrobe. Made the bed. Washed, dried and put away a sinkful of dishes using detergent from a half bottle of Fairy Liquid

I found while rummaging under the kitchen sink. Bailey hadn't been out of it after all.

As I stood at the sink holding the bottle of Fairy Liquid in one hand and a dishtowel in the other, I watched Tom, perched high in the driver's seat of his tractor, tow Stephen Bailey's damaged car past the kitchen window. I felt a chill, not entirely explained by the blast of air conditioning blowing on the back of my neck from the small window unit over the kitchen table. Scrapes and scratches cut a wide swath along the entire passenger side of the Prius, and the left front fender was curved around the tire. If Alison's father had staged the accident in an attempt to cover up damage to his vehicle from a hit and run, he couldn't have done a better job of it.

But what possible motive could he have had to mow Susan Parker down?

I shrugged, draped the dishtowel over the oven door handle to dry, and moved on to the farmhouse's single bathroom. Old folks were mistaking accelerator pedals for brakes every day of the week, I reasoned as I swished a rag around the rim of the bathroom sink. Add eighty-six-year-old Stephen Bailey to that statistic. I decided that cleaning the toilet was way above and beyond the call of duty, so I closed the lid on the offending rust stains and hoped for the best. Then I sat down to watch TV and wait.

By the time Alison returned with her father a few minutes after four, a butterfly bandage on his chin and his hand in a splint, I'd learned a whole lot about converting a garage into a granny annexe, but not a single estate agent or Hooray Henry from Manchester or anywhere had showed up expecting a tour of Three Trees Farm.

FOURTEEN

*'There were, inevitably, one or two who could not
understand – like the old man of over eighty who had
lived all his life in the cottage in which he had been
born . . . So when a messenger from one of the information centres called . . . he replied that he had heard
of some outlandish talk about moving people away,
but that he "didn't want no truck wi' it, thank 'ee".
"He's a nice old boy but obstinate [said a neighbor],
[but] he's lost touch with the world, really." When
moving day came, he watched the packing being done
as if in a dream, then sat on a packing crate outside
the gate and refused to budge.'*

Grace Bradbeer, *The Land Changed Its Face:
The Evacuation of the South Hams, 1943–44,*
Devon Books, 1973, pp. 59–60

'Help me, Hannah.'

It was inevitable. The old Beach Boys classic
'Help, Help Me, Rhonda' started running through
my head, and I knew the tune would stick with me all
day.

Alison was pushing a trolley down the dairy aisle of the
Sainsbury's superstore on the outskirts of Dartmouth, and
I'd just tossed three pots of full-cream yogurt into my
section of her cart. *Fruits des bois*, Paul's fave. Our husbands
were due home the following day, and I was stocking our
mini-fridge with treats.

'Hmmm?' I drawled, the wicked beat of a Beach Boys'
bass drumming hard in my head.

Alison turned a corner and brought the trolley squeaking
to a halt in front of a cold case of cheeses. 'Your dad is in
his seventies, right?'

I found a wedge of red Leicester and tossed it into the cart along with the yogurt. 'Yes.'

'Do you ever worry about him?'

'Well, sure, but he's been on the wagon now for almost ten years, Alison.'

'That's not what I meant. I'm talking about dementia, Hannah. Maybe even Alzheimer's.' She paused, and I saw that she was gripping the handle of the trolley so hard that the veins stood out, bold and blue, on the back of her hands.

My father spent his so-called retirement designing sophisticated missile tracking devices for the US Navy, so I presumed he was still operating with a full complement of brain cells.

Alison frowned. 'Dad's accident the other day?'

'That would worry me, too.' Her hand felt cold under mine, and it wasn't from the air conditioning. 'When we get older, our reflexes aren't what they used to be.'

'It's not just that, Hannah,' she rattled on. 'Those people from Manchester showed up, all right, but their appointment was for Friday, not Wednesday. He'd got it all mixed up. And when I went back to check on Dad's car this morning, Tom told me that he's been worried about Dad, too. He seems distracted, Tom says. Misplacing his tools. Tearing the house apart looking for his keys, only to find he'd left them in the ignition. And last week, he was supposed to take delivery of a shipment of seed, and he forgot all about it. When they got to the farm and found nobody home, the delivery men dumped the bags in the courtyard instead of stacking them in the barn.'

'Gosh, Alison, I'm so sorry.' We walked only a few more steps before I decided I needed to add to the misery by telling her about the Fairy Liquid, too. 'It didn't seem significant at the time, but I discovered he wasn't out of Fairy Liquid, either. I found a bottle half full of the stuff under the sink.'

'Christ on a crutch,' Alison said, giving the trolley a savage push to get it going again. 'Three Trees can't sell fast enough for me. I want him in that retirement home so *someone* will be keeping an eye on him. I can't do it from Dartmouth.'

'He shouldn't be driving, Alison,' I said gently.

'Don't I know it! But Tom says the damage to the Prius was mostly cosmetic.'

'If my face were as bunged up as that car, I'd need the help of a skilled plastic surgeon.'

'Yes, but like that car, you'd still be drivable, or so Tom says. Clever boots put it back together with duct tape and chewing gum.' She seemed to brighten. 'Well, if my father wants to drive around in a vehicle that looks like it's been through the wars, that's fine with me, as long as he stays on the farm. That way, nobody else is likely to get hurt.'

'If only you could guarantee that he'd stay on the farm.' I sighed. 'In the old days, we'd simply remove the distributor cap.'

'Cars don't have distributor caps any more.'

'Pity.' I engineered a detour down the aisle where they carried the Hob Nobs and snagged two packets of the chocolate-covered kind. 'What does your father's doctor say?'

'He refuses to see one.'

'His vicar?' I asked, remembering a cute little church in the village.

'Dad? Don't make me laugh. He hasn't darkened the door of a church since the day I was baptized.' She aimed the trolley for one of the checkout aisles. 'Mum was such a steadying influence. It's been very hard since she died.'

My stomach lurched. *Been there, done that.* 'Well, as you say, getting him into that retirement home is a number-one priority. Have you thought about lowering the asking price on the farm?'

Alison tossed a cello pack of tomatoes on the conveyor belt, followed by two heads of romaine and a bunch of radishes. 'Give it another week. I need to discuss it with Jon. Then we'll see.'

The following afternoon, a bright, sunny Sunday, we met Paul and Jon at the Dart Marina Hotel and Yacht Basin. The guys were sitting at a table outside under a blue umbrella, looking fit, tan and full of good cheer, primarily the amber liquid kind.

On the spot, Alison invited Paul and me to dinner,

allegedly to celebrate *Biding Thyme*'s triumph at Cowes, where our team came in first in three races out of seven, and placed second overall. But as soon as we arrived at the Hamilton home that evening, bottle of wine in hand, I knew that something else was on the agenda. A white damask cloth covered the table, candles flickered in silver candlesticks, a name card sat in front of each place – all that was missing was the paper streamers and party hats.

While Jon, with Paul assisting, twisted a corkscrew into the bottle of wine we'd brought to the party, I followed Alison into the kitchen, eyeing her suspiciously. 'OK, what gives?'

She smiled mysteriously, and handed me a plate of cheese straws.

When we got back to the sitting room, Jon reached behind the sofa and produced a silver ice bucket draped with a damask napkin. Holding the bucket in one hand, he removed the napkin with a flourish. 'Tah dah! Champagne all round!'

Champagne flutes materialized just as magically, and when all the glasses were full, Alison raised hers high. 'A toast!' she crowed, beaming in the direction of her father who sat, solemn as Buddha, in a straight back chair. 'We've sold the farm!'

'Hear, hear!' said Paul.

'Super!' said I.

'Fools!' growled Stephen Bailey. By tacit agreement, everyone decided to ignore him.

'To who? Whom?' I corrected.

'That pair from Manchester,' Alison announced. 'Offered the asking price for it, too.'

'Hobby farmers,' Bailey sneered. 'Don't know a bloomin' thing about farming. Turn up with a copy of *Pig Farming for Dummies* in their manbags, and think they know it all.' The way he said 'manbags' made it clear what he thought about men who carried shoulder bags. 'Just wait till winter sets in. They'll be driving out to Tesco soon enough.'

Jon raised his glass. 'Another toast! Goodbye to mud, muck, manure and misery!'

Alison punched him in the arm. 'It wasn't *that* bad!'

'So, what are they going to raise?' I asked, thinking that with all that acreage it could be anything.

'Bees or cheese,' mumbled Alison's father. 'Hard to tell with that Mancky accent.'

Paul raised an eyebrow. 'Mancky?'

'They're Mancunian, aren't they? Manc. From Manchester. Need bleeding subtitles crawling across their chests.'

I laughed so hard that I spit wine out my nose. Put my cocktail napkin to good use before I asked, 'So, Mr Bailey, what does a Mancunian sound like?'

'Ever seen *Life on Mars? Cracker*?'

'Yes. We had them on PBS or BBC America, I think. Enjoyed them a lot.'

'Like that.'

'They mumble, you mean?'

'Sound like they just stepped off the special needs bus.'

'Dad!' Alison flushed crimson, and shot me a you-can-dress-'em-up-but-you-can't-take-'em-out look of embarrassment.

Political correctness aside, I had to laugh. I found myself wondering if any nineteenth-century Mancunians had settled in rural Kentucky where a gas station attendant had once inquired, 'Youoioh?' My college roommate-slash-interpreter had informed me that he was merely wondering if we came from Ohio.

Paul eased the champagne out of the ice bucket. 'More bubbly?' As he topped off our glasses he said, 'So, when do you close?'

'It's a cash offer, and there's no chain, so it should happen relatively quickly,' Jon said.

Alison grinned. 'Then, as you Americans are wont to say, it's a done deal!'

But as anyone who has ever bought property in the UK will tell you, it's definitely not over until it's over.

FIFTEEN

'In the hierarchy of life forms on this, our earth, the British tabloid journalist lies somewhere between the hagfish and the dung beetle.'
Tunku Varadarajan, *www.Forbes.com*,
2 February 2009

The next morning after breakfast, I nipped back upstairs and managed to catch the news on the tiny flat-screen television in our room. Susan's death was still a major story, but there had been no progress on the case:

> *'Police have issued a fresh appeal for information leading to the identification of a hit-and-run driver who left a popular television personality dying on the North Embankment in Dartmouth, Devon, whilst walking her dog. Susan Parker, star of the television show,* Dead Reckoning . . .'

The news reader went on and on, but didn't tell me anything I didn't already know, so I switched the television off.

I was still sitting on the arm of an overstuffed chair, feeling that I ought to be doing something, but not knowing exactly what, when I felt Paul's hand on my shoulder. 'What we need, Hannah, is another medium.'

I managed to dredge up a smile. My husband, in his own backhanded way, was trying to be helpful. 'Good idea, Paul, but from what I understand, Susan wasn't on speaking terms with most of them in life, so I doubt she'd be dying to talk to them now.' I caught my breath. I'd not intended to be punny.

If you're lookin' for the bloke what done me in, his name is Greg.

Susan had been joking when she said that, right? And

yet, I found myself wondering where Greg Parker had been on Friday morning. Back home in California, presumably. Los Angeles, City of Angels. According to the CNN reporters hanging out at Heathrow Airport, Greg Parker would be stepping off a BA flight from Los Angeles – flying first class on Susan's dime, no doubt – at any moment.

'If Susan chooses to talk through a medium,' Paul was saying when I tuned back in, 'there's no shortage of them about.'

Janet kept a pile of daily newspapers on a side table in the dining room. Paul had liberated a copy of the *Daily Mirror* – the only tabloid Janet would allow in the house – from under *The Times* and now he handed it to me. 'Check this out.'

I scanned the headlines. Susan was already communicating with other mediums, it appeared:

Ghost Lady's Ghost Speaks!
Medium Murder Message!

'Well, they're both fakes, we can be sure of that.'

Paul squeezed my shoulder. 'Basingstoke,' he whispered.

'Exactly. When one of those charlatans comes up with the word Basingstoke, she'll have my undivided attention.'

The following morning, I visited the police station and, once again, found it locked. I seriously swore, using the big F-word. To be fair, solving Susan's hit-and-run was probably the highest priority on their blotter, so maybe they *were* all out hunting for Susan's killer.

I followed the *Dartmouth Chronicle*, the local weekly. High crimes that week had included the theft of twenty pounds' worth of groceries from an elderly lady while she was returning her trolley to its bay, and a woman who was evicted from her home for chronic 'anti-social behavior'. Playing loud music day and night was a crime that paled in comparison with what had happened to my friend Susan, so I'm sure the police had their hands full.

There's a newsagent on the corner near the boat float. On my way back to the B&B, I popped in and bought a copy of each of the tabloids – the *Sun*, the *Mirror*, the *Mail*, the *Express*, the *Star*. I do this at home on occasion, too, but for other reasons. Roll 'em up and tie 'em with a bow. Give them as gifts at office Christmas parties, or to patients in the hospital. *Hours* of entertaining fiction.

Back at our B&B, I went up to our room and spread the papers out on the bed.

As usual, sleaze was the story of the day. I learned who had been kicked out of the Big Brother house, what ailing actor hated his wife so much that he was divorcing her on his deathbed, and that Britney Spears was heading for rehab. Again.

'What is this endless fascination with Tom, Katie and Suri Cruise?' I muttered to Paul as I flipped through the pages of the *Mirror*. His lanky frame was sprawled on a chaise in the bay window, where he was editing the page proofs of his geometry textbook, *Geometric Proof: From Abstract Thought to CGI*.

'Dunno.' Clearly, he wasn't paying attention.

If what I read in the *Sun* was true, competition for Susan's ITV time slot was already heating up. Two episodes of *Dead Reckoning*, including the one we'd attended in Paignton, were already in the can, but after that, it'd be reruns from America, starting with *Everybody Loves Raymond*, temporarily filling Susan's hour-long time slot. I thought that episodes of *Medium*, starring Patricia Arquette, might be more appropriate, but network executives weren't beating down the door in the effort to consult me.

Perhaps they didn't take counsel from mediums, either, so candidates were auditioning for the job in the press.

'Look at this one, Paul!' I folded my copy of the *Mirror* and held it up. 'Natasha Madrid. If that isn't a made-up name, I'll eat my hat. And check out her getup!'

The last time I'd seen an outfit like that – white peasant blouse, flowered skirt, oversize gold hoop earrings, and heavy-handed eye make-up that would have made Tammy Faye Baker step back and say *whoa!*– it was being worn by a volunteer in the fortune-telling tent at the Stoke Fleming village fête. 'You weel ween big prize,' she had intoned. She was right about that, too. Hannah Ives, first place in the vegetable art competition for a herd of sheep assembled from cauliflower and black olives. But it didn't take a fortune teller to suss that fortune out, just a visit to the competition tent.

The *Mail*, *Express* and *Star* had zeroed in on Greg, who was a fairly attractive guy, if surfer-boys or Nazi youth turn you on. Caught by the camera as he emerged from airport security, he was hatless, his sun-bleached hair cut in a retro buzz. Greg was shaped like a triangle, with broad shoulders and narrow hips, and for his debut on the world stage he had selected dark pants and a pale yellow polo shirt that displayed his biceps and pecs to advantage. I flipped from one tabloid to the other, thinking that the photos were so similar that the paparazzi must have snapped their shutters at precisely the same moment. Or maybe the papers were owned by the same company.

'Greg Parker told the *Sun* that plans are in the works for a memorial service for his wife at Central Lutheran Church in downtown Minneapolis, sometime at the end of August,' I read aloud.

From the chaise, Paul spoke up. 'You think the WTL Guardians will approve of that?'

'Who gives a flying fig what they think?' I muttered.

Wait a minute. Back up, Hannah. Greg said 'wife'.

The story in the *Star* also mentioned the memorial service, but in that article, Susan Parker was described as Greg's 'estranged wife'. Had their divorce not been final?

I got my answer by turning to the *Express*. 'My wife and I were separated,' Parker told a reporter. 'Susan had filed for divorce, but I never stopped loving her, and had hoped for a reconciliation.' Greg, pictured standing in front of a white stretch limo, was wearing a little-boy-lost expression that could melt ice at the polar caps. Women were probably already queuing up to comfort the poor, grieving widower.

'Well, damn!' I tossed the paper on the carpet. 'It's an epidemic. *Everybody's* shading the truth!' First Alison, and now Susan.

'Chill, Hannah.'

I made a face. 'I've never even met the guy, but I already dislike him.'

The *Mail* reported that Greg had been playing golf in Palm Springs when news of the accident reached him. As much as I wanted to pin Susan's hit-and-run on the opportunistic so-in-so staring out at me from the front page of the *Mirror*, unless he could manage a round trip from Los Angeles to London and back at the speed of light, he had a rock-solid alibi. Or an accomplice.

Had one of Susan's readings hit too close to home? In that case, suspects were legion. All they needed was a car. A dark car, I reminded myself. Either blue or gray. Maybe black. A Ford, or a Vauxhall, or a Fiat. Everybody in England seemed to drive a Ford, Vauxhall or Fiat. How do you spell 'needle in a haystack'?

SIXTEEN

'There were men shouting, screaming, praying and dying all around them. The cold water was starting to take its toll. The minutes passed into hours and still there was nothing but darkness . . . After three hours he could no longer feel his legs. From the waist down he was paralysed by the penetrating coldness of the water . . . He also admits, with some candour, that one thing that kept going through his mind all night while he hung on to the raft, was that he had never had a woman, and he could not leave the world in that condition.'

Ken Small, *The Forgotten Dead*,
Bloomsbury, 1988, pp. 46–47

The rest of the day, I couldn't shake the feeling that Susan's murder was related to a reading, and that kept bringing me back to the mysterious disappearance of Jon's first wife, Beth. What if Jon had murdered Beth? What if he believed Susan Parker was getting messages from Beth, his victim, from the great beyond, and what if he thought Susan was going to rat him out?

There were a lot of ifs in that statement.

Even though Jon was married to my best friend, and as much as I liked him, Jon had – for the moment, at least – shot straight to the top of my suspect list. The only difficulty with this theory was my husband. Paul was Jon's alibi.

Lying next to Paul in bed that night, I said, 'Tell me about your sailing trip.'

Paul tugged on the duvet and tucked it under his chin. 'Well, the first race was Saturday . . .'

'Start before the race, when you left home.'

Paul turned his head on the pillow and studied me quizzically. 'We sailed to Cowes . . .'

'No, before that.'

'OK. Wednesday morning I got up, staggered to the loo, showered, shaved, brushed my teeth . . .'

'Not *that* early, silly.'

Paul propped himself up on one elbow. 'What's going on, Hannah?'

'I was just wondering, is all. After you sailed out of the Dart Marina, was Jon with you the whole time?'

'Of course he was! He was at the helm.'

'Thursday and Friday, too?'

'Where else would he be? We were stripping the boat of non-essentials, getting her ready to race.'

'Jon didn't slip away, even for a few hours?'

Paul's eyes widened, comprehension dawning. 'If you're asking me whether Jon had time to get himself from Cowes to Dartmouth and back again . . .'

'That's exactly what I'm wondering.'

'What are you smoking, Hannah? Jon didn't have a car, for one thing. And even if he'd rented a car, Cowes is on the Isle of Wight. It's an island, remember? Water all around? There'd be a ferry involved.' He pressed to my lips a finger that smelled like lavender soap. 'And before you go off on another wild tangent, we kipped aboard *Biding Thyme*, so there was no sneaking out of the hotel room at night, either.'

I sighed, stretched out my arm and began playing with a lock of his hair, twisting it around my finger.

Paul closed his eyes. 'May I go to sleep now?'

'Certainly.' I kissed the tip of his nose goodnight, lay down and stared at the concentric circles of light my bedside lamp was casting on the ceiling.

'Maybe Alison would have been more secure in her relationship with Jon if they'd been able to have a child together,' I mused, speaking more to the ceiling than to my husband.

Next to me, Paul stirred. 'Well, that would never happen, would it?'

'Didn't, but could have.'

'Not possible, Hannah. Jon had a vasectomy.'

I shot straight up into a sitting position, leaned over my husband. 'What did you say?'

Without opening his eyes, Paul repeated. 'Jon had a vasectomy.'

'That's what I thought you said.' I plopped back on to my pillow, my brain reeling. 'Are you sure?'

Paul nodded.

'One hundred per cent positive?'

'What's it going to take, Hannah? A signed affidavit from his surgeon?'

'When?' I asked.

'A year or so after Kitty was born.'

I sat bolt upright, stunned by the news. 'Jeeze, Paul! Jon told you that?'

'One night at the Cherub, when we were here on the exchange, in fact.' He turned on his side to look at me. 'Jon was feeling no pain at the time, and he let it slip. Frankly, I'd forgotten all about it until now.'

'From talking to Alison, I don't think she knows.'

'That would surprise me very much. Jon and Alison seem very close.'

'Maybe so, but take it from me, Alison's clueless.' I folded my pillow in half and propped it behind my back. 'OK, you're a guy. You tell me. Why would Jon keep his vasectomy a secret from Alison?'

'Perhaps he was afraid she would leave him if she found out he couldn't father her children?'

'Could be,' I agreed. 'But aren't vasectomies reversible?'

'Sometimes. But the surgery would have to be private, not on the NHS's dime. Maybe money was an issue.'

With Paul to alibi him, I was willing to scratch Jon off my list of suspects in Susan Parker's murder, but something still didn't compute. Why would a happily married man with only one child decide to have a vasectomy? Clearly, he didn't want to have any more children with Beth. So, maybe he wasn't as happily married as everybody thought.

Next to me, Paul began to saw logs.

I elbowed him awake. 'We have to ask him, Paul.'

'Ask who what?' he snuffled.

'Jon. Invite him to meet you at the pub. Ask him *why* he got that vasectomy.'

'You're not going to let me get any sleep until I agree, right?'

'I see you understand.'

'OK, I'll try.'

'Do or not do,' I quoted, channeling Yoda. 'There is no try.'

When Paul and I walked into the Cherub just before noon the following day, Jon was already there, sitting at a table in the corner, nursing a pint. When he caught sight of us, he shot to his feet. 'Hi, Hannah. I didn't know you'd be coming, or I'd have brought Alison along.'

He kissed the air next to my cheek. 'Name your poison, folks.'

While Jon went to the bar to fetch a shandy for Paul and a lemon and lime for me, we sat down. 'You go first,' I whispered.

After the arrival of our drinks and the usual pleasantries, Paul took the lead. 'Actually, Jon, we didn't invite Alison on purpose. There's something Hannah and I want to ask you.'

Jon sipped his lager, winked at me. 'Very mysterious.'

'Before we go any further,' Paul continued, 'I want you to assure me that you didn't have anything to do with Beth's disappearance.'

Jon's eyebrows shot into the stratosphere. 'Christ, Ives! How can you even think that?'

'I don't believe you did, but a couple of things that we've found out recently simply don't add up.'

Jon ran a hand nervously through what was left of his silk-fine hair. 'Like what?'

'Your vasectomy, for starters.'

'How did you . . .?' Jon looked genuinely surprised.

'You told me. Remember? Right here in the Cherub. After England won the Tournoi de France in 1997?'

'I did?'

Paul nodded.

'I must have been shit-faced.'

'You might say that.' Paul waited for that to sink in before asking, 'So, why does a perfectly healthy man decide to have himself fixed . . .?'

Jon seemed to crumple before us, his body shrinking two sizes within his freshly pressed Cambridge blue shirt.

I finally spoke up. 'Alison doesn't know, does she?'

Jon closed his eyes, wagged his head, confirming my suspicions. 'I always meant to tell her, but the time never seemed right.' He looked up, his pale eyes somber. 'It started out as just a little deception. I don't know how it got so out of hand. I may even have broken the law.'

Now I was really confused. 'Broken the law? Honestly, Jon, I don't see the connection.'

Jon took a deep breath, let it out slowly, making us wait. 'I didn't tell the police that Beth committed suicide.'

I looked at Paul and Paul looked at me, then we both stared slack-jawed at Jon.

'There was a note. It wasn't . . .' He sighed, shook his head. 'It wasn't addressed to me, it was for Kitty. But she was so young, just learning to read, really. I couldn't show it to her then, could I? And later? Well, I'd met Alison by then. Fell head over heels in love with her.' He smiled ruefully. 'Kitty took to Alison right away, too. How could I tell my daughter that her mum was a suicide, and that it was her fault?'

'Your pronouns are confusing me, Jon,' I said. 'Whose fault? Surely you don't mean that Kitty . . .'

Jon raised a hand, cutting me off. 'After Kitty was born, Beth had a severe case of post-partum depression bordering at times on psychosis. One day, I came into the nursery and caught Beth holding a pillow over the baby's face.' What little color remained in Jon's face promptly drained away. He gulped some of his lager, regained composure. 'We got Beth into treatment, of course, but I couldn't trust her alone with Kitty after that, not even for a minute. It took all the money we had, but I hired a nanny. When the nanny wasn't available, or I had to be out of town, Kitty stayed with her grandmother in Exeter, or my mother would come to us.

'We kept Beth's condition quiet, of course. In public, she'd appear to be fine, but at home, she'd sometimes sink into depression for days at a time. And when she refused to take her medication . . .' Jon let the sentence die, while I filled the silence with all kinds of horror scenarios gleaned from watching too many cop shows on television.

'I see,' Paul said. 'You couldn't take a chance of having any more children with Beth.'

Jon nodded glumly. 'Beth refused to have her tubes tied, so I had to do something.'

'Why didn't you tell Alison?' I wanted to know. 'Why did you let her go on believing it was *her* fault she couldn't have any children?'

'I'm not proud of it, Hannah. It's just that I loved Alison so much, I was afraid that she'd leave me if she knew.'

'I don't think you know Alison very well, then, Jon.'

'What happened to the suicide note?' Paul asked.

Jon stared at the ancient ship timbers that held up the ceiling of the fourteenth-century building. 'It was a horrid, rambling thing. Beth in full off-meds mode. "I'm going to kill myself before I kill my child." On and on and on. I was going to destroy the note, Ives, but in the end, I couldn't. It's in a safety deposit box at the bank.'

'But why keep the note secret from the police?' I wondered aloud. 'Was there a suicide clause in Beth's life insurance policy or something?'

'It was nothing to do with life insurance!' Jon exploded, slamming his fist on the table so hard that I had to grab my glass to keep it from toppling. 'Don't you understand? It was all about *Kitty*. I couldn't burden a six-year-old with the knowledge that her mother was so unsuited to mother-hood that she killed herself over it!'

Jon covered his eyes with his hands, breathing deeply. 'At dinner that night?' he continued in a calmer tone of voice. 'When Susan Parker said she felt a pain in her head, I knew that my suspicions were right.'

So, Susan Parker *had* gotten to him. 'What suspicions?'

Jon spread his hands out on the tabletop, fingers splayed.
'My father had a German Luger from the Second World
War. When he died, it came to me. I kept it in a box on
the top of the wardrobe in the bedroom. The gun went
missing the day Beth did.'

'Jesus!' In that instant, I saw it all. Beth, balancing on
the stern of *Biding Thyme*, aiming the gun at her head,
pulling the trigger. Beth and the gun toppling backwards
into the sea, leaving only the tiniest speck of blood to mark
her passing.

Paul reached out, squeezed his friend's shoulder. 'You
should tell the police.'

Jon blinked back tears. 'Why? It's not going to change
anything. Accident or suicide, Beth is just as dead.'

I reached out and covered one of Jon's hands with mine.
'But Alison needs to know, Jon. Tell her. Tell her *every-thing*. She thinks you're still deeply in love with Beth.'

'I've really fucked up, haven't I?' Jon lay his head on
his hands and began to cry.

SEVENTEEN

'The UK government annual statistics 2007 reveal that over 3.2 million animals suffer and die in British laboratories in experiments that "may cause pain, suffering, distress and lasting harm". An estimated additional 8 million animals are bred and then destroyed as surplus to requirements.'

www.Uncaged.co.uk

Another drink later, we left Jon, after extracting from him a promise that he'd have a heart-to-heart with Alison at the earliest possible opportunity.

Rather than return immediately to the B&B, Paul and I decided to hike to the medieval Castle that guarded the mouth of the Dart, hoping the spectacular scenery might lift our spirits. We were nearly there when my iPhone began to vibrate. I fished it out of the pocket of my jeans. I didn't recognize the number. 'Hello?' I said a bit breathlessly. Paul has long legs, and I have to work to keep up.

'Hannah, it's Olivia Sandman. I would have called you sooner, but I had trouble dialing the US number, and my calls didn't go through. Just got this weird buzzing. I'm at the Orange shop now, and they helped me out.'

I rested against the railing that separated me from a twenty-five-foot drop into the sea, and watched my husband's back disappear around a bend. 'I'm glad you called, Olivia. How can I help?'

'It's complicated,' she said.

'I'm listening.'

'Remember when you asked me about Alf and where he was the day that medium got herself killed? And I said we was in Glastonbury?'

'Yes.' My heart did a flop as I suspected (hoped!) I knew where Olivia was going.

'Well, we was, but he wasn't.'

'Where was he, then, Olivia?'

She waited a beat. 'Look, I can't talk now, but if you meet me, I can show you something.'

'Where will you be, Olivia?'

'Down in Kingsbridge. Today is when we picket the Biozencorp animal testing labs. We'll be just outside the gates. Like they'd let us in! Hah hah. You can tell Alf you're interested in joining us or something.'

I thought about Olivia's plan for less than half a second before realizing I'd have to come up with a Plan B. No way I wanted to look at, let alone carry, a picket sign with a photo of a rheumy-eyed rabbit, or a cat with electrodes screwed into its tiny skull, or a crippled dog. My stomach lurched.

'I'll think of something, Olivia.'

'OK. But be cool. And don't say much.'

'Why?'

'You know. Vancouver.'

Right. I was a Canadian.

I'd already hung up the phone when it occurred to me: I didn't have a car.

There was certainly a bus that went to Kingsbridge, but when I got back to the B&B and checked out Biozencorp on the Internet, I learned two things: it was a scientific research company claiming every major pharmaceutical company among its clients, and it was a good distance from the town center, on the Tacket Wood side.

Suddenly, like the Grinch, I got a wonderful, awful idea.

I told Paul what I was up to and invited him along. From his spot on the chaise lounge, he fanned the page proofs with his thumb and screwed up his face. 'I'm not even halfway there, Hannah, and now my damn fool editor wants to change the title.'

'To what?'

'*From Euclid to Riemann*. Idiot! You've got to throw

CGI into the equation if you want to grab the attention of high-school students.'

'Of course you do, sweetheart.' Euclid was the ancient Greek who invented geometry, so I figured Riemann was some modern dude, but otherwise I had no idea what Paul was talking about. Checking equations and formulas requires intense concentration and an eagle eye, I knew, so I gave my husband a swift kiss on the cheek, waved my iPhone under his nose so he'd know we would be tethered by AT&T and zipped out the door.

It took me less than five minutes to reach the car park at the Visitors' Center where – Hallelujah, there is a God! – Cathy's rental car was parked exactly where I'd left it.

I opened the back door, located the ignition key under the floor mat where I had been instructed to leave it, and climbed into the driver's seat. If Europcar hadn't picked the car up by now, I reasoned as I started the engine and pulled out on to The Quay, the little Corsa couldn't be an all-important cog in their enormous fleet. It would be rotten luck if Europcar decided to collect the car that day, of course. What if they reported it stolen? What if my image was captured on one of the CCTV cameras scattered about town, following my every move?

A light went on in the vast, empty attic of my brain. CCTV!

In true Big Brother style, the UK has one CCTV camera for every fourteen persons, or so they say. Did the police have a videotape of the vehicle that ran Susan down? If so, they were keeping mum. I hadn't noticed any cameras on the Embankment or in the Gardens, but that didn't mean they weren't there. As I turned south on the familiar road toward Torcross, I adjusted my sunglasses, pulled my ball cap a bit further down over my eyes, and made a mental note to look into it.

At Torcross, I turned west, heading inland toward Kingsbridge. I had entered Biozencorp's address into Cathy's GPS, and followed the voice she'd chosen – John Cleese. Does a GPS get any more trustworthy than that? On the outskirts of Kingsbridge, 'John' directed me with confidence down a narrow paved road that ended at a compound of concrete block buildings surrounded by a ten-foot-high chain-link fence, topped by coils of barbed wire. A sentry box stood to the left of a sliding electric gate, which was closed. Two private security guards wearing brown uniforms, arm patches, and humorless expressions appeared to be on duty.

I pulled to the verge behind a passenger van and several other cars, parked, and climbed out. Keeping the cars between me and the road, I strolled along the narrow verge, casually checking each one of them for damage.

Alf's much-decorated car was at the head of the line. As old as the car was, it seemed to have all its parts, and there appeared to be no damage to the left front fender. The finish, once a metallic blue, was now so bleached that any repair would have stood out like the proverbial sore thumb. It would have taken a body shop mechanic with the skills of Michelangelo to match that weather-worn, sandblasted blue.

Olivia, the youngest of the picketers by far, was easy to spot. Her red headband had been replaced by one in blue, which matched a tailored blouse tucked into a pair of white jeans. She stood to one side of the gates along with the usual WTL suspects, their number augmented that day by half a dozen representatives – according to their picket signs – of organizations called Uncaged and the British Union for the Abolition of Vivisection.

I needed to draw Olivia away from the pack.

I leaned against the bonnet of Alf's car, warm against my bum, and thought. Did Kingsbridge have a newspaper? I pulled out my iPhone, opened the Google app and tapped in a search. Yes! The *Kingsbridge and Salcombe Gazette* came out weekly, and was owned by the same family that published the *Dartmouth Chronicle*.

I would be a reporter, then, but what would I do about my accent? I'm lousy with accents. The price one pays, I suppose, for being born in Ohio where our accents are about as nondescript and boring as we are. If I tried on a fake one, I'd be no more successful than those British actors who play Americans on TV and seem to suffer from the delusion that all Americans drawl and come from Texas.

I should begin with the tall guy, I thought, the one with the rasta braids, the one waving the sign declaring 'To Animals, All People Are Nazis'. Definitely the Alpha Dog. *Excuse me, sir – work the eyelashes overtime, Hannah – but I'm wondering if you have a moment to answer a few questions for the Kingsbridge Gazette?*

I was rehearsing the dialog in my head when, out of the corner of my eye, I saw Olivia shift her picket sign nervously from one hand to the other. No Bible chapter and verse for Olivia today. This time the message she carried was unambiguous – a picture of a sad-eyed, brown and white spotted dog bearing the caption, in red letters dripping blood, 'Born To Die'. By the rigid set of her jaw, I knew Olivia was clenching her teeth, probably fretting that I'd blow her cover.

I was scrabbling in the depths of my handbag for the little notebook and ballpoint pen I keep in there somewhere, when I heard Olivia shout, 'Oh my God, if it isn't Mrs Wingate! What the heck are *you* doing here, Mrs W?'

My head snapped up in time to see Olivia prop her picket sign against the chain-link fence. She turned to Alf, who was standing next to her holding a sign that said, 'Stop EU Chemical Tests', and said something to him. Alf shrugged, then went back to waving his sign. Olivia retrieved her handbag from the ground and hurried over to join me.

'Quick, let's get out of here.' She kept her voice low, husky. 'I told him you were my sixth-form science teacher. L-O-L.'

'Don't you think he'll wonder what a former teacher was doing way out here?' I asked as I hustled Olivia back in the direction of Cathy's rental car.

'That's why I said *science*,' she explained.

'Olivia,' I said, keeping my voice steady. 'I checked Alf's car just now. There's not a sign of any damage.'

Olivia reached for the car door and wrenched it open. 'Not *that* one, Hannah. Alf drives a BMW. Keeps it in a garage, like. Doesn't let nobody drive it but him.'

'Have you seen the BMW recently?'

'No.'

'Where does Alf keep the car?'

'That's what I want to show you.'

Now that I had a real live girl to issue driving instructions, I turned 'John' off via the GPS. Olivia directed me west through Kingsbridge for what she said would be a twenty-, thirty-minute drive, max, to Totnes. At the Palegate Cross Roundabout, we headed north on the A381 and when I got to the main road I asked, 'What reason could Alf have had to run Susan Parker down?'

'Well, they had words.'

'Words?'

'You know. Shouting, like.'

'It's hard for me to imagine Susan Parker shouting,' I commented as I slowed to let the car that was tailgating me pass.

Olivia colored. 'It's Alf doing the shouting, I guess you'd say.'

'What were they arguing about, Olivia?'

'She said one shouldn't take what it said in the Bible literal like.' Olivia swiveled in her seat to face me. 'I know the Bible isn't saying to stone girls what aren't virgins, or it's OK to keep slaves. But Alf? He don't like to be contradicted. Couldn't talk no sense into him, neither. Miss Parker, she buggers off to the theater, but he won't stop yelling about witches and harlots, the lot, and almost straight away, the police show up and charge him with breach of peace, pack him up and take him off. He comes home the next day spitting mad.'

Olivia folded her arms and pouted. 'Now Alf won't go back to London.' A wistful sigh escaped her lips. 'I so fancy London. Used to skive off and look at the shops. Not like I had the money to buy more than a cuppa.'

'Do you live with Alf, Olivia?'

'No, never done. I share a flat in Brixham with some girls from school. Kayleigh, she works at night as a barmaid, and I'm thinking there's more money in drawing pints than working for Alf and holding up his bleeding signs.'

On the outskirts of Totnes, Olivia directed me to a quiet neighborhood of red brick, semi-detached homes built sometime at the beginning of the last century during the reign of Edward VI. Rather than park out front, she instructed me to proceed to the end of the street, turn left, and drive down an alley. 'Alf keeps the car in a garage in back.'

I drove slowly, watching walled-off back gardens crawl by to my left and a row of wooden garages, painted white, to my right, each marked with a number.

'It's this one,' Olivia said, pointing.

I parked the car and we got out.

There was a small, high window in the garage door. I stood on tip-toe and peeked in, but couldn't see much through the grime. I huffed on the window and cleaned a small spot with my sleeve, but all I got for my efforts was a dirty sleeve. It was still as dark as the inside of a Goth's closet on the other side of the door.

'I don't suppose you have a key, Olivia?'

'I'm just an employee. Full stop.'

'Is there a Missus Alf?' I asked.

Olivia laughed out loud. 'Used to be, but she ran off with some bloke from Australia round fifteen years back. Alf didn't seem too upset about it, though. He has a char do the cooking and the washing-up, but Alf, he's good about hoovering.'

'Sounds like you know him well.'

She shrugged. 'Since I was twelve, but if Alf had anything to do with running Susan Parker down, I'm finished with him.'

I considered the stout padlock that secured the door against intruders like Olivia and me. 'Must have left my picklocks at home in my other pair of pants,' I told her.

'You're pulling my leg.'

I grinned. 'Well, yes, I am.'

Olivia shrugged. 'So what do we do now?'

'I used to be good at picking locks, but I need a bobby pin.' I grabbed the lock and yanked it in frustration. To my amazement, it came open in my hands.

I scarcely had time to pat myself on the back before Olivia gasped, 'That's *amazing*! How did you *do* it?'

'I'd like you to think it was my talented fingers, but I'm afraid Alf slipped up. He must not have pushed the shank all the way in.' I removed the lock, and with Olivia's help, raised the door about halfway so the two of us could slip inside. I closed the door behind us.

The BMW was clearly Alf's pride and joy. Even though it was garaged, he'd protected the vehicle with a canvas cover. 'Is there a light?' I asked, squinting into the darkness and seeing nothing but a car-shaped hunk of fabric.

Olivia disappeared into the dark. 'There's a switch over here somewhere.' She found the switch and a bank of overhead lights blazed on, nearly blinding me.

When my eyes got adjusted, I called Olivia over. 'Here, help me get this off.'

Soon the cover lay in a heap on the concrete floor, and we were staring at a late model BMW sedan. 'Blue or black, do you think?'

'Blue. Leastwise that's how it looks in the daytime. Looks perfect, too,' she added, sounding disappointed.

I ran my hand slowly over the left front fender, bending to study the finish as closely as I could, looking for imperfections. 'Wish I had a flashlight . . . torch,' I corrected.

'There's a torch on the workbench. I'll get it.'

When Olivia handed me the torch, I shone it on the fender, angling the beam, looking for tape lines, overspray, anything that might indicate the car had been repainted.

I opened the passenger door wide, inspected the inside of the door and the frame of the chassis. Was that overspray on the manufacturer's information plate? Or a figment of my imagination?

When I straightened up, slightly dizzy, I noticed that Olivia had circled around the car and climbed into the driver's seat. The center console stood open, and she was sorting through papers she had obviously found inside. 'Olivia, what are you doing?' I asked, although it was perfectly obvious what she was doing.

'I'm looking for evidence, like.'

'Evidence of what, pray tell?'

She shrugged. 'Will know when I find it, won't I?'

I was beginning to suspect that Olivia had it in for Alf, and was anxious to pin something, anything, on the old fellow, when her next move confirmed it. 'Lookit this!' she whooped. Olivia was holding a thin leather portfolio and, as I watched, she began sorting through its contents, which appeared to be a series of receipts. 'Petrol, petrol, petrol, insurance, oil change . . .' She paused, unfolded a piece of A4 paper that looked like a computer printout. 'This here's a ticket reservation for the Eurotunnel!' Her jaw dropped. 'God's knickers! It's for the day Susan Parker snuffed it.'

I slid into the passenger seat and held out a hand. 'Let me see.'

According to the contents of Alf's chronologically arranged portfolio, he'd visited the continent six times over the past several months, once on the very morning that Susan Parker was run down. The Eurotunnel reservation was for one p.m. Forty-four pounds. A two-day return. Susan had been struck and killed shortly after eight in the morning.

I stared at Olivia. 'It's at least a five-hour drive from Dartmouth to Folkestone. Could Alf run Susan down and still make it to Folkestone in time to make the train?'

Olivia's eyes did a slow roll. 'In *this* car, he could.'

'What would he be doing in France?' I wondered aloud.

'Hell if I know. Alf don't drink wine.'

I was still puzzling over that, putting the receipts back in order, when Olivia reached out, punched a button on the dash, and hopped out of the car. 'Let's see what the old goat's got in the boot!'

Before I could tuck the portfolio back into the center console where she'd found it, Olivia disappeared. Like a two-year-old, she was everywhere all at once. After half a minute I heard her say, 'Bloody, bloody hell!'

I returned the portfolio to the console, slammed it shut, slid out of the car, and went around to the boot to see what all the fuss was about. I expected to see cartons of WTL Guardian literature like Alf carried in his everyday vehicle. Instead, Olivia was leaning over a gray-green carpet bag, its mouth yawning open, and running her hands through what looked like hundreds and hundreds of ten, twenty and fifty pound notes.

'Beautiful, beautiful money!' She picked up a fistful of bills, put them to her nose and inhaled deeply. 'There must be millions here!'

'Not millions, but tens of thousands, that's for sure.'

'Well, the lying old sod. Said he couldn't afford to give me a rise in salary.' Pouting, Olivia helped me stuff the money back into the bag. As we did so, I noticed that the loot consisted mostly of pounds, but there were several fat bundles of Euros, and an envelope of currency with Arabic writing on it from Da Afghanistan Bank. Was Alf being paid to convert Muslims to Christianity? If so, Osama bin Laden might have a thing or two to say about that. The idea of anyone issuing a fatwa on Alf Freeman almost made me smile.

'Where did Alf get all this money?' Olivia's eyes were wide.

'Are they contributions?' I asked.

'Nobody *ever* gave us that much money. Never!'

Alf was a flake, his theology even flakier, so that I could believe. 'Could Alf have collected it over a long period of time? Saving it up?'

'What we collect in the can? What comes in the mail? *I* take to the bank. There's five, maybe six hundred pounds in the bank right now.'

'Where do you think the money came from, then, Olivia?'

'How should I know?' Her eyes narrowed. 'Not legal, and that's a fact.'

I closed the lid to the boot, resisting the urge to wipe off my fingerprints. 'I think we better clear off before Alf comes home.'

Olivia checked her watch. 'He won't be home for hours. Won't leave till Derrick leaves, and Derrick won't miss the workers heading home.'

'Derrick the tall bloke?' I asked as Olivia helped me ease the cover back over the BMW and tie it down.

'Right. Ah-maze-ing. Got arrested once for breaking into this lab up in Essex and letting all the animals out of the cages.'

'My kind of guy,' I said as I closed the garage door, replaced the lock and shoved the U-shaped shackle home.

I drove Olivia to the nearby bus station where she could catch a coach directly to Brixham. There was time to spare, so we sat in the car park with the windows open, enjoying a pleasant afternoon breeze.

Olivia stopped gnawing on her thumbnail long enough to ask, 'What do you think I should do about Alf?'

'Well, as much as I'd like to pin Susan's accident on somebody, the fact that his car isn't obviously damaged, and he has receipts that show he was probably on his way to the Chunnel at the time . . .' I let my voice trail off.

'But the money?'

'I don't know about the money, Olivia. There could be a perfectly reasonable explanation for why Alf keeps a big bag of money in his car. He's no spring chicken. He could have been saving it up for years.'

Olivia climbed out of the car, closed the door. She leaned through the open window, resting her elbows on the sill. 'If you believe that, Hannah, then I have a bridge that I can sell you real cheap.'

I had to laugh. 'Well, take care, Olivia. You still have my phone number, right?'

She patted her handbag. 'Know what?'

'What?'

'I think I can wait to start being a barmaid. Alf wants watching, don't you think?'

EIGHTEEN

'Gazump is a Cockney corruption of gezumph, a Yiddish word that means to swindle or overcharge.'
Simon Clark, 'Gazumping London',
www.Bloomberg.com, July 26, 2007

*H*annah, you are totally screwed.
Although I drove around for several minutes, I couldn't find a single available parking space in the Visitors' Center car park. My hopes were raised when the tail lights of a green Vauxhall flashed white and the vehicle began to back in my direction. I had already turned the steering wheel, preparing to slip into its space, when another car zipped around the corner and beat me to it. The smirk on the driver's face as he aced me out made me wish I carried a box cutter so I could put it to good use on the young jerk's tires.

So I waited, idling, still fuming, near the entrance. Eventually, a woman entered the car park from Flavel Place, carrying two shopping bags. I followed her to her parking space, positioned the car strategically and waited while she stowed her purchases in the boot. She gave me a friendly wave, pulled out, and I slotted my car in, thinking, whew, dodged that bullet.

I walked the long way around to Horn Hill House, scanning light poles, eaves and rooftops along the way, checking to see if there were any CCTV cameras installed anywhere in the vicinity of the spot on the Embankment where Susan had been struck down.

Zero, zip, nada.

Other than a webcam on the roof of the Royal Castle Hotel (was it even operational?), Dartmouth didn't seem to be a town that was overly concerned about serious crime.

Even the pint-sized police station appeared devoid of closed-circuit recording devices.

That night at dinner I asked Janet and Alan Brelsford about it.

Alan crossed his knife and fork on his plate and scowled. 'Don't get me started!'

'We petitioned for the cameras,' Janet said. 'We don't have much trouble here on Horn Hill, but there have been a number of problems with hooliganism and vandals at Royal Avenue Gardens. However . . .' She drew out the word. 'The town council, in their infinite wisdom, voted the proposal down.'

'They think they can handle the vandalism and petty crime with better street lighting.' Alan picked up his silverware and began sawing on his lamb chop. 'Idiots!'

'What happened to Susan Parker had nothing to do with the presence or absence of street lighting, though, did it?' I sighed. 'It was daylight. If there'd been a camera down there, the person who ran Susan down might even now be cooling his or her heels in one of Her Majesty's fine prisons.'

'What you fail to understand, my American friend, is that installing CCTV cameras is an invasion of privacy. It might even contravene the Human Rights Act.' Alan drew quote marks in the air with his fingers.

'In which case,' Janet huffed, 'there needs to be a massive effort to pull them down all across the country. How many at last count? Forty-two million?'

'To be fair,' Alan said, chewing thoughtfully, 'the town council did consult the police, who weren't entirely on board. Said, and I quote, "it wouldn't help in the legal process", whatever the hell that means.'

'Stingy sods. They just don't want to spend the money!'

'It's the same in the States,' Paul complained. 'We bend over backwards to protect the guilty, always at the expense of the innocent.'

'Makes me tired,' I said.

'Me, too,' Paul said. 'So, let's change the subject.' He smiled apologetically at our hosts, then affectionately at me. 'Once you turn Hannah on, it's sometimes hard to turn her off.'

Five minutes later I was really 'on,' telling the tale of my adventures with Olivia. I'd reached the part about the BMW and discovering the money in the boot, when the house phone rang.

Janet pushed her chair away from the table and hurried off to take the call. 'Sorry, but that's probably a booking. They always call at night, for some reason.'

When Janet returned, she was grinning. 'Guess who's coming back tomorrow?'

Back? I thought for a minute. 'Cathy Yates?'

'Yup. By train, this time. I'm collecting her at the station in Totnes.' Janet reclaimed her chair, helped herself to more runner beans, then sent the bowl on another circuit around the table.

'Had I but known,' I said, piling some beans on my plate, 'I could have picked her up in her very own rental car.'

'Oh, you squeaked by on that one, Hannah Ives.' Janet waggled her brows. 'While you were in the shower, Europcar called saying they'd collected it. Cathy'd left them our number.'

Paul shook his head. 'Hannah sometimes skates on very thin ice.'

I stuck out my tongue at him. 'Better to be lucky than smart.'

Alan laughed. 'Who said that?'

I shrugged. 'I don't know, but it seemed appropriate.'

Janet turned to me. 'Cathy says she has exciting news.'

'Gosh, I wonder if she's found out more about her father?'

'I asked her that, but she just laughed and said I'd have to wait until she got here.'

When Cathy arrived, she didn't make us wait long for her news. She dragged her bag into the entrance hall, parked it next to the newel post, and plopped herself down on a chair in the lounge. While five minutes out of Dartmouth, Janet had given me a head's up on her cell phone, so Paul and I were waiting for them.

'You'll never guess in a million years, so I'll tell you.' Cathy slapped her hands on her knees. 'I've just bought the Bailey farm, Three Trees.'

That can't be right, I thought to myself. I glanced from Paul, to Janet, and back to Cathy again. 'You bought Three Trees Farm?' I repeated dumbly.

'Abso-flipping-lutely! Isn't that a gas?'

I was still trying to process the information when Paul said, 'I thought it sold to a couple up in Manchester.'

Cathy grinned slyly. 'Well, it did, but I outbid them.' She all but pulled the tablecloth out from under what remained of the tea things with a flourish and a cry of 'Tah-dah!'

'My offer was accepted several days ago.' She pressed her hands together, raised her eyes to the ceiling. 'Thank you, Jesus!

'We'll be exchanging contracts in a couple of weeks,' Cathy rattled on, 'and my solicitor thinks that since it's a cash deal, and there's no chain of sales, we can go to completion on the same day.' She paused to take a breath. 'Don't you just *love* British terms? Anyway, I don't know why there have to be so many steps, but with such an old farm, I guess they have to check out the boundaries, and rights of way and . . .' She waved a hand. 'Makes my head hurt. That's what I pay the solicitor for, right? So *he* can buy the aspirin!'

As Cathy talked, Janet had been stacking the cups and saucers on the tea tray, but she stopped for a moment to ask, 'Whatever made you decide to buy the Bailey farm, Cathy?'

Instead of addressing Janet, Cathy looked directly at me. 'Remember when I told you that I had a private reading with Susan Parker, Hannah? I gave her a watch that used to belong to my father, and almost right away . . .' Cathy took a deep breath. 'You know how she always used to see a letter, like in someone's name? Well, in my case, she saw a number. Three. Isn't that amazing?'

'Amazing,' Paul said, using a tone of voice I recognized. I inched my foot closer to his and got ready to stomp.

'Then she got all shivery,' Cathy continued. 'She put her

hands on her neck, and started gagging. Said she couldn't breathe, like she was strangling. Right away, I knew I was on the right track.'

'You did?' I had absolutely no idea what Cathy was going on about.

'Didn't you ever wonder how the farm got its name?' Janet stopped fiddling with the tea tray and sat down. 'Would it be stating the obvious to say that perhaps at one time, there were trees there, and that the trees were three in number?'

'That's right!' Cathy said, a proud teacher commending a student. 'But not just any trees, Janet. In the seventeenth century, those trees served as an unofficial gallows!'

I thought it was a stretch, and Paul did, too. Before I could stop him, he commented, 'Three trees and a hanging could just as well apply to the crucifixion of Christ.' Anticipating objection, he raised a hand. 'Just saying.'

Cathy ignored him. 'My father's body lies on that farm somewhere, Hannah, I can just feel it. And Susan could, too. Honest to God, when I saw on CNN that somebody'd run her down, and she had *died*, I cried buckets. Buckets! She was the real deal, wasn't she?'

'I like to think so, Cathy, but Susan was always the first to admit that she could occasionally be wrong.'

Cathy flapped a hand. 'Yeah, yeah, yeah. I've heard all that. But you know what?' She leaned forward, as if her words were only for me. 'That means that some of the time, she's gonna be tee-totally right!'

Claiming jet-lag, Cathy eventually left, heading up to her room to settle in.

As soon as she was out of earshot, I telephoned Alison, playing it casual. 'How's your father?' I asked. 'How's he dealing with the sale?'

'Wait, wait, wait!' Alison said. 'You're not letting me get a word in edgewise!'

'Well, OK,' I said. 'Over to you!'

'I was just about to call you, Hannah. Have I ever got news!'

'News?' I was playing dumb.

'You'll never, ever guess who bought the farm.'

'Is this a trick question, Alison? I was there, remember? When you told Paul and me about the buyers from Manchester. Champagne? Party hats?'

'Well, they got gazumped.'

'That sounds ominous.' Visions of the Mancs sprang to mind, felled in their prime by a rare, African disease contracted while on holiday in Kenya. 'What's gazumped?' I honestly didn't know.

She laughed. 'A London company trumped their offer by a good ten thousand pounds. There was a bidding war, actually, and the poor Mancunians kept upping their offer in thousand-pound increments, but eventually they had to drop out and the London people won.'

'Who would want Three Trees that badly?' I asked, feeling guilty about playing Alison along.

'You'll never guess.'

I hate playing Twenty Questions. 'Is it bigger than a bread box?'

'Oh, Hannah, you crack me up! As soon as I tell you this, you will guess for sure. The buyer is American!'

'Could it be . . .' I paused for dramatic effect. 'Cathy Yates?'

'Exactly! I was gobsmacked.'

'I'm gobsmacked, too,' I told her truthfully. It's just that I had been smacking my gob about ten minutes earlier. 'Does your father know?'

'We're not going to tell him until after we complete.'

'Alison, that could be weeks! How can he not know?'

'Well, the offer was made through a limited partnership in London. Cathy's the only partner, of course, but Dad won't know that.'

'Crimenently, Alison. Your father will have a stroke when he finds out!'

'So what? At the end of the day, the only thing that matters is the money. And after we've completed, there'll be nothing Stephen Bailey or anybody else can do.'

NINETEEN

'The American military police were called Dewdrops
because their helmets were white.'
Pat Kemp, *Ministry of Food: Women's Land
Army: Index to Service Records of the Second
World War 1939–1948, Series: MAF421*,
National Archives, Kew, Richmond, Surrey

While Paul was soaking in the tub, I kicked off my shoes, climbed on to the bed and reached for my iPhone. Olivia hadn't given me her phone number, but when she called me earlier in the week, the number had been captured in my 'Recents' folder. I scrolled through the list of incoming calls, tapped her number, adjusted a pillow behind my back, and waited while it rang.

No answer.

I left a brief message asking Olivia to call me back, then joined Paul in the bathroom, a place, Paul always claimed, where he did some of his finest work. The toilet lid was up, so I put it down and sat on it.

Paul glanced up from the paperback he was reading to ask, 'So, how was your day, sweetheart?'

Paul had bugged out on me at tea time, leaving me alone in front of the television screen with Cathy and the dirty dishes, so I hadn't had the chance to tell him about an unnamed person from Totnes who was presently, according to a police spokesman on BBC1, helping police with their enquiries in the Parker case.

'There are a lot of people living in Totnes,' Paul reasoned after I'd finished. 'Why are you so eager to pin the hit-and-run on poor old Alf?'

'He gives me the creeps?'

'Hah! Take that to the police and they'll act on it right away.'

'I'd sure like to know where he got all that money.' I smiled, remembering Olivia's reaction when she opened the bag. 'Olivia calls it wonga. I looked it up, by the way. It comes from "wanger", a Gypsy word for coal which was apparently used as currency at some time in the past.'

'Dough, moolah, cabbage, bread, bacon . . . whatever. Maybe he doesn't trust banks to take proper care of his wonga.'

I giggled. 'When you put it that way, it sounds mildly off-color.'

Paul feigned wide-eyed innocence. '*Moi*? Hannah Ives, you have a dirty mind.'

I plucked a wet face cloth off the rim of the sink and tossed it at his head.

After a few more seconds, I said, 'Olivia claims she makes regular deposits to Lloyds of the charitable contributions they receive, so Alf trusts banks to that extent.' I leaned my head back against the wall and closed my eyes, suddenly feeling very tired. 'The only reason I can think of for not putting my money into, say, the Navy Federal Credit Union, is if I didn't want anybody, especially the IRS, to know that I had it.'

'Well, duh.' Paul folded down a corner of a page to mark his place, closed the paperback and dropped it on to the bathmat. 'There must be a million ways to launder money when you collect donations on the street.'

'True, but Paul, you didn't see it. To quote Olivia, it was a whacking great wodge of wonga. If Alf spent a century standing on a folding chair in Speakers' Corner at Hyde Park, he couldn't collect that much money. It's ill-gotten gains. I'm sure of it. And so is Olivia. Alf pretends that he's only a fiver away from going on the dole, yet he hasn't given her a raise in over a year. She's really fuming.'

'Well,' Paul drawled, 'I could spend the rest of the evening lolling in the tub, discussing Alf and his finances, but if I'm taking you to dinner, I'd better get a move on. What's your pleasure?'

I whipped a towel off the warming rack and handed it to him, watching appreciatively as he stepped out of the tub, tall and trim, water droplets glistening on his slightly graying chest hairs and trickling down his recently acquired tan. 'I'm thinking we should skip dinner.'

Paul wrapped the towel twice around his waist, tucked it in. He padded over to where I was sitting, took my hand and pulled me to him. 'How about we just postpone dinner,' he whispered into my hair. 'We have reservations at Spice Bazaar at eight.'

I wrapped my arms around his waist, hardly noticing as the bathwater soaked through my sleeves. 'Sounds like a plan,' I mumbled as his lips found mine.

Twenty minutes later, I lolled in his arms, gazing out the window and across the Dart where the last rays of the sun were turning Kingswear into a photo opportunity – if I had a camera handy and even the remotest inclination to get out of bed. 'Do you think Olivia turned him in?' Paul breathed into my ear.

I rolled over to face my husband. 'Could be. When I put her on the bus, she was fit to be tied.'

Five minutes later, I would find out how pissed off Olivia Sandman could be.

I had just started dressing when Olivia returned my call.

'Hannah. Guess you heard.'

'Someone from Totnes is helping police with their inquiries?'

'It's Alf. Serves the bastard right.'

I buttoned the last button on my shirt, one-handed, and sat down on the edge of the bed. 'Did he do it, do you think? Did he run Susan Parker down?'

'I don't know and I don't care. Hope they lock him up forever.'

'How did the police get on to him, Olivia?'

'Somebody might have called Crimestoppers?'

'Was that somebody, you, Olivia?'

'Not saying I did, not saying I didn't. But do you remember how I told you Alf pays me a salary? What

I shoulda said is I get an allowance. When my mum died, she left a bundle, but it's in trust, like, with my mum's brother, Uncle Alf, as trustee. I get the lot when I'm thirty.'

I had figured that Olivia was about the same age as my daughter, born in the same decade anyway, but I had never asked her. 'When's the magic birthday, then?'

'November fifth. It's Guy Fawkes Day. I was planning to splash out on a party for my mates. Had the restaurant laid on and everything. So I go to the bank where they got my trust, and you know what I find out? The money's gone. Most of it, anyway. One hundred pounds and some pence is all that's left. My bleeding uncle spent it, the son of a bitch.' Olivia took a deep, shuddering breath, and I could tell that she was crying.

'Olivia, that's terrible! You need to see a lawyer. What your uncle did is illegal.'

'What I need is to knock his bloody block off, and take that bleeding bag of money. Should have done it when I first saw it,' she snuffled. 'Now the police got it, I s'pose, cos they got the car.'

Paul made a production of checking his watch, tapping the crystal, putting it to his ear to see if it was still running. If I didn't hurry, we were going to be late for our reservation.

But, there was something puzzling me. 'Olivia, when we looked at your uncle's car the other day, it didn't appear to be damaged.'

'It wasn't.' She paused, and I could hear her breathing. 'Not then.'

'What the hell are you talking about, Olivia?'

'You think I just go along like a daft dog? When he had my money, I had to dance to his fooking tune. Yes, Uncle Alf, no, Uncle Alf. But that was going to be all over once I got what was mine by rights. So, me and Kayleigh, we drive to Alf's and I'm going to tell him I know what's going on, and where's my money, you bastard. But Alf, he's not home, and I see the Beemer's in the garage.' She paused to take a breath. 'Not sure I should say anymore.'

Paul was making circular, hurry-up motions with his

hand. I countered with my hand up, palm out: hold-your-horses, bucko. 'So, what happened next, Olivia?'

'It was Kayleigh's idea.'

'What was?'

'She had a screwdriver in her car. She unscrewed the hinges t'one side of the lock, and we got in, easy like. I was gonna get my money, see, but damn that Alf, he had the car locked tight.

'So I picked up a big stone, and I wrapped it in my cardigan, and I was going to smash one of his fooking windows so I could open up the boot . . .' She started to giggle. 'Then I had a brilliant idea. I told Kayleigh what I was about and we fell about laughing!'

While Olivia was busily confessing to a B and E, Paul had given up on me. He brushed aside my hair, kissed the nape of my neck and walked over to the window where I could hear him speaking into his cell phone, telling the Spice Bazaar that we'd be a few minutes late.

'If I busted the windows,' Olivia continued, 'Alf'd just get them fixed. But what if he got a bit of aggro from the police? So I wound up and gave his left front wing a good whack. Pranged it good, I did. Oooh, it was brilliant! Then Kayleigh and me, we put the garage door back together and scarpered.'

I pressed my hand to my mouth, stifling a laugh. It *was* brilliant. Wicked, completely illegal, of course, but brilliant. 'And then you called Crimestoppers?' I asked again.

'It's anonymous, right?'

'Right.'

'No way they can find out who called?'

'None.'

'Well, OK then.'

'Olivia, you didn't answer my question.'

I could practically hear her smile coming down the line. 'What question?'

Paul had started to pace, so I changed course. 'So what's happening with Alf, do you know?'

'I guess he's screwed. Alf called me on my mobile and asked me to get the name of a good lawyer.'

'Do you think he *was* responsible for Susan's hit-and-run, had the car repaired, and then you, well, un-repaired it?'

'Dunno. But they musta stitched Alf up good and proper. He says he's not coming home for a while, and I should "carry on".' She snorted. 'As if. WTL can go fook itself.'

I laughed out loud. 'I figured you didn't totally buy into Alf's theology.'

'Too right,' she said. 'So you know what I did? I got that lawyer's name and number, all right, but Alf? He can whistle for it. I'm hiring the bloke myself. He says he's gonna help me get my mum's money back.'

TWENTY

'When they left Torcross their means of transport to Chivelstone was a meat lorry . . . After the household effects were loaded, the chicken sheds came next and lastly, bags of coke on the tailboard with Reg sitting on top. Reg's father had to leave the family car, a Rover, behind, and when they returned to Torcross it was discovered in the Ley.'
Robin Rose-Price and Jean Parnell, *The Land We Left Behind*, Orchard Publications, 2005, p. 78

Early the next morning, in spite of enjoying a full English breakfast at the B&B, I walked up the hill to Alison Hamilton's with the taste of lamb rogan josh making an occasional, but not unwelcome appearance – a hint of ginger, a tinge of red curry – at the base of my tongue.

While Paul and Jon were attending a seminar at BRNC, Alison and I planned a second trip from Three Trees Farm to Coombe Hill carrying a small load of household goods that her father had packed up with the assistance of his right-hand man, Tom Boyd.

A few minutes before ten, I was dropping a detergent tab in the dishwasher, while Alison was scurrying around her kitchen, turning over newspapers, napkins and the previous day's mail searching for her car keys, when the telephone rang. She snagged the receiver with one hand, and said 'hello' while moving cereal boxes around on the sideboard.

'Oh, hi, Tom. We're running a little late, but we should be there to pick up the boxes shortly.' Alison paused, and I watched her expression change from mild annoyance to shock. 'Stolen? You have *got* to be pulling my leg! Dad's car is a wreck!'

I closed the dishwasher door, set the dial to normal wash,

and focused my full attention on Alison's end of the conversation.

'Who would want it, Tom? Who? It looks like the last vehicle standing after a banger race.' She leaned against the countertop, nodding. 'Yes, yes, I understand, but are you sure he didn't just drive it to town and forget where he parked it?'

Alison pantomimed an exaggerated eye-roll. 'He could have walked home, couldn't he, or someone could have given him a ride? Everyone knows my father . . . What? Of course you should, right away. And Tom? This time, we're really going to take away his car keys. Right?'

Alison dropped the phone into its cradle, closed her eyes and massaged the bridge of her nose. 'Did you hear that?'

'Hard not to.'

'Tom had to ask me whether to call the police. My God.' She took a deep, calming breath and let it out slowly. 'Now, where the *hell* are my car keys?'

As my friend continued to rant, I spotted what looked like a Lucite sunflower peeking out from behind the electric kettle. 'Fob shaped like a sunflower?'

Alison nodded.

I pointed.

Alison scooped up the keys, tugged on the hem of her T-shirt in a let's-get-down-to-business way. 'I swear, Hannah, the sooner I get that impossible old man into Coombe Hill, the better. When Tom showed up for work this morning,' she elaborated, 'Dad reported that he'd left the car where he usually does, in the courtyard, but when he came out this morning, the car was gone.'

'Priuses are popular right now, hard to get.' I'd read something of the sort recently in *The Times*. 'Maybe they weren't interested in the body, just the parts?'

Alison spread her arms wide. 'That's me! Body a wreck, but, oooh the parts!'

'Nut!' A tiny fact stored somewhere in my brain surfaced and began to wave hello. 'Alison, didn't you tell me that Tom worked part-time in a body shop in Plymouth?'

'I know where you're going, Hannah, but Tom's worked

for my father for more than ten years. There's no way he could have been involved in something like that.'

'How about Tom's mates?'

'Possible, I suppose, but not likely.' Alison paced from the Aga to the pantry to the sink and back again, nervously tidying counters that looked perfectly tidy to me. 'I told Tom to go ahead and report it to the police. Now, *where* did I put my handbag? Other than informing the insurance company, I don't suppose there's much more we can do.'

That tiny thought was now waving and shouting, *you-hoo!*

Was Alison's father trying to scam his insurance company? He had been reluctant to file a claim for the damage from the accident, but if the car were reported stolen instead, who would be the wiser?

None of my business, of course.

I returned to an earlier, slightly less thorny topic. 'Do you have to wait until the completion date to move your dad off the farm?'

'No, thank goodness. We've had the flat from August first, so as far as I'm concerned, Cathy Yates can move into Three Trees Farm at any time, fancy New York interior designer and all.' She winked. 'Although that would be illegal, of course.'

By then she had collected her keys, her handbag, and a lightweight jacket, and we were headed for the front door. 'What's kept him on the farm until now was the cows. How he loves those cows.' She grinned. 'Feckless is Daddy's little girl, I'm afraid. Did I tell you they were sold to another farmer?' When I nodded, she continued, 'Well, the transport lorry's coming for them later this morning, so my father's in mourning, everything but the black armband.'

Olivia Sandman, on the other hand, was far from mourning, if I interpreted the punctuation on her text message correctly:

Unc Alf confessed!!!! 8-O

'Well, that's that,' I commented to Alison after sharing the news. I switched off my iPhone and dropped it back into my bag. 'I suppose it will be all over the news tonight.'

Alison apparently feels compelled to look at you while

talking, which is not particularly compatible with conversation while driving. I lived to see another day, because she pulled into a lay-by on the outskirts of Dittisham before facing me to say, 'I'm glad they caught the fellow, of course, but there must be more to it than a simple exchange of words on a London street.'

'Back where I come from, Alison, people kill people simply because they won't hand over the North Face jacket they're wearing, or give up a pair of one-hundred-eighty-five dollar athletic shoes, so anything's possible. But, I agree, it's puzzling.'

'Maybe Susan did to Alf what she did to you.' Alison touched my hand where it rested on the console between us. 'You know, an off-the-cuff reading that hit close to home.'

'A dark secret from his past, you mean? Something incompatible with his holier-than-thou persona?'

'Exactly. Or maybe he was all fired up with religious indignation, saw her walking on the Embankment as he drove by and something snapped.' She brought her hands together with a crack. 'Stranger things have happened, Hannah.'

'I'm sure. Remember the Crusades.'

Alison checked the wing mirror, then eased the car back on to the road. 'Don't have to think back that many centuries. Osama bin Laden springs immediately to mind.'

'I'd rather not think about that madman, Alison.' Two young naval officers, Paul's former students, had been killed when terrorists flew an airplane into the Pentagon. It was a difficult subject.

Alison took her eyes off the road for a moment. 'But that's exactly my point, Hannah. Madmen are not governed by logic!' After looking both ways, she turned right from The Level on to Riverside Road. 'So, trying to understand or explain them is futile.'

'If so, a lot of psychiatrists would be out of work.'

'Boo hoo,' Alison said.

Ten minutes later at Coombe Hill, I found myself unpacking dishes in the kitchen, while Alison worked on installing a small flat-screen television in the adjacent lounge. It was to be a surprise for her father.

I leaned around the bookshelf that divided the two rooms and yelled, 'Do I need to wash these dishes before putting them in the cabinets?'

The floor around my friend was littered with boxes, cables and instruction manuals, one of which she held up for my consideration. 'It's written in English, French, Spanish and Arabic, but does it tell me where to attach this damn wire? In *any* language? It does not.' She tossed a cable that terminated with three plugs – banded in red, yellow and white – aside. 'I'd like to tell them where they can shove their bleeding wires!'

'Does that mean I don't have to re-wash the dishes?'

She flapped a hand. 'Never mind. I'll figure it out.' She picked up the manual, flipped over a few pages and began to read, eyes narrowed and brow furrowed in concentration. 'Who drew these illustrations, anyway? Three-year-olds?'

Back in the kitchen, dust motes danced in slants of sunlight streaming through the window. My nose began to itch, and I felt a big, juicy sneeze coming on. I twitched my nose like Samantha in *Bewitched*, but not even magic would stop that sneeze from coming.

I slipped the platter I'd been holding back into its protective nest of crumpled newspaper, and plunged my hand into the pocket of my cotton jacket, hoping I'd find a tissue. What I came out with was a wad of newsprint.

Oh, right. I'd forgotten about that. It had fallen out of Alison's car the other day, and since I firmly believed in Keeping Dartmouth Green, I'd picked it up off the street fully intending to throw it away.

I started to pitch the scrap into the bin with the rest of the packing trash, but as I closed an eye and lined up the shot, a single word leapt out at me: Parker.

Curious is my middle name, so I took the scrap of paper over to the kitchen counter and smoothed it out on the granite:

Police Seek Help of Public in Solving Hit-and-Run

Forensic analysis of clothing worn by the victim of a hit-and-run on the North Embankment nearly two weeks ago has revealed that a blue coloured vehicle was involved.

Sergeant Barry Evans, Dartmouth Police, said finding the vehicle with this coloured paint is crucial in helping to find the driver who was responsible for the hit and run.

Popular medium and television personality Susan Parker was walking her dog on the Embankment when she was struck from behind, killing her instantly. The hit-and-run happened around 8.15 in the morning.

'We hope that the paint analysis from fragments on the victim's clothing may focus public attention to a blue vehicle that has recently been damaged.

'From the extent of the victim's injuries and the paint fragments on her clothing we know that the vehicle involved will have some body or paintwork damage. The driver or owner may have taken it to a panel beater for repairs. They may have tried to fix it themselves or have parked it up out of sight.

'If anyone has any information about a vehicle with blue paint that has recently been damaged then we would like to hear from them,' he said. 'The driver who struck Ms Parker must know what happened. We urge that person and anyone with information about the hit-and-run to contact police.'

Why did Stephen Bailey go to all the trouble of tearing that particular article out of the paper, then crumple it up and save it? Thinking about the trials and tribulations of Bailey's car lately, the man couldn't be acting more guilty than if he'd run Susan Parker down himself.

Blue car. Check.

Body damage. Check.

Out of sight. Check.

But Alf Freeman had motive. And he'd confessed to the crime, hadn't he?

I dragged a chair out from under the dainty bistro-style table I'd helped Alison pick out at the IKEA store in Bristol and sat down to think.

Stephen Bailey knew that Susan Parker had been planning a visit to Slapton Sands, but even if that visit were to lead to the location of the remains of American soldiers some sixty years dead, the only thing she'd prove was that Ken Small was right and Stephen Bailey was wrong about the disposition of some of the victims' bodies following the disastrous training exercise.

At her live show in Paignton, Susan had called on Bailey, saying she had a message from somebody named Rose, but she'd been wrong, hadn't she? Or had Bailey lied about ever knowing a woman named Rose?

I couldn't make the pieces fit. Unless . . .

My bag was on the table, so I pawed through it until I found my cell phone. A few taps later, I reached Olivia. 'Got your text, Olivia. So, tell me. What's up with Alf?'

'Oh my God, Hannah! Him and Derrick got arrested for human trafficking!'

'What? You mean he didn't kill Susan Parker?' If Alison hadn't had the television and its paraphernalia spread out in pieces on the carpet all around her, I would have rushed right out to click the set on.

'Coulda knocked me over with a feather, and that's a fact.'

'But, but . . .' I'm seldom at a loss for words, just ask my husband, but human trafficking was the last thing that came to mind when I thought about Alf God-Loves-Me-Better-Than-You Freeman. Sex slaves? Prostitution? Diminutive Alf with the pasty skin and thinning hair, dressed in the height of last year's fashions from the Men and Boys department at Walmart? I tried to reconcile that image of Alf with the burly, dark-haired, gold-chained Mafioso so recently popularized on HBO. Fuhgedaboutit.

As Olivia rattled on, however, the penny dropped. Calais, she said. Chunnel. A BMW that was even more 'special' than the manufacturer intended, with an undercarriage compartment that was impervious to heat sensors and infrared cams.

Alf had been smuggling illegal immigrants from France into the United Kingdom at £1000 a pop.

'Strange occupation for a man of God,' I huffed.

TWENTY-ONE

'Important meetings. The area described below is to be requisitioned urgently for military purposes, and must be cleared of its inhabitants by December 20th, 1943.'
Notice, Mortimer Bros. Printers and Publishers, Totnes, November 12, 1943

'The Chairman of the Devon County Council, Sir John Daw, was ordered to requisition an area of 30,000 acres [including] the villages of Torcross, Stokenham, Chillington, Blackawton, East Allington, Slapton, Strete, Frogmore and Sherford. It also included 180 farms and many small hamlets. It affected 750 families and totaled 3000 men, women and children.'
Robin Rose-Price and Jean Parnell, *The Land We Left Behind*, Orchard Publications, 2005, p. 10

'The trouble is,' I said to Paul as we were getting ready for bed that evening, 'I like Stephen Bailey. It's hard for me to believe that he'd deliberately run anybody down.'

Paul rinsed his toothbrush and dropped it brush-end up into a drinking glass. 'How would you feel if he were just an ordinary Devonian farmer and not the father of one of your closest friends?'

'I'm trying to keep that out of the equation, darling.' I crawled into the bed, propped some pillows behind my back, and pulled the duvet up to my chin. Maybe I could think better that way.

A few minutes later, Paul joined me under the duvet. 'So, what are you going to do with the information?'

'What information? I don't have information, just

hunches. The police aren't going to be interested in my unsubstantiated theories.'

He rolled over and started to trace circles on my upper arm with the back of his index finger. 'Which are?'

'Whatever it is, it's rooted in the past. Susan either sensed it, or Bailey was afraid she would come to sense it. Maybe Alison's father had a beef with one of the American soldiers. Maybe they fought, the soldier got killed, and Bailey buried him on the farm.' I sat up a bit straighter. 'Yes! That explains why Bailey has this love-hate thing going on with Yanks.'

'The trouble with that theory, Hannah, is that Bailey wasn't here during the occupation. He and his family had been forced to move their farm lock, stock and barrel to someplace near Dittisham, right?'

'Right. And security was tight.' I folded my arms across my chest and pouted. 'But there are first-hand reports in some of those booklets I bought of farmers sneaking back into the American zone to check on their property, to collect fruit, search for family pets. Maybe Bailey was able to slip past the patrols. Maybe . . .' I was making it up as I went along. 'How about this. He makes his way back to the farm, discovers some soldiers lounging about in his sitting room, laughing, drinking his father's elderberry wine, breaking up his mother's furniture for firewood. It was winter.'

'And?' By the way he lifted one eyebrow, I could tell my husband was unimpressed.

'Something snaps. He clobbers them with a fire iron or something.'

'All very interesting, Hannah, but I don't know how you are going to prove any of this.'

'Frankly, neither do I.'

Paul picked up the remote. 'Mind if I turn on the television?'

'Just as long as it's something mindless, like Big Brother. I've heard all I care to hear about Alf Freeman and Derrick What's-His-Name today. Hard to believe they were part of a smuggling ring. Just goes to prove that all thugs aren't big, burly goodfellows from Russia or Bulgaria. Primordial slime, the pair of them. Preying on hundreds of poor, desperate people hanging out in a squalid tent city in the woods near Calais. You'd think the French police would swoop in and clean it up.'

'Do you think that there was anything legitimate about the Guardians of Way, Truth and Life?' Paul asked when I paused to come up for air.

'I doubt it. I think the organization was a massive smoke screen to explain his frequent trips to the continent. We still tend to trust men of the cloth, even though in case after case, they've proved themselves unworthy of that trust. Alf wasn't so much "of the cloth", though, was he? More of a self-styled prophet.'

'A prophet of profit?' Paul grinned.

I punched him in the arm. 'Don't get me started!'

On the TV, Siavash was sweet-talking Sophie in the garden now that Noirin had been evicted from the Big Brother house. 'How can people watch this drivel?' Paul aimed the remote and switched the channel.

'Paul?' I asked as the channels flickered by. 'You're a farm boy. If you had a car you wanted to get rid of, what would you do with it?'

'Does Three Trees Farm have a pond?'

'It certainly does.'

'Then that's the first place I'd look.'

I turned on my side, punched the pillow into submission, and snuggled down under the duvet. 'Before I call Crimestoppers, however, I think I need to talk to somebody about wartime in Devon.'

Paul's face was inches from mine. 'Who?'

'The woman that Cathy says is going to help with her museum project. I met her at the charity lunch at St Saviour's. Her name is Lilith Price. She knits, Paul.'

'She knits? Well, that explains everything.' He kissed the tip of my nose.

'Shut up and cuddle, Mr Ives.'

And Paul, being the obedient husband that he is, promptly obliged.

*   *   *

The following Tuesday, I gathered up my knitting and hurried off to St Saviour's, hoping that I'd find Lilith there. I'd just settled down at a table by myself, wondering if I'd have to eat alone, when Lilith appeared. I motioned her over. 'When you get your lunch, do join me.' I indicated my knitting bag that was sitting on the empty chair next to me, the needles I'd borrowed from Janet sticking out of the top like antennae. 'Did you bring your knitting today?'

Lilith patted her bag. 'Never go anywhere without it! You never know when you'll be stuck waiting for something with time on your hands. Some people carry paperback books. For me, it's knitting.'

I knew what she meant. I'd once been a card-carrying member of the paperback club, but recently I'd found myself wasting vast amounts of time in doctors' offices and airport terminals playing Bejeweled on my iPhone.

Before long, Lilith was back. She seated herself across from me. I had planned to show her the shawl I was making, using our mutual love of knitting as an ice-breaker, but I found myself diving right in instead. 'I heard a rumor about you the other day, Lilith.'

Lilith glanced up from her cucumber sandwich, a bemused look on her face. 'Oh? I hope it was a good one. I could use a little excitement.'

I grinned. 'I understand that once she gets it going, you're going to be curator of Cathy Yates' museum at Slapton Sands.'

Lilith nodded. 'Fascinating project, don't you think? Although I hadn't been born yet when it happened, I've always been interested in the evacuation. I've written several articles about it for some of our better historical journals. You can find them in the public library here, if you're interested, and at BRNC, too, of course.'

I reached into my bag, rooting around under the knitting until my hand closed on a yellowish green pamphlet. 'I have one of them here. I bought it at the Harbour Bookshop the other day, and was pleased to see your name in it.'

'Lovely bookshop, isn't it? Did you know that for many years it was owned by Christopher Milne, the son of A. A. Milne who wrote the Winnie the Pooh stories?'

'Christopher Robin, yes, I did.'

'He disliked Americans, you know.'

'That I didn't know.'

'I gather the Winnie the Pooh stories were much more popular in America than they ever were over here. And after the Disney movie came out?' She cast her eyes toward the sturdy, fourteenth-century rafters. 'Americans kept coming in and asking for Christopher Robin. Eventually, whenever he heard an American accent, poor Chris would scurry upstairs and hide out until they were gone.'

I laughed, and tried to use the opportunity to get Lilith back on track. 'My friend Alison Hamilton's father doesn't think much of Yanks, either. I figure it has something to do with the American occupation. Stephen Bailey, do you know him?'

'Of course. Until Cathy Yates bought it, Three Trees Farm was owned for centuries by Stephen Bailey's family.' She paused, chewing thoughtfully. 'Stephen must have been, what, sixteen or seventeen when the war broke out?'

'That's right. Tragically, his older brother was killed at Dunkirk, so he stayed home to work the farm. Even so, my friend Alison says that after Teddy's death, her grandfather was often ill. She thinks the old man died of a broken heart.'

Lilith had finished her lunch, and pushed her plate aside. 'I can understand that. If anything happened to one of my sons . . .' She shivered. 'It doesn't bear thinking about.'

I'd finished eating, too. I picked up my knitting, arranged the nether end of the shawl on my lap, and began working a row. 'What I'm wondering, Lilith, is how one boy and one sick old man were able to manage such a large farm by themselves?'

Lilith hauled out her knitting, too. 'There were a couple of local lads helping out, of course. Fourteen or fifteen years old, too young to be called up.' She held up a needle like a baton. 'Do you know about the Women's Land Army?'

'A little. Wasn't it like our Civilian Conservation Corps in America?'

'Not exactly. During the war, so many young men were called up that there was a severe shortage of labor on farms all over England. As a rural community, Devon was particularly hard hit. So, the government called on women to fill the gap.' She smiled. 'As they tend to do.

'A lot of the girls were sent out here from the cities,' Lilith continued. 'They were just sixteen or seventeen, leaving home for the first time. Manual labor from daybreak to dusk was a new thing for them.' She studied me thoughtfully. 'As I recall, four Land Army girls were assigned to Three Trees Farm. They were billeted along with half a dozen other girls at a small hotel in Strete.'

'So, what happened to the girls after the evacuation?'

'In general, they either transferred to some other area of the country, or they went back home, if they had a home to go back to.' She shook her head. 'Much of London had been destroyed, as you probably know.'

'I did.'

'But, lighter note! After the war, one of the girls who had been assigned to Three Trees Farm came back to Strete. She'd fallen in love with Adam Wills, you see, whose father owned the farm adjacent to Three Trees. Eventually they married, and she stayed in the area.'

Like a bird taking flight, my spirits soared. 'Is she still alive?'

'My, yes.'

'Do you think I'll be able to talk to her?'

'I don't see why not. She's widowed, living in Stoke Fleming now. I'll get you her number, shall I? Her name's Audrey. Audrey Wills.'

'I'd really appreciate it. I first heard about the Land Army girls while watching an episode of *Foyles War*, and since then, I've been fascinated.' I tapped the pamphlet that lay on the table between us. 'And I've read your article, of course.'

She beamed, accepting the compliment. 'Fortunately, Audrey's farmer was able to move himself, his family and his livestock to another farm outside the American Zone, up near Harbertonford.' She shook her head. 'Many farmers weren't so lucky. They had to sell everything, and you can imagine with everyone selling their livestock all at once, the prices were at rock bottom.'

I thought about Stephen Bailey's cows – Feckless, Graceless, Pointless and Aimless – and how hard it must have been for him to see them go.

'They were only given six weeks to clear out,' Lilith continued. 'Six weeks! Can you imagine? And just before Christmas, too.'

'I can hardly pack for a two-week vacation in that little time.'

Lilith shook her head. 'Isn't that the truth? Now, don't let me forget to get you Audrey's number.'

'I won't!' I gave Lilith my cell-phone number, and the telephone number at the B&B.

'Now that that's settled, Hannah, it's time to show me what you're working on so industriously.'

TWENTY-TWO

'There were a lot of Americans stationed in the area and we were often invited to the dances at their camps ... They would send a lorry for us and would bring us back. When it was time to leave the camp the lorry was stopped at the gate and the military guards would shine their torches and ask if there were any GI's on board and everybody chorused "no" and when we were out of the gates the GI's would come out from under the seats.'

Pat Kemp, *Ministry of Food: Women's Land Army: Index to Service Records of the Second World War 1939–1948, Series: MAF421,* National Archives, Kew, Richmond, Surrey

I arranged to meet Audrey Wills at the Singing Kettle Tea Shoppe in Smith Street, just around the corner from St Saviour's. She was already there when I arrived, chatting with one of the owners – Darren, or it could have been Brian – at the foot of a narrow wooden staircase that led up to the first floor.

I recognized her at once from Lilith's description. Tall, impossibly thin, with cropped hair the color of tar – a color that would have been startling on a woman half her age – sticking out in spikes like an electrified hedgehog.

I introduced myself to Audrey and to Darren, who showed us to a small round table near the window, covered with a scrupulously clean white tablecloth. After studying the menu, and consulting with Audrey, I ordered the cream tea for us both.

'Thanks so much for seeing me, Mrs Wills,' I said, after Darren left with our order. 'Since my visit here, I've become very interested in the evacuation of the South Hams during the Second World War. Lilith Price told me that you were one of the Land Army girls stationed here. I was hoping you could tell me what it was like.'

Audrey laced her fingers together and rested her hands on the table. 'The Land Army, yes. It turned out to be a life-changing experience for me, but I really wanted to join the WAAF.' She winked. 'My father wouldn't let me.'

'The WAAF?'

'The Women's Auxiliary Air Force. It's part of the RAF now. Back in 1943, to a young girl barely seventeen, it sounded like the most exciting thing in the world. Some of the WAAFs worked on codes and ciphers, which I thought would be much more interesting than slaving away as a seamstress in a sweatshop like my mother.'

Brian brought our tea – Earl Grey – along with warm, homemade scones served up on a crystal cake stand decorated with whole strawberries, segments of clementine, and slices of kiwi. Pots of proper Devonshire clotted cream, lightly crusted with yellow, and strawberry jam were delivered on a separate plate.

Brian set a silver egg timer on the table in front of me. 'When that's done, your tea will be perfectly brewed.' He waggled a finger. 'And not one second before!'

While we waited for the sands of time to tell us that the tea was ready, Audrey continued with her story. 'For some reason, Father didn't object to my joining the Women's Land Army, so I went off to be interviewed.' Audrey picked a strawberry off the plate and ate it in three tiny bites. 'They quizzed me on my experience, of course, and I had to admit to the woman who interviewed me that the only thing I knew about country life was what I'd read in books, but that it had always appealed to me. So she asked me what books I had read, and I had to invent something on the spot. "Friendly Animals of Forest and Fen", I told her.' Audrey giggled like the schoolgirl she had been at the time. 'She had to know I was green as grass, Hannah, but in spite of that, I was accepted and they dispatched me off to Herefordshire for training.'

'Tea's ready,' I said, with an eye on the egg timer. 'Shall I pour?'

She nodded.

'Black or white?'

'White, with,' she said.

I passed the milk and the sugar bowl.

'I didn't get on with the first farmer I was assigned to,' Audrey told me. Using the tongs, she dropped a lump of sugar into her tea, then stirred it vigorously. 'There was never enough food for one thing, and I had to sleep in an unheated loft.' She shivered. 'I've never been so cold in all my life.'

She wrapped her hands around her cup and took a long sip of tea, as if even the memory of the cold needed warming. 'But the last straw came when I was asked to hold the piglets while he castrated them. That was no job for a woman, and he knew it. I can hear them squealing to this very day! So I hopped on my bicycle and cycled away!'

'The Women's Land Army was very cross with me, of course, but I already knew how to hoe, dig ditches and milk cows, so they forgave me and transferred me to Devon. I was bivouacked in a hostel in Strete, but I worked primarily on Three Trees Farm, along with three other girls.' As she spoke, her eyes lit up. 'I loved the work, the fresh air, the sunshine. And even digging potatoes was fun when there were others to share the task.'

'What can you tell me about the girls you worked with, Audrey?'

'As I said, we were billeted in Strete, in a hostel with ten other girls.' She chuckled. 'With all the American soldiers in the area, we were having the time of our lives. Dances every weekend. Big band music, jitterbug and jive. We taught the Yanks how to do the Lambeth Walk and the Paul Jones, which they must have found hysterical. And, oh, how we used to put it over on our supervisor!' She leaned forward and whispered, 'There was a curfew, you know.'

Audrey reached down and retrieved her handbag from the floor. She pulled out a small packet of black and white photographs, held together by a rubber band. 'I've brought photos along, if you're interested.'

'I love looking at other people's pictures.'

Audrey removed the rubber band from the pack, cleared a small space on the tablecloth between us and laid down the first photo. It showed four girls standing in front of a tractor, arms thrown around each other's shoulders. Each girl's right leg was extended, as if they were executing a dance routine.

'We wore uniforms, as you can see,' she said, pointing to each item as she named it. 'Olive green gabardine breeches, a cream-colored shirt, green pullover, a tie.' She tapped one of the ties, which was askew as its owner leaned against her companions. 'If you look closely, you can see the Women's Land Army insignia on the tie.'

In a second photo, it was winter, and the same group of four smiling girls stood in a village square wearing heavy double-breasted overcoats, beige knee socks and sensible brown shoes. Two of the girls wore soft felt hats at jaunty angles, strings tied in loose bows just under their left ears.

A third photo showed one girl riding a tractor pulling a reaper, while another stood just behind holding a pitchfork. In the far background, a farmer looked on. 'The girl on the tractor is me,' Audrey said with a slight smile. 'The supervisor was none too pleased when I cut the legs off my dungarees so I could get a good tan.'

I bent over the table to study the photo more carefully. 'Is that Mr Bailey Senior in the background?'

'Stephen's father? Yes. He was a handsome man in his day. Stephen favors him, I think.'

I had to agree. The abundant hair, high cheekbones, ruddy complexion, and laughing eyes that seemed to say: *Life is good in the country.*

I slid the photos around on the tablecloth, until the country chorus line was again uppermost. 'The girl on the left is you, I can see that now. Who are the others?'

Audrey smiled wistfully. 'That's me, as you said, then Flo, Vi, and Mary.'

'I know you married Mr Wills, but what happened to the other girls after the South Hams were evacuated?'

'Mary got transferred to a farm in Exeter, and Flo went

home to Birmingham. I don't know what happened to Vi. I've managed to keep up with Mary and Flo over the years, though.'

'More tea?' I wanted to keep Audrey talking, and her cup was empty.

Audrey scooted her cup in my direction and I topped it up. 'We had a reunion of Land Girls in Totnes in April of 2005,' she continued, testing the temperature of the tea with a cautious sip. 'The mayor was there, and they had a cake. It was good to see Mary and Flo again, but like me, they'd lost track of Vi. We always figured that she married her Yank, and went home with him to America after the war.'

Audrey leaned back in her chair. 'The British boys were jealous of the Yanks' success with local girls. They found it hard to compete with the luxuries the American boys could offer, like cigarettes, silk stockings and chocolate.'

'What can you tell me about the Yank?'

'A couple of months before they announced the evacuation – that would have been August, or early September of 1943 – Vi met him at a dance in Totnes. Oh, he was a handsome devil!' She closed her eyes for a moment, as if trying to picture the young man more clearly. 'Tall and lanky. Curly hair the color of wheat. A US Navy pilot, from somewhere in the north-east, as I recall. Is Connecticut in the north-east of America?'

I grinned. 'The last time I looked at a map.'

'Vi was crazy about Rocky.'

'What was Rocky's last name?'

Audrey shrugged. 'Ever since you telephoned me, I've been trying to think of it. The American lads all seemed to go by nicknames: Tex, or Mac, or Buck. There were a lot of Texes.' She chuckled. 'We used to joke that half the American Army came from Texas.'

'What if Vi didn't end up marrying Rocky? What might she have done then? Gone back home to London?'

Audrey shook her head sadly. 'I doubt it. Poor thing. Her whole family – mother, father, younger sister – they were wiped out during the Blitz. She had nobody but us.' She crossed her fingers and held them up. 'We were that

close. Like sisters. That's what makes it so hard to understand why Violet didn't stay in touch.'

My heart started doing somersaults in my chest.

She's showing me a flower.

Many women were named after flowers: Daisy, Iris, Lily,
Pansy, Petunia . . . even Marigold. What if Susan Parker
had gotten it *wrong* that night in Paignton? What if the
flower she'd been thinking of had been a violet, and not a
rose?

Ask her, Susan Parker seemed to be whispering in my
ear. *Ask her about the ring*. 'Did Rocky give Violet a ring?'

Audrey looked blank. 'Could have done, I suppose, but
if he did, she never wore it while we worked. We dug potatoes, mostly, so you'd lose a ring, wouldn't you?'

'Tell me something, then. You said the British boys didn't
get along very well with the Yanks. How did Stephen Bailey
feel about the relationship between Violet and Rocky?'

'Oh, well, you've put your finger on it there, Hannah.
Vi might have been a little flirtatious, she might even have
allowed Stephen the occasional cuddle, but it was always
light-hearted, never serious. Not so for Stephen. He made
it clear that he didn't like it when she started stepping out
with that American. But then the evacuation came, and just
like that . . .' She snapped her fingers. 'The Land Girls were
gone.'

'And six months later, D-Day happened, and the
Americans were gone, too.'

'Yes. After all the hubbub leading up to the invasion, the
land was eerily, almost spookily quiet. No people, no cattle,
no birds signing. A few abandoned dogs and cats, that was
all. Except for the rats.' She shivered. 'They were so hungry
they were eating the putty out of the window glass because
it had been mixed up with fish oil.'

I shivered, too. We'd had fruit rats in the Bahamas, and
even though they wiggled their ears and twitched their
whiskers like Disney mice, I didn't like them one bit. 'When
did you get to return home, Audrey?'

'Most of us were eager to go back, but we couldn't
because of all the unexploded bombs. Once the Americans

returned the area, the Government brought in the mine sweepers, then the surveyors and the photographers came through to assess the damage so the government could pay compensation.' She stared out the window for a moment, deep in thought. 'The first viewing permits were issued in August, as I recall, but the residents didn't actually start returning until October.'

'Do you remember when the Baileys came back?'

'Not until spring, I imagine. In any case, it would have been in time for the plowing and planting.'

During our conversation, I had been neglecting my scone. I slathered the second half with cream, topped it with a generous dollop of strawberry jam, and took a big bite, using the opportunity to think about what Audrey had told me.

Stephen Bailey had been sweet on a girl named Violet who spurned him for another man.

Violet had disappeared.

Susan Parker said to Stephen: *She's showing me a flower.*

Now Susan was dead.

One crime to cover up another?

If so, what was I going to do about it?

TWENTY-THREE

*'The area seemed to lie as if under a spell, beautiful
still but neglected and forlorn, waiting for the touch
of a magic wand to revive its normal life. But nature
is never still . . . and gradually the flowers and ferns
helped to hide the ravages of war.'*
Grace Bradbeer, *The Land Changed Its Face:
The Evacuation of the South Hams, 1943–44*,
Devon Books, 1973, p. 94

S tephen Bailey's car, I decided, was key. It would have
to be found.

With Stephen Bailey living at Coombe Hill full-
time, I'd have time to poke around on Three Trees Farm.
I knew Cathy wouldn't mind.

I hadn't heard from Alison in a couple of days, but after
what I'd learned about her father from Audrey Wills, I was
almost relieved. I felt guilty about keeping secrets, of course,
but how could I tell her what I suspected, especially without
any concrete evidence?

I'd just stepped out of the shower when Alison finally
called, but her news took me entirely by surprise.

'Hannah, I'm sorry. It seems I'm always calling you for
help, but I really need you this time. Dad's gone missing.'

'What? I thought he was happy at Coombe Hill.' I
wrapped the towel around my body, and sat down in a chair.

'He *seemed* happy enough. But I just got a call from the
administrator, and they can't locate him. His room is empty,
and they say his bed hasn't been slept in. How can they
have been so careless?'

'Alison, it isn't a nursing home. Your father's free to
come and go as he pleases, right?'

Her only answer was a whimpering sound.

'Too bad they don't have any granny cams,' I added, 'but that's one of the reasons you picked the place, remember? Because it seemed dignified, more like a resort hotel than a retirement living facility.'

She sighed. 'I know, I know. They do have a security camera at the main entrance, though, and it shows him walking out the front door and turning right. It's time-stamped at ten minutes past two. He could have been heading for the bus station, or even the ferry. Neither one is too far a walk for a man in good physical condition like my father.'

'Do you have any idea where he could have gone?'

'He's old and confused. He could be wandering around Dittisham somewhere, feeding the pigeons in the park, or chatting up barmaids. Oh . . . I don't know!'

'Have you checked the farm?'

'But that's miles away, and he doesn't have a car.' She paused. 'Do you really think he would have gone back to the farm?'

'Alison, for his whole life, that farm was the center of your father's world. That's where I'd go. When my mother died,' I continued, 'my father held on to the home they had shared for the longest time. Even after he moved into a smaller place and put the big house on the market, he'd show up at every viewing. It was as if he had to *audition* the buyers. If they made sarcastic remarks about the wall-paper, well, scratch that couple off the list!'

I was relieved to hear her laugh.

'How would your father get back to Three Trees Farm?' I wondered aloud.

'Dead easy,' she said. 'The number one-twelve bus goes from Dittisham to Dartmouth, and he could catch the ninety-three from Dartmouth to Strete. Or he could have caught the ferry. Once he got to Strete, he'd walk the rest of the way, or hitch a ride with a local.'

'Have you telephoned Cathy Yates?'

'Why? She hasn't moved in yet.'

'I know she hasn't. But when I saw her at breakfast, she had a sheaf of paint samples clutched in her fist. She said something about calling a cab and a meeting with contractors, so I just put two and two together. Does she have permission to be out there?'

'She does. With Dad in Dittisham, I told her she could visit any time she wanted.'

Carrying my iPhone, I returned to the bathroom. I lay the phone on the toilet lid, set it to speakerphone, and began to towel dry my hair. 'Look, give me a few minutes to get dressed, then come pick me up. We'll drive around Dittisham. Maybe he's having a pint in a pub somewhere. If we don't find him in Dittisham, we'll drive down to the farm. OK?'

Needless to say, we ended up at the farm.

As we climbed out of her car, Alison said, 'I'll check the house. Hannah, why don't you go around to the barn?'

With a wave of agreement, I left Alison and wandered through the courtyard from which Stephen Bailey's Prius had (or had not) recently been stolen, making my way, as instructed, toward the barn. Ahead of me, the barn door yawned open. Chickens scratched around in the dirt and gravel, and somewhere, a rooster crowed.

In the near distance, a flash of red distracted me. I didn't recall ever seeing Stephen Bailey wearing red – he tended to favor clothing in the blue and yellow spectrum – but it could have been Tom Boyd, the man-of-all-work who Cathy had agreed to keep on, at a generous rise in salary.

But the red sweater didn't belong to Alison's father, or to his former handyman. It was worn by Cathy Yates, bent over a long-handled spade.

I called out to her. 'Cathy!'

She looked up from whatever she was doing, resting her hands one over the other on the handle of the spade. 'Hannah! What brings you all the way out here?'

'Alison and I are looking for her father. He's run away from Coombe Hill, and this is the first place we thought of to look.'

'I've been here over an hour, but I haven't seen him. I'll keep an eye out, though.'

The noon sun was hot, and sweat glistened on Cathy's

brow. She peeled off her sweater and tossed it aside. A bottle of spring water sat on the ground near her feet. She unscrewed the cap, took a sip, and dabbed her mouth daintily, considering she was using her sleeve.

'Why are you digging?' I asked.

Cathy pointed with the spade. 'What does that look like to you?'

'A concrete slab?'

'No. It's the remains of a brick and concrete air-raid shelter with steps leading down to it.' I recognized the quote from a passage in Ken Small's book.

'It doesn't look like an air-raid shelter to me,' I said gently.

'It's here! It fits the description perfectly, Hannah!' She thrust the spade repeatedly into the dirt at the base of the concrete slab. 'These are the steps, I'm sure of it.'

They were, indeed, crumbling steps, but the steps weren't attached to anything, in my opinion, that remotely resembled an air-raid shelter.

'Hey!' somebody yelled.

Cathy and I turned to see Stephen Bailey striding toward us. He was waving both arms over his head, as if attempting to flag down a runaway train. 'I wouldn't go digging around there if I were you, missy.'

Cathy stared the old man down. 'Why not?'

'Unexploded shells,' he said simply. 'Time was we let bullocks out to roam the fields as mine detectors.'

Cathy's eyes narrowed. 'Were *you* the farmer that Ken Small mentioned in his book?'

Bailey's smirk was tinged with amusement. 'Not me. I told you you'd not find American bodies here in Devon.'

'Isn't this the remains of an air-raid shelter?'

'No. Used to be my dairy barn. More than a hundred and twenty years old, it was. Blew away in a wind storm back in October 2000.'

Cathy stuck her spade into the ground, mashed down on it with her foot. 'I'm thinking that the steps went down about here.' While we watched, she turned over another spadeful of earth and added it to a growing pile to her left.

Bailey scowled. 'This is still my property, Ms Yates, and I'll thank you to put down that spade and leave, right now.'

Cathy glanced up from her digging. 'No, it's not, Mr Bailey. You agreed to sell the farm to me, contracts were exchanged, and I gave you a sizeable deposit.' She looked pointedly at her watch. 'In point of fact, my solicitor just called to say that everything's moving along very smoothly. For the money I'm paying him to settle things as quickly as possible, he'd better be right.' She waved a dismissive hand. 'You're welcome to stay, however. I know how hard it must be for you to let go of something that's been in your family for so long.'

Bailey blinked rapidly. 'You can't have done. It's too soon.'

In point of fact, Stephen Bailey was right. Until formal completion, he still owned Three Trees Farm, but Cathy was thinking like an American, not a Brit. Contracts had been exchanged, money had changed hands. In Cathy's mind, it was a done deal.

'If you don't believe me, ask your daughter,' Cathy said. 'Here she comes now.'

I glanced over my shoulder.

Alison was indeed chugging up the drive. 'There you are, Dad!' Her tone was cheery, impossible to tell that she'd just spent the last four hours worrying about her father, searching bus, train and ferry terminals that offered service from Dittisham to points out in all directions. 'Hi, Cathy,' she added with a friendly wave.

Her father looked like a little boy lost in a large department store. 'She says I don't own the farm anymore, Alison.'

Alison reddened, but skirted the issue. 'You sold it to Mrs Yates, remember?'

'I did no such thing!' he blustered. 'I agreed to sell it to some bloke in London, going to grow organic vegetables or something daft.'

'Agrishare Limited is my company, Mr Bailey.'

Bailey froze, back ramrod straight, his arms dangling. He glared at Cathy, then turned to his daughter and gave her a look so malevolent that if looks were arrows, she'd have dropped dead on the spot.

'Busted!' I teased.

Alison grinned sheepishly, and we watched her father slump and stalk off to the barn.

'Do you . . .?' Cathy began. 'Maybe somebody should go and talk to him? I might have been a little harsh just now.'

Knowing, or rather suspecting, what Stephen Bailey had been up to lately, I had no inclination to raise my hand. He could pout in the barn forever, for all I cared, or at least until the police came to cart him away.

'No, no,' Alison told her. 'He'll sulk for a bit, then he'll be fine. And who knows? The way his memory's been lately, he may forget that the whole thing ever happened.'

With Stephen Bailey temporarily out of the picture, Cathy hefted her spade and began another assault on the foundation of the old dairy barn. 'I can tell there used to be steps here.' Her spade took another bite out of the soil.

I had a very good idea why Bailey didn't want Cathy, or anybody, digging in this particular spot, so when Cathy looked up and said, 'Hunt up another shovel, will ya, Hannah, and lend a poor working girl a hand?' I spread my arms helplessly and shrugged in a *who-me?* sort of way.

I was saved by the reappearance of Stephen Bailey.

At first, I was relieved. Then I saw he was carrying a shotgun over his arm, almost casually, break action open. As he walked, he fed a shell into each chamber, then flipped the gun closed with an ominous clack.

Bailey was closing with single-minded intent on Cathy Yates who had her back to him and was digging with such concentration, accompanied by her own incessant chatter, that she was oblivious to the danger he represented.

Her spade bit into the ground. 'Well, what's this?' She tossed the tool aside, bent at the waist to get a closer look, and peered into the hole.

'Dad!' Alison's voice was low, urgent.

'You stay out of this, Alison.' He took several more steps in Cathy's direction, but she still didn't see him. 'Stop digging. Now!'

Cathy jumped into the hole, bent over for a moment, thrust her hand into the dirt. 'There's something down there,

Mr Bailey, and I . . .' Her head came up and she sucked air, finally noticing the shotgun pointed straight at her chest.

'Climb out, and move away from the hole,' Bailey instructed, motioning her aside with the business end of the gun. When Cathy didn't budge, he tugged on the bolt and slammed the shell home.

She raised a hand in surrender. 'Now look, Mr Bailey . . .'

'I said *move!*' His finger twitched where it rested on the trigger.

Cathy's fists migrated to her hips, her arms akimbo. 'You lied to me, Mr Bailey. You told me there were no bodies here. But what am I looking at right now, huh? Tell me that?'

The woman had chutzpah, but I already knew that.

She held out a fist, slowly uncurled her fingers. 'What's this, then?'

From where I stood, something glittered like a cat's eye on her open palm. I moved my head slightly to the right. Another flash.

'And down in this hole?' Cathy continued, her eyes still locked on Alison's father. 'There's a bit of khaki fabric in that hole, that's what. I don't know what else I'll find down there, but if that fabric is a piece of uniform, then it could belong to somebody's son, or husband, or father.'

'Alison, where did your father get the gun?' I whispered.

'Oh, God, he kept one in the barn,' she whispered back, her voice quavering. 'I completely forgot about it.'

I grabbed her arm and squeezed reassuringly. I touched my lips with an index finger, then indicated that I was going to work my way around behind her father. His attention was so focused on Cathy that I hoped he wouldn't notice me.

'Put the spade down,' Bailey ordered.

Cathy obeyed, thrusting the tool into the pile of dirt. 'You don't really want to hurt anybody, do you, Mr Bailey? Why don't you put the gun away?'

Suddenly, the shotgun exploded. Alison's father staggered back with the recoil, his eyes wide in astonishment.

Alison screamed.

Cathy seemed paralysed with shock. She clutched her left arm, hugging it against her body as a scarlet stain began to leak through her blouse and between her fingers. 'Well, got down sat on a bench! That crazy old fool just shot me!'

Even with blood running down her arm, Cathy Yates managed to keep her profanity clean.

'I – I – I . . .' Bailey stammered, drooping like a rag doll. 'I didn't mean . . . my finger just . . .'

I shoved past him, heading straight for Cathy, peeling off my jacket as I ran, thinking I could use it as a tourniquet. Lessons learned at Girl Scout camp die hard. 'Call 999!' I yelled at Alison whose shoes seemed riveted to the ground.

'Dad?' she wailed.

'Your cell phone, Alison! For Christ's sake, call an ambulance! Your father can wait.'

I was ripping Cathy's sleeve open to check the seriousness of her wound, and Alison was busy punching numbers into her phone, so neither one of us noticed when Stephen Bailey, still carrying the shotgun, disappeared into the barn.

Alison charged into the house to fetch some clean cloths, while I stayed with Cathy. 'Do sit down, girl. You've got buckshot in your arm.' I propped her up against the pile of dirt, using her sweater as a cushion.

Alison was back in a moment carrying some dishtowels and a can of Coca Cola. 'I can't believe my father . . . Oh, God, Hannah, is she going to be all right?'

'I think so,' I said as I wrapped my jacket tightly around Cathy's arm in an attempt to staunch the bleeding.

Alison held out the Coke.

'What's that for?'

She shrugged. 'I thought Cathy could use the sugar or something.'

Cathy forced a smile. 'Thanks. Maybe later. First, I've got something to show you.' She uncurled her fingers. A man's signet ring, set with a red stone that reflected the sun like tiny tongues of fire, sat on her open palm, both stained with blood.

It's a signet ring of some sort, with a red stone, Susan

had said. Once again, Susan Parker had been tee-totally right.

'You should recognize this, Hannah.'

I bent down to get a closer look. 'May I?' When Cathy nodded, I picked the ring off her palm and examined it.

'It's from the Naval Academy,' I explained to Alison. 'Class of 'thirty-nine. See here on this side? It's incised with the initials USNA. And on the other, there's a thirty-nine.'

In spite of her wound, Cathy was still on task, her face bright with victory. 'Ken Small was right all along! Americans *are* buried here!'

'No, I don't think so. That bit of fabric you found in the hole? Land Army Girls wore khaki uniforms, too.'

Cathy and Alison exchanged glances that suggested that I'd lost my mind.

I turned the ring, now drinking up the sunlight for the first time in sixty years, so they could read the inscription I suspected I would find inside: Anthony J. Rockefeller.

'Rocky,' I said aloud.

'Who?' Cathy sounded confused, and I couldn't blame her.

'I'll have to explain later,' I said. 'But in the meantime, if he's still alive, I think Rocky would like to know that a beautiful young girl named Violet didn't simply walk out on him.'

The keening of sirens split the air. Followed by a deafening boom.

Stephen Bailey had sat on a milking stool in Feckless's stall, put the barrel of the gun under his chin, and used the remaining shotgun shell on himself.

TWENTY-FOUR

*'Perhaps I should believe in a hereafter, in a conscious-
ness that zips through the air like a Simpsons rerun,
simply because it's more appealing – more fun and
more hopeful – than not believing. The debunkers are
probably right, but they're no fun to visit a graveyard
with. What the hell. I believe in ghosts.'*
Mary Roach, *Spook*, Norton, 2005, p. 295

After an overnight stay in the hospital, Alison was
released to the care of her husband, daughter Kitty,
and a competent therapist, all of whom encouraged
her to take a long vacation with a drastic change of scene.

After her father's funeral, of course.

Alison and Jon and been secretive about their trip, but
we volunteered to drive them to the airport. From
Heathrow, we'd head north to the outskirts of Cambridge,
to the American Cemetery at Madingley. Cathy Yates
would come along, too, although her arm was still cradled
in a sling.

Just before leaving, we learned that Violet Johnson's
body had been positively identified from her ration book
and identity card contained in the brown leather handbag
that had been found with her body on Three Trees Farm.
Violet had been claimed by a distant cousin living in Kent
and would be buried there, next to her entire family, all
of whom, it turned out, had perished in the war.

'Was there anything else in her handbag?' I wondered
aloud.

Alison glanced at Jon, as if seeking his approval. When
he nodded, she said, 'There was a letter, addressed to my
father, but apparently it never got delivered.'

'You were right, Hannah,' Jon said, continuing the story.

'It was a Dear John. Violet was throwing Stephen over for a Navy pilot from Connecticut.'

'How did she die?' Cathy wondered from the back seat as we hurtled north up the M5.

'Strangulation,' Jon said, reaching for Alison's hand. 'Her hyoid bone had been crushed. Alison and I are still having a hard time coming to terms with the idea that her father was capable of such a violent act.'

Cathy tugged on her seatbelt, easing it out a few inches and arranging the strap more comfortably across her injured shoulder. 'What I don't understand is why your father agreed to sell the farm at all, Alison. He must have known it increased the risk of Violet's body being discovered.'

Alison shivered, leaned closer to her husband who wrapped his arm around her, drawing her close.

'That's why he went AWOL from Coombe Hill,' Jon explained. 'He needed to move the body. When the police searched the property, they found a little flatbed trailer behind the barn, hooked up to the tractor. There was a tarp in it, and a pickax and a shovel.'

I turned around to face our friends. 'Your father wasn't senile at all, was he, Alison?'

She shook her head sadly. 'Nothing was wrong with Dad's noodle, I know that now. He staged that whole "accident" for our benefit, simply to hide the damage sustained to his car when he drove it up the Embankment and mowed Susan down.'

'So the people coming for a viewing were a lie just to get us there. The Fairy Liquid a bogus errand.'

'Right. My father set us up – two perfect witnesses.'

'Are you going to be OK, Alison?' I asked.

'In time. Yes, I think so.' Alison smiled up at her husband. 'Jon and I have had a long talk, and I think we can *both* lay the past to rest now.'

Jon caught Paul's eye in the rearview mirror. 'You were right, Ives. I was the luckiest man in the world the day this woman walked into my life.'

Alison rested her head on Jon's shoulder, smiling modestly. 'Did you tell them where we're going?'

'I thought you'd like to, Al.'

'Well, Gretna Green being totally out of fashion, we're going to . . .' She paused for dramatic effect, like those irritating shows on the House and Garden channel: if we were to list this house today, we'd list it for . . . long pregnant pause, then cut to an ad.

'Alison, you are going to make me rip off all my clothes and run around the countryside screaming and tearing out my hair!'

'I'm surprised you can't guess, as it was your suggestion.'

I drew a blank. 'How about a hint?'

'The Bahamas? Eleuthera? Something special on a pink sand beach?'

I sat up straight. 'You're getting married!' I threw kisses through the air into the back seat.

For the first time in weeks, Alison actually laughed. 'Jon suggested we elope to Las Vegas and be married by an Elvis impersonator. I quickly vetoed that.'

'Oh my God, I almost wish you had. I would have paid anything to see the videos!'

Jon launched into the chorus of 'Love Me Tender', but was quickly subdued by Alison's hand clamped firmly over his mouth. When he was free to speak again, he asked, 'When do you and Paul go home, then?'

I answered for both of us. 'The day after tomorrow.'

'Safe travels,' Jon said. 'And come back again soon.'

Paul's eyes cut to the rear-view mirror. 'You mean we haven't worn out our welcome?'

'Never!'

The sun came out for our drive to Cambridge.

After a tour of the cemetery grounds, Paul and I stood inside the Memorial and watched through the Memorial Door as Cathy strolled alone along the reflecting pool, then crossed over to the Wall of the Missing, searching for her father's name among more than five thousand other names, including Joseph P. Kennedy, Jr and bandleader Glenn Miller whose bodies also had never been found.

I was no medium, Lord knows, but the place seemed tranquil, with no restive spirits hovering about.

'Do you think Cathy's at peace?' Paul asked, slipping his hand into mine.

'No. I think she'll be back, accompanied by a Congressional fact-finding team, and Nancy Pelosi will be carrying her bags.'

'Poor Devon.' He squeezed my hand.

'Oh, they can handle it, Paul. They'll stay at the Royal Castle, eat breakfast at Alf Resco's, share a pint at the Cherub, keep the restaurants open past their closing time. They'll collect a lot of facts, then go home and order their aides to churn out a two-thousand-page report that says exactly what Stephen Bailey said all along. No bodies washed ashore at Slapton Sands. No bodies remain in temporary graves in Devon.

'Not even Violet Johnson's.'

I turned to my husband and looked straight into his eyes. 'It gives me the creeps to think about it, but, yes, thanks to Susan Parker, Violet's voice was finally heard.'

Leaving Cathy to mourn in private, we wandered over to a relief map of the Normandy Landings, where each wave of men that sailed from Devon to Utah Beach stood out in bold relief. As I traced the lines with my fingers, I thought how it all came together – the evacuation, the disaster at Slapton Sands – and how years later, our lives would become entwined with those long dead, just like the intersecting lines on that map.

That night as we prepared for bed back at Horn Hill House, I opened the window and pulled back the curtains, closed my eyes and let the gentle evening breeze wash over me. Feeling sorry for myself because our visit was coming to an end, I had self-medicated with an overdose of wine. I'd do penance in the morning, for sure.

Paul handed me an aspirin and a glass of water, waited until I'd swallowed both down, then tucked me into bed beside him.

I dropped into a fitful sleep.

It was still dark when somebody called my name. 'Hannah!'

I clawed my way up through a cotton-wool world, willing myself awake.

'Hannah!'

After struggling for what seemed like eternity, I managed to open my eyes.

A figure stood at the end of the bed. I could see her plainly in the light spilling in from the street lamp outside our window. Susan Parker, dressed the way she had been on the day I first met her on Foss Street.

My heart flopped, began to flutter. Susan was dead. I had seen her body. I was dreaming, I had to be. But if so, how could I feel Paul lying next to me, hear him softly snoring, see the breeze actually lifting the curtains?

I tried to sit up, but I was paralysed. A great weight pressed down on my chest. Air, I needed air! My heart raced and I tried to call out – *Susan!* – but my vocal cords seemed to be paralysed, too.

Susan beamed. 'Basingstoke,' she said. 'Does that mean anything to you, Hannah?'

Suddenly, my little finger was free. I nudged Paul's thigh with it, trying to get his attention, calling his name. 'Puh, Puh, Puh.'

From the foot of the bed, Susan began to sing, her purple forelock quivering over her brow. '"Abba dabba dabba dabba dabba dabba dabba said the monkey to the chimp. Abba dabba dabba dabba dabba dabba dabba said the chimpy to the monk."' She paused, cocked her head in the listening posture I knew so well. 'Your mother tells me this song makes her smile.'

It made me smile, too. I hadn't thought about it for years, but when I was a toddler, Mother had to sit in the chair next to my bed and sing 'Abba Dabba Honeymoon' three times through exactly before I would agree to go to sleep.

What's the message? My brain screamed, but nothing came out of my mouth.

'"Then the big baboon, one night in June, he married them and very soon . . ."' Susan sang in a clear, high soprano.

The message! Tell me! Please!

Susan pressed her hands together, rocked back and forth on her toes. 'Tell your father he should marry Cornelia. It's been a long time, your mother says, and he deserves a little happiness.'

As I watched, working my pinky as hard as I could – 'Puh, Puh, Puh' – Susan Parker faded away, the last lines of the song – *they went upon their abba dabba honeymoon* – lingering in the air while I lay there like a rock, struggling to breathe.

'Puh, puh, puh!' After what seemed like hours, I felt my husband stir. His hand found my shoulder and jostled me. 'Hannah, wake up. You're having a bad dream.'

My body relaxed at his touch. I could move my fingers, my hand, my arm. 'Paul . . .' I was hot and cold all at the same time. Sweat beaded on my forehead.

Paul caressed my cheek. 'Jeesh, Hannah, what's wrong? Are you having a hot flash or something?'

I lay there in confusion, trying to sort it out. What *had* just happened? Visitation or dream? I shivered. Either way, Susan's advice was sound, and I planned to share it with my father.

Grateful that I could move again, I got up and closed the window, rubbing my arms briskly for warmth. I scurried across the carpet and climbed back into bed, snuggling close as Paul wrapped his arms around me.

'I just had the weirdest dream,' I said, matching the curve of his body with my own.

'Mmmmm.' He nuzzled my neck.

'Do you think the spirits can see us when we're naked?' I asked.

'I suppose so.'

'When we're on the toilet?'

'Sure.'

'How about when we're making love?'

Paul kissed my forehead, my nose and my lips, tickling them with his tongue in the way that drives me crazy. 'Our last night in Dartmouth, Hannah.'

When I came up for air, I said, 'But we'll come back, won't we? I just love it here.'

'Of course. And we'll stay at Horn Hill House, too.'

'Paul?' I asked as he began to nibble on my earlobe. 'Do me a favor?'

'What's that?' he mumbled

'When we come back, let's ask Janet for a different room.'